The Strange Files
of Fremont Jones

The Strange Files
of Fremont Jones

DIANNE DAY

DOUBLEDAY
NEW YORK   LONDON   TORONTO   SYDNEY   AUCKLAND

PUBLISHED BY DOUBLEDAY
a division of Bantam Doubleday Dell Publishing Group, Inc.
1540 Broadway, New York, New York 10036

DOUBLEDAY and the portrayal of an anchor with a dolphin are
trademarks of Doubleday, a division of Bantam Doubleday Dell
Publishing Group, Inc.

Book design by Gretchen Achilles

Library of Congress Cataloging-in-Publication Data

Day, Dianne.
    The strange files of Fremont Jones / Dianne Day. — 1st ed.
        p.   cm.
        1. Women detectives—California—San Francisco—Fiction.   2. Femi-
nists—California—San Francisco—Fiction.   3. San Francisco (Calif.)—
Fiction.   I. Title.
    PS3554.A9595S7   1995
    813'.54—dc20   94-15170
                                                                            CIP

ISBN 0-385-47549-7

Printed in the United States of America
April 1995
First Edition
1   3   5   7   9   10   8   6   4   2

For Harvey Klinger,
gratefully

Contents

The Strange Files
of Fremont Jones

1.

No More Caroline

I KNOW WHAT people say about me: that I am willful and opinionated, shockingly eccentric in my manner of dress (this because I will
not wear a corset), altogether a trial to my father. These things are true
except the last. I am not a trial to my father because he gave up on me
long ago. For the past few years he has been reduced to muttering, "If
only your mother were still alive . . ." or alternatively, "If only I
hadn't allowed you to go to that seminary for females . . ." by which
he means Wellesley, where I received an excellent education and had a
few ideas put into my head, in addition to the ones I seem to have
been born with.

In spite of my father's mutterings I expect I would have got round
him eventually, had he not succumbed to the calculated charms of the
seemingly docile, completely conventional, properly corseted widow
Augusta Simmons. I realize my father needs companionship, as he is
only forty-seven, still rather handsome and robust; but after the first
excruciating hour of tea that I spent with Augusta (she called it High
Tea—she has pretensions), I knew she meant trouble for me: the end
of such freedom as it was possible for a female of a proper Beacon Hill
family to glean for herself, even at the beginning of a new century, in
the year 1905.

Therefore, I was not unduly surprised recently to overhear a conversation between my father and Augusta that went like this:

Augusta: "We really must do something about Caroline, Leonard." (My father is the Hon. Leonard Pembroke Jones.)

Father, with an audible sigh: "I know. If only her mother—"

Augusta, interrupting: "Never you mind, my dear, I'm here now. I shall take the young woman in hand. What she needs is a husband, although at twenty-two the bloom is off the rose, if you know what I mean; indeed, Caroline is not far from spinsterhood! It won't be easy to find her a husband, but it's not impossible; for example there is my nephew—"

I didn't stay at my post outside the library door to hear about Augusta's nephew, whoever he might be. My cheeks were flaming. Really, I thought, she might at least have waited until they were married before poking her nose into my life! I wanted to burst in on them and give the woman a lashing of my opinionated tongue, but I knew it would have done no good. Father was besotted. I went upstairs instead, and began to make plans.

Actually, what I did was make some new plans, as it now appeared the ones I had already made would not work with Augusta installed permanently on the scene. After allowing myself a few moments of delicious fantasy, in which the widow Augusta fell out of a swanboat in the Public Garden and drowned among the ducks, I got down to business. I believe I am good at getting down to business; my business sense is almost—but not quite—as good as my imagination. Business, in fact, was the essence of my plan.

You see, I did not want to marry. Not that I have anything against men—I do like men, and have often fantasized that sex (yes, I dare to think the word though not even I would utter it aloud) must be more pleasurable than women are supposed to think, otherwise kissing would not be half the thrill that it is. Rather, I object to the institution of marriage with its trappings of subservience for women, and I do not intend to participate in it. What I want to do is *work*. I want to have my own business, and if it were not for the advent of the widow Augusta, I would have talked my father around to it.

So . . . I lay on my stomach across my bed, with my chin on my fist, and thought. Before very long, I leapt up and shouted, "Eureka!" Most appropriately, as that is a California-type exclamation. The new plan had sprung, like Minerva from the head of Zeus, full-grown from my mind: I would have my business, just as I'd intended, but far from the nosy reach of my soon-to-be stepmother. In San Francisco rather than Boston!

I whirled around my bedroom with my arms outflung and my skirt belling about my ankles, too excited to keep still. Yes, yes, yes! Yes, I could do it, and what was more, it was perfect! What could be more perfect than that I, who bore my mother's surname Fremont as my own middle name, should go to California? I would take my female eccentricities to the state where my distant relation, John C. Fremont, had made a large part of his own eccentric reputation. Yes!

I stopped whirling and went to my desk. Composing myself, I closed my eyes and silently said a few words of thanks to my mother, whose legacy made this possible. Then I took pen in hand and began to figure. The sum of money that mother had left to me was modest, but it would do. I would *make* it do. I wrote a list of things to be done and divided them up into a timetable. Everything fell into place—on the paper and in my mind—so easily that I knew this was right. The hard part would be keeping my mouth shut and all my plans secret for the two months until my father's wedding.

Father would not give his consent to a move across country, of course; I would simply have to leave when he and Augusta were away on their honeymoon. Nor, to be honest, would Mother have approved —the adventurous genes that had made John C. Fremont an explorer had not infected his second cousin, my mother. Like most Bostonians —though she was one only by marriage—Mother had thought Boston was the Hub of the Universe, and a trip West meant to Framingham. The adventurous genes had skipped a generation, to pop up in me.

I had never met my famous cousin Fremont; he'd died some ten years previous, a few years before my mother. But as I behaved with uncharacteristic docility at home over the next weeks, all the while pulling together my secret arrangements, I felt more and more a kinship with him. How brave and unconventional he had been! Admirable qualities, I thought, that I would do well to emulate. The unconventional part came effortlessly to me; I hoped the bravery would also come, when and if it were required.

Going to purchase my railway tickets, I had a sudden inspiration: I told the ticket master to make them out not to Caroline F. Jones, but to C. Fremont Jones. I was going to have a new life in a new place—why not a new name as well?

From that moment on (though until I left Boston it was only in my own mind) I called myself Fremont. No more Caroline!

The sign painter had just left the large, one-room office I had rented over a bookstore on Sacramento Street, and I surveyed his work with approval: FREMONT JONES, TYPEWRITING SERVICES. I'd seen no need to keep the C before my name any longer; I'd never felt much like a Caroline anyway. Plus which, it made good business sense not to advertise my gender. The sign appeared twice: on the window that faced the street and, of course, on the office door.

I went out into the corridor, closed the door behind me, then turned and read the sign as if I were an approaching customer. FREMONT JONES, TYPEWRITING SERVICES. A little thrill went through me. Still pretending to be a customer, I opened the door—the little bell I'd affixed to it jingled—and went into the office. I approved the big, solid oak desk in the center of the room and the matching (well, for secondhand they were a good match) oak file cabinets against one wall. On the desk, in addition to the usual paper and pens and such, were a brass lamp with a green glass shade, and a telephone—my first of these modern instruments. My father hadn't thought we needed to be on the telephone at home, but I considered it a prudent business investment.

At a right angle to the left of the desk, sitting on a table I'd had especially designed for it, was my pride and joy, the typewriter. It was a handsome thing, with a high, shiny black carriage and silver-rimmed round keys. The typewriter was new, ordered months before, when I'd thought I would be opening my business in Boston, and carried with me on the long train trip across country.

My office furnishings were completed by my own chair, fitted with wheels so that I could move from typewriter to desk and back with ease, three additional wooden chairs set in strategic locations about the room, and a long worktable in front of the street-facing window. The oiled floorboards were bare and would remain so for now; I intended to add an area rug for color and to muffle the clacking sound of the typewriter, when I could afford one.

I smiled. Yes, this did very well. Now, all I needed were the customers. There was no question of being idle, though; while I waited, I would practice my typing. I was self-taught—the operation of typewriters not being in the Wellesley curriculum—and I needed all the practice I could get!

My first customer came in the afternoon of my second day at the office. I was clacking away furiously, transcribing for practice from Jane Austen's *Pride and Prejudice,* when I heard the jingle of the bell above the door. I turned and looked up with what I judged to be a professional-type smile on my face.

I said, "Good afternoon."

"Good afternoon," said the man as he entered, letting the door close behind him. "Ah, is Mr. Jones in?"

"I'm Fremont Jones," I said with satisfaction, "have you something to be typed?"

He was looking me over critically, so I did the same with him. I knew what *he* saw: a fair-skinned woman with straight reddish-brown hair (the color some call chestnut but I just call brown) pulled back and tied with a black ribbon at the nape of the neck, and green eyes under eyebrows too thick to be fashionable (I refuse to pluck them because it seems a silly thing to do and besides, it hurts); a woman not too generously endowed beneath her pleated white shirtwaist—and also not corseted, which I presumed he would not know though other women invariably seemed to. What *I* saw was a man who could not be much older than I, tall and thin, with a bit of a stoop to his shoulders, as if he had gained his height too quickly for his own comfort. His thinness emphasized the bone structure of his face, which was fine, as were the straight nose and large blue eyes. He had hair the color and texture of corn silk; no doubt he wet it down in the mornings but by this time of the day it was sliding down over one eye. Likewise his tan suit and white shirt, while they must have started out the day crisply enough, were now rather crumpled.

He said dubiously, *"You're* Fremont Jones?"

I maintained my professional smile. "As I said."

Now he too smiled, but his was genuine, curving his lips and crinkling and lighting his eyes. "How unusual, and how pleasant! My name is Justin Cameron. I saw your handbill posted downstairs in the bookstore. May I?" He cocked his head toward the chair at the right of my desk.

"Please do be seated, Mr. Cameron."

He sat, crossed one long leg over the other, and balanced a manila folder on his knee. "I'm a lawyer just starting my own practice. My office is a couple of buildings up on Sacramento. I can't afford a clerk yet, so I was hoping . . ."

"That's exactly what I'm here for," I said, extending my hand for the folder. But he didn't give it to me and there I was with my hand out, feeling a bit foolish.

Justin Cameron had opened his folder and was frowning at the papers within. "Penmanship was never my strong point. I hope you can read it." He riffled through the pages, his frown increasing. "The first thing is a letter, I suppose that's straightforward enough. But the rest is a brief, a lot of legalese, with, you know, uh, words in Latin . . ."

I had folded my hands together on the desk, no longer smiling. "I assure you, Mr. Cameron, that I am well educated. I can read Latin. Not to mention Greek, and a few modern languages. Now if you'll just let me see your papers, I can tell you if I am able to read your handwriting, as well."

"Oh, sure thing. You bet. Here." He had the grace to look embarrassed as he shoved the now-untidy folder across the desk to me.

Justin Cameron's handwriting was loose and loopy, a style of penmanship that suited him, and that somehow made the corners of my mouth want to turn up, but I did not allow it. I said, "I'll have no trouble with this. But if you'd like to be sure, I'll read some of it back to you."

"No, no"—he dashed fine strands of hair out of his eyes—"that's not necessary. Look, I didn't mean to be offensive about the Latin and all that, but I haven't known any, uh, ladies who, uh, do what you're doing here."

I hoped that he, with his open, vulnerable expression and tangling tongue, was not the kind of lawyer who might often have to argue before judge and jury. I instinctively liked Justin Cameron. "No offense taken," I assured him, smiling. "I suppose my situation is unique. I have a college degree, Mr. Cameron, but I did not want to teach or do any of the usual things women do with such degrees. I wanted to have my own business. I judged that as an independent typist I would be providing a new and much-needed service."

"Oh, absolutely!"

I stacked the pages neatly and returned them to their folder. "I can have this typed for you by noon tomorrow. The charge will be ten cents a page."

He wrinkled his brow in a way that made me wonder just how much the starting up of his practice had impoverished him. I said, "I hope you don't think the charge is too high. After all, I have my equipment to pay for, and the office to maintain . . ."

"No, that's not what I was thinking. I was thinking that, as you just said, with the cost of setting up an office you're going to need an awful lot of customers at ten cents a page! I ought to know, having recently set up my own office. You can't have been here long or I'd have noticed. You must be new at this typewriting business."

"Yes, I am new, but I'm not worried." I wasn't, much. "I've studied the market, and I know the customers will come."

"Umm." He got up out of the chair with gangling grace. "Well, Fremont Jones, I for one plan to come back. Often."

I stood up and shook hands with him across the desk, because it seemed the thing to do, and then he took his leave.

I knew it wasn't very professional of me, but the tone of Justin Cameron's voice when he'd said he would come back often, and the look in his eyes, and the touch of his hand, made me feel warm all the way down to my toes.

I got to work right away on Mr. Cameron's letter—I could not allow myself to begin thinking of him as Justin—and proceeded to the brief. It was interesting, and my heart skipped a beat as I realized that he would indeed have to present this in court. He was filing suit on behalf of a fishmonger who believed he'd been cheated out of his traditional vending place on the wharf. I gathered, from the way the legal argument was proceeding, that the practice of law in San Francisco was a complex affair. Due no doubt to the fact that until recent decades this city had been a lawless place, Justin—that is, Mr. Cameron—was having a hard go at establishing precedents.

I became engrossed. When daylight faded I lit the lamp and one of the gaslights on the wall, and kept on with my work. The noise of my typewriter prevented my noticing how quiet the building had become.

The bell on the door jingled—a small sound but so unexpected that I jumped.

The man who stood in the doorway was dressed in black. The open door yawned on more blackness behind him, so that his face and hands stood out starkly white by contrast. He had a face like a cadaver: sunken cheeks, pale popping eyes, and long, unkempt hair as black as his clothing.

I wheeled to the desk and clasped my suddenly trembling hands firmly out of sight in my lap. I made a mental note not to stay in the office alone after dark in the future. But my voice was firm as I asked, "May I help you?"

"Yes, yes!" he cried, coming into the room in a rush. He left the door open, which gave me a certain amount of courage. "I have a manuscript"—he pulled out from under his arm a battered portfolio that once had also been black but was now so worn that it had a greenish tinge—"that I want to have typed. You do that, don't you? I was passing, and I saw the lights, and the sign, and I thought, Oh, this is a godsend. A godsend!"

I might be a godsend, but he looked as if he'd been sent from the other place. I wondered if he ever went out in the daylight, or whether at the touch of the sun's rays he might burst into flame. Half-seriously I speculated whether he would or would not cast a reflection in a mirror. Mr. Bram Stoker would have loved this man, but I didn't think I could, not without several necklaces of garlic around my neck and at least one cross in my pocket. Nevertheless I said, "I was working late. Have a seat, Mr. ah—?"

"Partridge. Edgar Allan Partridge." He scrambled over to the chair and perched his stick-like body on its edge. He clutched the thick portfolio tightly to his chest; his bony wrists looked too thin to hold such a burden. "These are my stories. I write in the style of my chosen namesake, Mr. Poe. You know, Edgar Allan Poe. I'm told I bear him a physical resemblance, as well."

"Ah!" I said, enlightened. Mr. Partridge had an unusual voice, thin and grainy yet slightly musical.

"I used to be a newspaper reporter. I'll tell you a secret." He stretched his scrawny neck toward me and I felt obliged to bend to him. He whispered, "My stories are better than Mr. Poe's, because mine are true!"

"Is that so?" I asked, pulling back.

"Yes indeed, yes indeed!" The popping eyes rolled. "That's why they're after me, you see, and I have to hide my stories from them. So I thought, when I saw your sign, that I could hide my work by giving it to you to type. Here, you'll do it, won't you?" Mr. Partridge dropped the portfolio on my desk with a thump.

Then an expression of absolute horror came over his emaciated face as he turned his head toward the black rectangle of the open door.

2.

Quoth the Raven . . .

"THE DOOR," Edgar Allan Partridge shrieked, "the door is open! What if they followed me?"

Merciful heavens, I thought, the man is paranoid! On the other hand, paranoia is an extremely contagious condition, and I was in danger of catching it. Paradoxically, given my initial reaction, I was not sorry to see him dash across the room and close the door. Now he stood, panting, leaning his back against it, looking the perfect picture of insane panic.

"The key," he said, "you must have the key! We must lock ourselves in!"

While observing his remarkable consistency of syntax, I tried to keep my senses. I said firmly, "On no account will I lock myself in a room with a man I have only just met. Use your head, sir! If someone had followed you and seen you come up to my office, he would have had more than sufficient time by now to join us. I suggest you return to your chair and try to calm yourself."

He rolled his eyes a few more times, took out a crumpled handkerchief, and mopped his face. Finally, he resumed his seat. In the meanwhile, I'd opened the portfolio and removed a great many loose pages, closely written in a small but fine hand. A significant amount of work—I thought I had best find out how serious he was about my typing it, and how well able to pay.

"Let us go about this in a more professional way," I suggested.

"Yes, yes," he nodded. "Do you have a safe?"

11

The question took me aback. I blinked. "A safe?"

"You know, to lock up the manuscript when you aren't working on it. For safekeeping. I have no other copy."

"I do not have a safe. But this drawer"—I pulled out a deep bottom drawer in the desk, currently empty—"has a lock. Will that be sufficient?"

Edgar Allan Partridge leaned over and peered into the empty drawer, nearly falling off his chair in the process. "I suppose it will have to do."

"Very well. Now, you said that your manuscript is stories, so I presume you would like it typewritten for submission to a publisher? You do wish to publish your stories, Mr. Partridge?"

"Yes, I do. The sooner the better." He nodded vigorously, stringy black hair flopping about his head. "That is, if I live long enough." He looked nervously over his shoulder at the closed door.

Clearly, the poor man really believed that someone was after him and intended to do him harm. However, I had scanned some of his pages as we talked, and what he had here was fiction of the flowery, fantastical, gothic variety. I couldn't believe anyone would kill for that!

I assumed a brisk manner. "Your manuscript looks to be several hundred—"

He leapt in to clarify, "Three separate stories totaling three hundred and twenty-three pages, to be exact."

"Thank you, three hundred and twenty-three pages of manuscript. My charge is ten cents per typewritten page. Is the charge acceptable?"

"No problem, no problem. Money is no object." Mr. Partridge was looking over his shoulder again.

"I can have it done in, say"—being new to this, I made a wild guess—"a month. Have you a card, sir, with an address where I may contact you, or are you perhaps on the telephone?"

Edgar Allan Partridge stood up, still casting nervous glances at the door while he searched one pocket after another of his ill-fitting black suit. I assumed he was looking for his calling cards, but instead he was emptying his pockets of money. "I'll pay in advance," he declared. "Here, take this. And this, and this. Oh, here's another." He flung bill after rumpled bill onto my desk without looking to ascertain their denomination.

"Really, Mr. Partridge, I—"

"I have to go. Can't stay any longer. Have to run!"

"Come back!" I insisted, bolting to my feet. "You haven't told me how to get in touch with you!"

"You type it, that's all," he called from the doorway, "Miss, Miss—"

"Jones. Fremont Jones. But—"

Edgar Allan Partridge, white hands flapping, thin body dancing with anxiety, sent a hoarse stage whisper through the air to me: "Take care of my true stories, Miss Jones. I'll come back in a month." And off he ran.

"Well!" I exclaimed, going weak in the knees. I did not like the look of that door open upon the blackness of the unlit corridor, nor the sudden cold dampness of my palms.

I forced myself to be sensible; I must avoid catching his paranoia. The first order of business was to close that open door. When I had done it, I glanced at the small gold watch—a twenty-first birthday gift from my father—pinned to my blouse. The time was seven-thirty, and if I did not want a long walk back to my flat, all of it uphill (San Francisco had given me a new appreciation of uphillness), I had best be going while the cable cars still ran.

I went back to my desk and looked at the several green wads scattered about. I felt an odd reluctance to touch Mr. Partridge's money. Nonsense, most unbusiness-like! But still . . .

I sat down and smoothed my hair, which did not need smoothing, and my waistline where blouse was tucked into skirt, which did not need smoothing either. I disliked the uneasiness I felt. For the first time, I had encountered the underside, the dark side, of my venture into independence. Never before in my life had I needed money. But now I did. Not desperately, not yet; but enough that I could not afford to turn down any work that came my way.

With this in mind, I began to open up and smooth out the green dollar bills: a one, a ten, two fives, another one, a twenty, and a fifty. Edgar Allan Partridge had tossed ninety-two dollars on my desk, far more than I would ever need to charge for the typing of his stories. Carefully, thoughtfully, I locked both the money and the manuscript in my desk.

The electric lighting that had found its way into some of San Francisco's houses and most of its public buildings had not yet reached its streets. The streetlamps on their tall poles were gaslights—they glowed with eerie haloes in the fog that rolled in most evenings as the sun went down. I had not known about the predominance and pervasiveness of San Francisco's fog; in fact, I had known almost nothing about this city before so precipitously choosing it as my new home. I was having to learn everything the way a child learns, through a series of first-time experiences that were usually wonderful. But not always.

Tonight, being out alone after dark in a city I had not yet learned to trust, was not so wonderful. Tonight's lesson was about darkness and fog, how the thick white mist obscures and distorts sight, yet carries sound. I stood on the corner, waiting for the cable car that would carry me up Van Ness to Vallejo Street where I lived, and felt all my senses excruciatingly alert. I could hear approaching footsteps long before I was able to see the dark shapes of the people who produced them. I heard rumbles and thumps of traffic, yet no vehicles passed; and from who could tell how far off came the ear-piercing whinny of a startled horse. Much closer, a door slammed open and let out the sound of voices raised in anger before it slammed closed again.

My winter coat was too heavy for March in San Francisco, yet I felt cold and clammy, as if the fog had made its way beneath the fabric and crept along my skin. I shivered.

The cable car came, and this bit of familiarity gave me back a sense of balance and perspective. I climbed aboard, dropped my fare into the box, and commenced to enjoy the ride as much as always.

The flat I had rented comprised the third floor of a narrow side-hall type Victorian house on Vallejo Street. When I left the cable car I still had a steep climb of two blocks, plus part of a third, for the house, like most of San Francisco, was on a hill. Since I had been in town only two weeks, I had not gotten the names of all the hills straight yet, but I believed mine was called Russian Hill. The view from the very top (my curiosity had compelled me to climb it even before I had finished my unpacking) was spectacular. I would have liked to live on the top of Russian Hill, or Nob Hill, where I might look out across the Bay with its sometimes blue, sometimes gray waters, many boats, and few islands. Already I could identify Alcatraz, which was small and rocky and had a beacon tower; and Angel Island, which was larger and less rocky; and Yerba Buena, largest of all, with trees and houses.

But it was not likely that I would ever live on top of one of San Francisco's hills, because that was where the mansions were. Huge houses, ornate and elaborate in their architecture. With my Boston-bred eyes, used to plain brick exteriors of Federal Style buildings, I did not know quite what to make of these mansions' show of wealth. I wondered who had built them, who lived in them, what kind of people they were, what went on behind those opulent facades.

The owner of the considerably more modest house in which I dwelled was Mrs. O'Leary, and when I had climbed the steps and unlocked the front door, she was waiting for me.

"Out late, ain't cha, Fremont?" she said. Mrs. O. was long on heart and short on grammar. The first time I'd told her my name she'd had me repeat it, then said, "Ain't that a hoot!" and she'd called me Fremont ever since. She was a widow, like Augusta, but there the likeness ended. Thank goodness!

"Yes," I agreed. "I got my first customers today and lost track of the time."

"Payin' customers already, that's good, ain't it?" she beamed, and I assured her it was. I liked Mrs. O'Leary and did not mind her interest in me. She wasn't intrusive, just genuinely warm and friendly. She had a rosy, square Irish face and an ample body, and was, I guessed, in her fifties. Her late husband had been a policeman.

She patted my arm and said, "Well, I won't keep ya. I'm just glad to see ya home safe and sound. You bein' so new here and all, I was just a mite worried when I didn't hear ya come in the usual time. *Himself*, now, God only knows when he might show up. Not that I'm no nosy parker, but this is still my house even if I got ta rent it out, and I notice how my tenants comes and goes. Now go on, git up them stairs and fix yerself a hot drink!"

"I will." I smiled, taking the stairs lightly, as glad to be home as she apparently was to see me. Mrs. O'Leary lived on the first floor of her house. *Himself* was an older man named Archer who rented the second floor, and was either shy or standoffish; I'd met him once on the stairs and introduced myself but he'd never even looked at me, just mumbled something and scurried away. I gathered from Mrs. O. that he was hardly ever at home—a source of some consternation to her. Mr. Archer seemed an enigma.

My flat, being at the top of the house, had sloping ceilings and a lot of windows with deep sills that made fine window seats. There were four rooms, all of which opened onto a long side hall: living room, two bedrooms, kitchen with an eating area, and a small bathroom that was mostly taken up by a big claw-footed tub. The flat was sparsely furnished, but what there was, was of decent quality. The rugs, all Persian and barely worn, were especially fine; when I'd remarked on them Mrs. O. said she'd bought them "for a song" at a fire sale when one of the mansions on Nob Hill burned. She'd confided that the owner "was in over his head, if ya know what I mean," and was suspected of burning down his own house for the insurance. My landlady was a fount of local knowledge—though how much was fact and how much was gossip I had no way to ascertain.

A plus about Mrs. O'Leary's house was that it had been electrified. My father's house still depended on gas and spirit lamps, and at first the electric lighting had seemed harsh to me. But I'd quickly grown used to it, and it was now a welcome treat to have bright light at the flick of a switch. I lit the hallway right up and hung my coat on the clothes tree. Then I went into my living room; leaving it dark, I crossed to one of the windows and drew the curtains back. I could see nothing of the Bay, of course. I was on the wrong side of the hill for that, but all around me in a gauzy veil of fog lay the houses and buildings and streets of the City. San Francisco, the City by the Bay.

My heart stirred. Here on the hillside the fog was thinner, pierced by glimmering lights. I had been here for only two weeks, but I knew I loved this place. I loved being here, on my own; I felt I belonged here even more than in the city where I was born and had grown up.

From the very first I sensed in San Francisco an openness, high-spirit-edness, an appreciation and acceptance of the differences in people that welcomed and embraced me.

Yes, I was *home*.

"Oh, this is fine. Yes, superb!" said Justin Cameron the next day, reading through the pages I'd typed for him.

"I hope you win your case," I said earnestly.

"Oh, I won't," he shrugged.

"How do you know? You don't seem very concerned about it."

"I'm not. This is a stage we have to go through, that's all. There's no such thing as squatter's rights on the wharf, and these vendors have to learn that. After a few cases like this one, they'll all realize they have to pay rent for their spots, and that will be that. Precedent established. We'll move on to something else."

"But the poor man!"

"Cisneros, the fishmonger? I won't charge him much, and the rent will be reasonable. He'll keep his spot and he'll be fine. Speaking of charges . . . ten cents a page, right?"

I nodded, and Justin Cameron counted. I'd done nine pages for him, and he handed me a dollar. He grinned and said, "Keep the change."

"No, thank you," I demurred, reaching into the middle drawer of my desk and extracting a dime from my change purse, "it would mess up my bookkeeping."

"No, it wouldn't. All you have to do is add a page for bonuses. Ten cents isn't much of a bonus, but it's a start."

"Somebody, sometime must have taught you that you don't tip the owner of a business, Mr. Cameron," I said, holding out the coin. "Will you please accept your change?"

He stepped right up to the desk and held out his hand with the palm up. "I wish you'd call me Justin," he entreated.

I placed his dime in his hand while my heart gave a little skip. I admitted to myself I was pleased. "All right. Justin. And you may call me Fremont."

"That's such a weird name for a girl. A lady."

"A woman," I said, looking up at him. He looked as if he might have taken some pains with his appearance today, in a dark blue suit and lighter blue tie, his fine blond hair combed neatly back from a high, rather noble forehead. I had taken some pains of my own, having chosen to wear a green dress with white collar and cuffs, whose predominant color I knew enhanced my eyes.

"Woman," said Justin in a tone of voice that managed to suggest all the mystery of the difference between the two sexes, as if he'd just discovered it.

In the small silence that fell between us I cast down my eyes, but not before I noticed that his fair skin had turned a faint shade of pink. He was embarrassed, which I found endearing.

Justin stepped back from the desk, shoved the manila folder with the work I'd typed under his right arm, took out a pocket watch, and checked the time. "It's near the noon hour," he announced. "I'd like to invite you to have lunch with me, Fremont."

I wanted to have lunch with him, in fact, when I'd dressed that morning I'd been hoping he might ask me to do something of the sort. But now all the lessons I'd learned growing up, about proper introductions and knowing people's backgrounds and things like that, suddenly clamored inside my head. I heard myself say, "No, thank you. I can't today."

"Oh, come on. I see you have a lot of work to do," he gestured at the pile of Mr. Partridge's manuscript pages beside my typewriter, "but you have to take a break sometime!"

"Perhaps we could do it another day," I said firmly, turning away and beginning to gather up those manuscript pages so that I could lock them away in the bottom drawer. "I have to go shopping."

"Great. Mind if I tag along?"

I had to smile at his persistence. "I don't think you'd be very interested." I had a sudden burst of inspiration: "I'm going to buy a coat. The one I have isn't right for this climate."

"I *knew* you were new in town! But I've lived here for years. Well, not here but across the Bay, in Berkeley. My dad's a professor at the

University. I go shopping with my mom all the time. Really. The City of Paris—that's a department store—that's where you want to go. And then, when you've got your coat we can eat, there's a great little restaurant right in the store. Come on, what do you say?"

I laughed; I had to. He'd given himself enough of an introduction to satisfy the clamorous voice of decorum inside my head, and besides, he was almost irresistible. "All right. I guess I could use a guide."

Justin was a good guide, and good company, and he must have told the truth about accompanying his mother on shopping trips because he kept up a running commentary on all the stores we passed.

I liked best the flower vendors who sold their colorful wares from carts on the street corners. The streets themselves were noisy and crowded with horse-drawn vehicles of every size and description, with here and there an occasional one of the new automobiles. Justin was fascinated by them, but I thought them ungainly and ugly, certainly without the personality of a horse, or even a cable car—and said so. He replied that the automobile was just as much the coming thing as the typewriter. I found it hard to argue with that, being so devoted to my own machine. However, while Justin nattered on about the virtues of the automobile, I was thinking that the electric streetcars (which in Boston we called trolleys) were quite modern enough for me.

There was so much to see that I almost forgot the purpose of our trip downtown. But Justin guided me to the City of Paris where I bought not a coat, but a cape with a hood, in a color the saleswoman called "aubergine." It was precisely the shade of an eggplant. She assured me that it could be worn year-round in San Francisco, where the temperature varied little from one season to the next. I decided to wear the cape immediately, and had her put my too-heavy coat in a box.

Being so newly conscious of money, I said over lunch, "I have a feeling that neither you nor I can really afford this, Justin."

He stopped with fork midway to mouth. "You have a refreshingly different attitude, Fremont."

I felt my cheeks turn pink. Now I was the one who had embarrassed myself. "I spoke without thinking. I'm sorry, I—"

19

"Never mind. I didn't mean that as a criticism. In fact, you're right—but we're friends, aren't we? We'll work things out. Now, tell me about your unusual name."

I told him; in fact, I told him almost everything, and all the while I thought how kind he was, how easy to be with, and how glad I was to have made a friend like Justin Cameron.

Other customers came to my office that afternoon, one attracted by the handbill in the bookstore and another by the same advertisement I had posted in the Public Library. Their jobs were small so I got right to them. It was around four o'clock before I again unlocked the drawer and removed Mr. Partridge's manuscript.

He had given no overall title to his collection—a fact I would have to remember to mention to him when he came to pick up the work. I could easily do a title page while he waited. The first story was called "The Man in the Glass Tower." I found the place where I'd left off typing that morning, and went on from there.

The book from which I'd learned the operation of the typewriter had advised that one not actually read as one typed, but concentrate on reproducing the individual letters and spaces without regard to their meaning. This method was supposed to improve one's speed while reducing the number of typographical errors. I had found this to be true and so I tried to adhere to it in spite of the fact that it had been almost impossible for me, an addicted reader, at first; that was why I practiced by typing novels while not allowing myself to read them. Therefore I was some ten pages into "The Man in the Glass Tower" before I realized, with growing unease, what the story was about.

Subliminally, I had known. My hands were so wet with perspiration that my fingers slipped on the keys. The very air of my office seemed to have taken on the story's atmosphere of tense foreboding. I felt a pricking along my spine, as if someone were there behind, someone unwanted, looking at me.

"Foolish!" I said aloud, but my voice did not sound like my own, which made it worse. I turned around slowly, and looked behind me. I turned full circle, searching the room. Of course there was no one.

No person, but a small dark shape that must have been manufactured by my feverish imagination. It looked like a raven, and it said *Nevermore*.

Mr. Partridge, emulating the style and subject matter of Edgar Allan Poe, wrote convincingly of a man who was losing his mind.

3.

Curiouser and Curiouser

LOOKING AT THE page I was typing, I became quite disgusted with myself—which had the immediate healthy effect of banishing my fear *and* the imaginary raven. The page was full of mistakes, proof that I had, without meaning to, slipped into reading rather than pure typing. There was a cure for this: I would read the story through first, and then return to typing it. I pulled the page out of the typewriter with a satisfying whoosh! and wheeled to the desk with the manuscript pages in hand.

It occurred to me then that I had never asked or looked for a sign to see what time the bookstore downstairs closed. By my pendant watch it was nearly five o'clock. I didn't particularly want to be alone in the building as I'd been the night before, but I really did want to know what was going to happen to the poor man in the glass tower. Surely they would stay open until six, to have the business of people on their way home from work? I didn't dare take Mr. Partridge's precious manuscript home with me . . . I decided to read on.

Mr. Partridge was not quite as skilled a writer as his namesake, the other Edgar Allan, but he had a way with words. The man of the story's title was not given a name, he was simply called "the Man," which had the curious effect of making him a universal figure, like Everyman . . . or woman. I was having no trouble putting myself in his shoes! The glass tower of the title was made of glass only at the top; it seemed to be a lighthouse—but no ordinary lighthouse.

Suddenly I remembered Mr. Partridge's insistence that his stories were true. The unpleasant cold pricking along my spine came again. Surely they were true only in his mind, in much the same way that the raven had briefly materialized out of mine? True or not, the Man's tower was by the sea, on the Point of the Wolf. I wasn't yet familiar enough with the geography and place names of this area to know if there was such a place or not. I began at the beginning and read, fascinated, from "The Man in the Glass Tower," page 5:

> The great lens, like a highly polished and magical prism, ate light. All day it ate and ate, gobbling up the sun; on cloudy days, and when the fog came in a thick blanket to cover everything, the Man had to feed it. Up hundreds of winding steps, up and up and up he went, carrying lamps. When he had given it all the kerosene lamps from his miserable living quarters below, the Lens demanded more. The Man knew from its pulsing and throbbing and pulling at his mind that the Lens was still hungry. He was very tired; the muscles of his legs quivered, his knees ached, there were blisters on his feet from all the climbing. But if he did not give the Lens what it wanted, he feared it would eat his soul.
>
> So down he went, in search of matches and candles, and back up again. And again, and again. And all the while he prayed for the sun to come out, so that the Lens would be satisfied and let him rest for a while in peace.

That poor man! I read on, turning pages in haste.

Page 8:

> The Man bought every lamp he could obtain. He spent all his money on lamps and oil, and went without food. He became thin as a skeleton, and let his hair grow, and his nails, so that more and more he resembled a thing from the grave. Now he had to watch the Lens all the time, even on sunny days. He would sit among the many lamps (he no longer took them away when the sun shone, for he would only have to bring them back again) with his bony arms wrapped around his scrawny legs, rocking back and forth, and watch the Lens eat the sun.
>
> Once the Man had liked the Lens, been proud to be its keeper.

Then he had enjoyed polishing its many mirrored facets, loved to look upon its shining face. Now he dreaded to touch it, afraid of being pulled inside by all that power, afraid that the Lens might snatch what little the Man had left of himself to call his own. But when the Lens demanded, the man would get out his cloth, and rub, and rub, and rub . . .

Page 12:

He could leave the Lens at night, when it turned in awesome, brilliant majesty, throwing out the light it had eaten by day. The Man could rest then. He would go and sit upon the rocks, looking down at the sea. Sometimes he thought of throwing himself down from the rocks and drowning in the sea. But he could not, for who would feed the Lens then? Who could deal with its terrible anger? Surely as soon as his soul left the Man's miserable body, the Lens would throw out its awful, magical beam and gobble the Man's soul for all eternity!

The night came when a wonderful thing happened. The Man was sitting on his rocks above the sea, and a full moon rode like a great white ship across the black sky. The moon was so bright that even the Lens's sweeping light could not rival it. The Man thought, if I give the moon to the Lens, then it will leave me alone.

The Man stood upon the Point of the Wolf and yearned upward toward the moon, stretching out his arms. With his head back he stared at that glowing white orb, he opened his mouth and began to howl . . .

I knew then what would happen, of course: The Man was going to turn into a wolf. A werewolf. Not a very original idea, but I was hooked. I read on, and Mr. Partridge surprised me. Not only did he accomplish the Man's transformation in a particularly chilling way, but the Man did not meet the tragic end I had supposed he would. Instead, in the madness of his wolf-self he believed that by obtaining a beautiful woman he was obtaining the full moon. And by killing her in the presence of the Lens, he was giving the moon to the Lens.

Everything turned out well for the Man: he regained a twisted type of sanity, in which he was convinced that as long as he continued to give the full moon to the Lens every month, the Lens's great hunger for light would be satisfied. He no longer feared the Lens. He started eating again, put on weight, cut his hair and his nails, and became so handsome that he had no trouble attracting women. He was no longer lonely, except that every month or so he would have to make a new woman-friend.

Whew! I thought as I stacked the pages neatly, that was quite a story. And it left a lingering after-effect, like an odd taste in the mouth. I wasn't sorry that it was high time for me to go home.

Rather than restore Mr. Partridge's manuscript to the disreputable-looking (and feeling) black portfolio, I put it in a clean file folder and placed it in the deep drawer, where it fit perfectly. Of course! I thought, a little embarrassed by my lack of office experience, it *was* a file drawer. Thus Edgar Allan Partridge's manuscript became the first of my files.

Something continued to bother me, though. Something about the story, about the Man, something unfinished . . . As I swung off the cable car at Vallejo Street, I realized what it was: Mr. Partridge had left a loose end hanging. He had never said what the Man did with all those women's dead bodies!

I had not seen much of Justin for about a week. We had developed a habit (well, I had developed it; he might very well have been doing it all along) of bringing our lunches from home and eating them in each other's company at the noon hour. We did this out of doors when the weather was fine, in one of a variety of pleasant places to which he introduced me; if the weather were poor, we ate in his office or mine. Mine, usually, because it was larger. Justin's office had the virtue of being right on the street, which was good advertising, but in size and shape it resembled a long, narrow closet.

I missed his companionship, but only at noon. I had customers coming out of my ears! Justin himself gave me a good bit of work, and through him other lawyers came. Academics who frequented the bookstore downstairs soon found their way to me. A lovely, shy librarian who'd seen my handbill brought me a stack of poems to type—love poems!

Through my landlady, Mrs. O'Leary, I developed an unexpected clientele: people who either could not read or write, or could not read or write English though they could speak it, or who, like Mrs. O., just did not write a legible hand. On my first Saturday morning in the office I had typed a letter for her while she sat in a chair by my desk and told me what to say—which started it all. Most of the people she referred for similar services were older, and most were women; all were interesting characters. I liked doing their letters, but they did take a lot of time. I should have charged them a higher fee, but I did not have the heart. Ten cents a page probably represented a sacrifice for most of these folks.

I thought Justin was probably in court, which was why I hadn't seen him for so long. He specialized in business law, and business was booming in San Francisco. He wouldn't be an almost-penniless young lawyer for long!

Nor was I worried anymore about money; what I worried about was time. Nearly three weeks had whizzed by and I hadn't seen hide nor hair of Mr. Partridge—which was just as well, because I hadn't finished his manuscript. I would be hard-pressed to do so in the month I'd specified. I assumed he would make his strange cadaverous appearance on a month to the very day.

I had typed the second story; it was a straightforward ghost tale concerning a Spanish woman named Elena who haunted the Mission Dolores. Supposedly she had loved a priest there and he had loved her—physically, that is, perhaps spiritually too (the story didn't say, although it said a lot about the physical part; I got the idea that this priest was rather a randy type), and out of guilt and grief the woman had hung herself in the bell tower. The priest found the body and, feeling some guilt of his own, secretly buried it in consecrated ground, in the Mission garden. Thereafter, he went off his head (Mr. Partridge was at his most convincing in descriptions of men off their heads) and became possessed by the Devil.

There were no untidy ends in this story: The possessed priest committed suicide by throwing himself out of the bell tower onto the pavement below. Elena's ghost still walks the Mission garden, and climbs the steps to the bell tower, and some people (or so Mr. Partridge said, if one believes that his are true stories) have seen her standing there. The priest left no ghost behind—I presumed that was because the Devil got his soul and keeps him safely locked up in Hell.

The third story was as long as many novels. I had read it, and the truth was that I kept putting off the typing of it. I went ahead with other, more recent work instead, always finding some excuse . . .

Today, a Friday, was no different. I could have worked on that third story of Mr. Partridge's for an hour before breaking for lunch, or I could even have worked on it through lunch (previous experience when pressed for time had proven that it was possible to eat a sandwich with one hand while typing with the other), but I didn't. I suddenly, absolutely, had to have a bunch of daffodils from one of the flower vendors—no, two bunches. I would take one home to Mrs. O., to cheer her up. She continued to be terribly worried about Mr. Archer, which made little sense to me. I knew the man was around, I'd heard him walking down below me, which undoubtedly meant that she could hear him even better, as he would be walking over her head. But anyway, the daffodils . . . I grabbed my aubergine cape, and was off.

In the afternoon, with two bunches of daffodils keeping fresh in a jar of water on my desk, I was able to work without interruption and so got a great deal done. As I covered my typewriter and prepared to go home, I decided that tomorrow I would work a full day. (My practice had been to close at three on Saturdays.) And, without fail, I would begin on Mr. Partridge's third story; even working the whole day I would not be able to get through it.

Involuntarily, I shuddered. I thought of the ninety-two dollars he'd paid, and of the trust he'd demonstrated by leaving the work with me in spite of his paranoia. I had a commitment to the man, there was no way around it—in spite of the fact that his third story was so strange and bloodcurdling that I wished I'd never seen—much less read—the first word!

———

28

"Mrs. O'Leary?" I called out, knocking for the second time on the closed door of her drawing room. Still she didn't come, and then I remembered: she would be at the Friday Fish Supper in the parish hall of her church where she went every week. I was disappointed. Feeling the joy of spring, I wanted to share it with someone else—hence the daffodils—and since Justin seemed to have dropped out of my life . . . I sighed. I hoped Justin's absence was only temporary. I tried not to trudge as I ascended the stairs, but the lightness was gone from my step.

From the stair's turning on the second floor I saw a figure walking down the hallway. On sudden impulse I called out, "Mr. Archer!"

He stopped and turned. "Yes?"

"Might I speak with you a moment? It's Fremont Jones, your upstairs neighbor." I stood tentatively on the landing, hoping he would not detest me for interrupting his privacy.

He approached slowly, and as he drew near I saw that he was taller than I'd thought from our one previous encounter. He said, "Good evening, Miss Jones."

"Good evening." Still carried by impulse, I held out the bunch of daffodils I'd intended for Mrs. O. "I seem to have an extra bunch of daffodils, and I thought you might like them. A touch of spring, from one neighbor to another."

"Why . . ." He looked baffled for a moment, and then he smiled. I thought I understood why this man so occupied our landlady's thoughts: he was strikingly handsome, in a rather exotic sort of way. He had close-cropped dark hair, a small mustache, and a beard neatly trimmed to a point below his chin. The beard was streaked with white, which suggested that he was older than I, but possibly younger than Mrs. O., who I now suspected had a crush on him. His eyes were light, either blue or gray, and so very dark-lashed that they could not help but be captivating. He accepted the flowers I offered, then put his heels together and made a little bow, in the European manner. "Thank you! Such a charming gesture, and so unexpected when I have been a neglectful neighbor."

"Not at all. I can tell that you are a busy man, and I don't mean to intrude. I hope you have a pleasant evening." I continued up the stairs but did not get very far.

"I should like to remedy my neglect, Miss Jones," he called after me. "Perhaps, when you've had a few moments to refresh yourself, you will come down and join me for tea. Or perhaps a glass of light sherry?"

An intriguing idea! "Yes, that would be pleasant."

"Then I shall see you shortly."

No more trudging; I skipped up the remaining steps. Hanging up my cape, I decided to change my clothes. The plain blouse and skirt that had become my self-imposed work uniform did not seem the proper thing to wear for tea—or sherry—with an enigma. Especially a handsome enigma.

I chose a dress of pale mauve wool challis, brushed out my hair and hastily coiled it on top of my head. The whole process took little more than five minutes, including the one during which I stared in the mirror and wished there were something strikingly handsome about *me*. Comparative youth and green eyes and a complete lack of enigmaticness were all I had to offer.

"You've provided your own furnishings," I remarked a few minutes later. The arrangement of Mr. Archer's rooms was different from mine. The two center rooms adjoined one another through an archway, from which he had removed the sliding door to make a single large space. It was a wholly masculine stronghold which, clearly, no hand of woman had ever touched. I felt both honored and odd.

"That is true," he agreed, "with one charming exception." His gesture indicated my daffodils on a table in front of an upholstered couch, their brave yellow trumpets nodding over the rim of a diamond-patterned drinking glass. Excessively masculine enigmas probably didn't own vases.

"So I see." I smiled, determined that he would not remain an enigma much longer.

"Will you have tea or sherry, Miss Jones?"

"Sherry," I said boldly, "and please call me Fremont."

"Ah! Yes." He turned away without offering his own first name, and went to a large cabinet of dark wood set into a wall of bookshelves. He had hundreds of books. I longed to go close enough to read their titles, but remained standing near the edge of the rug.

"Your sherry, Fremont. Sit wherever you'd like."

I chose a leather wing chair, one of a pair with a low table between them. He took the other, and the lead in conversation.

"Fremont is a famous name in California. How do you come to be so called?"

"It was my mother's maiden name. She was John Charles Fremont's second cousin."

"Which, if I am correct, makes you his third cousin. And did you know the famous man?"

"No." I shook my head. "I always wanted to meet him when I was a child, but he was something of a black sheep in the family. Too controversial. Which was precisely why I wanted to meet him."

"You must have been an unusual child." Mr. Archer smiled, giving me a little salute with his glass before he raised it to his lips and sipped.

I too sipped my sherry, which was light and crisp and went down with a pleasurable sensation. I did not say anything, I was too busy trying to figure him out. He had a slight accent, but I couldn't place it.

"But then," he continued, "you are also an unusual young woman. No one has ever given me flowers before. No one."

I blushed; I couldn't help it. But still I held my tongue. And so did he. At length I said, "Mrs. O'Leary worries about you."

He arched one dark brow. "Is that so?"

"Yes." I decided to be direct. I have often found this to be the most effective way to obtain information, despite the fact that we women are trained to approach topics sideways or by a devious, circuitous route. "How long have you lived here, Mr. Archer?"

"I've been impolite. Since you have given me the use of your name, I should give you mine. It is Michael."

"How long have you lived here, Michael?"

"Three years." His eyes glittered, as if he sensed we were beginning to play a game and he expected to enjoy it. "And why do you think it is that Mrs. O'Leary worries about me?"

"Because you are gone for long periods of time. Or perhaps it's more than that. I really don't know, and I admit I am curious."

"Ah." That seemed to be his favorite comment. His lips curved in a knowing smile—a smile that said *I know and you don't.* I thought of the Cheshire Cat, except that Michael's lips were so beautifully shaped. One might say sensual.

To my surprise, he continued, "And is your own curiosity, Fremont, about me, or about Mrs. O'Leary's interest in me?"

"Oh," I replied, enjoying this game myself, "I think I know why she's interested in you. So I am curious on my own behalf. What do you do for a living, Michael?"

He laughed, throwing back his head and showing even white teeth. When he had finished laughing, he said anticlimactically, "I am retired."

"Oh, really?"

"Yes. Really."

"My experience of retired persons is that they stay home a good deal, which does not fit your pattern. Nor, if I may say so, do you look quite the age of most retired persons I have known."

Michael Archer placed his empty sherry glass on the small table and leaned forward with his elbows on his knees. I noticed his hands, long-fingered and white, hands that had never done hard work. But then, I knew that from the quality of his furnishings and from the velvet-collared smoking jacket he had donned when I, likewise, was changing my clothes.

He said, "You have the makings of a detective, Fremont."

"I am an admirer of Mr. Sherlock Holmes," I replied.

"As am I." The expression on his face showed that he liked me, and enjoyed our repartee. "Suppose, Fremont," he continued, "that a man had worked for a number of years at a profession not of his own choosing. And then suppose he had reached a stage in his life where he no longer had to pursue that profession."

"Yes . . ." I said. This had been more fun when he did not seem to like me quite so well.

"Would he not then have time, for the first time in his life, to

32

pursue his own interests? And to pursue them in depth, and at a pace that was nobody's concern but his own?"

"Of course," I nodded. Part of me wanted to ask what those interests were, but another part said it was time to leave. Undecided, I sipped the last of my sherry.

"Perhaps you would be so good as to tell me why you think our landlady has an interest in my comings and goings."

As devoted as I was to the truth, it wouldn't do to tell him that I thought Mrs. O. had a crush. So I said, "As you probably know, her husband was a policeman. She's a good person who seems genuinely to care about the welfare of her tenants; I expect being married to a policeman has made her more aware than most people that when someone is not where he, or she, is expected to be, something may have happened to him. Or her." Which was also true, I realized as I said it.

Michael drew his dark brows together. "I didn't know that about her late husband. I've scarcely spoken to the woman. True, she would be glad enough to talk to me, but—" He dismissed Mrs. O.'s attempts at friendliness with a wave of his hand.

I put my empty glass on the table and said, "Thank you for the sherry, and for putting up with my questions."

"Don't go yet. Have another."

"No, really, I—"

"The glasses are very small, and in all fairness it is my turn with a few questions. Other than how you acquired your name, you have told me nothing of yourself."

I could not deny an appeal to fairness. So I accepted a second glass of sherry and told him about my typewriting business. I relaxed and let him charm me, which he did very well.

The next morning on my way to the office, I stopped and gave Mrs. O'Leary the daffodils I'd bought for myself, since I'd given hers to Michael Archer. Of course I didn't tell her I'd done that, but I did tell her that I'd had "tea" with him.

"Did you now?" she asked, her round blue eyes opening wide. "Well ain't that something!"

"It was very pleasant," I said, "and I really don't think you have to worry about him anymore."

"And why is that, dearie?"

"Because he's a retired gentleman. He worked for years at a profession he didn't much like, and now he pursues his own interests, which do take him away from time to time."

"Stuff and nonsense! Retired? In a pig's eye he's retired!"

"What do you mean, Mrs. O'Leary?"

She looked up the stairs and then pulled me inside her flat and shut the door. "That man's not retired. He's a spy!"

4.

Spies and Black Toads

———⊰∘∘⊱———

"A SPY?" For a moment I scarcely comprehended the word.

"Sure as you're born, that's what he is."

"Is this something you know for a fact?"

Mrs. O'Leary chewed on her lip and clasped her hands together under the flowing apron she wore around the house. She was thinking, I suppose trying to be fair. At last she said, "Well, dearie, to be honest I can't say for sure. O' course, I didn't suspect anything like that when I let him have my second floor. I thought he was just a handsome gentleman, well enough off, who wouldn't give no trouble. Quiet-like, you know, with all them books and such. But then I got to watching how he comes and goes, and the way he acts. The kind of quiet that man is ain't normal. I seen men like that when my husband the captain of police was alive, always watching their step and what they say and kind of making themselves invisible, and I says to myself: I seen this before. Cultured and refined the way he is, he ain't no common criminal, so I figure he must be a spy."

"Well for heaven's sake!"

She nodded her head and chewed on her lip some more. "That's why I keep an eye on him, I feel like it's my bounden duty."

What she had said made a certain amount of sense. "If he really is a spy, who would he be spying on? And for whom would he be doing it? The government?"

"I don't know, but I can guess. Our Mr. Archer—if that's his real name—is a Russian. Could be one of ours, could be one of theirs."

"But we're not at war or anything, and the Russians are friends of the United States."

"There's all kinds of spies, dearie. There's the diplomatic kind, and the ec-o-nomical kind, and the criminal kind, and who knows what-all other kinds."

A Russian—no wonder I hadn't been able to trace the accent; I'd never known a Russian before. Perhaps I should have been alarmed, but I found it rather exciting to think that Michael Archer might be a spy. Then I had an idea: "What if Mr. Archer really is retired, just as he said, and he only *used* to be a spy?"

She took her hands out from under her apron and scratched her head thoughtfully. "Could be. Them habits, the sneaking around and all, is hard to shake."

I found I wanted to mediate on the man's behalf, although I couldn't have said why. "Mrs. O'Leary, I have to get to work—I've fallen behind and I'll have to be in the office all day instead of just a partial day. But before I go, I think I should remind you of what Mr. Archer said to me last night: that for most of his life he'd had to work at a job he didn't really like."

"You did tell me that, didn't you, dearie? That's a right interesting bit of information. That's a new twist on Mr. Archer, Fremont, and I'll think on it. You ain't gonna worry none about what I said now, are you? Because if I thought he was really dangerous, or if I ever do, you can be sure I'd have him out of my house like a shot."

"I'm sure you would." I smiled at her earnestness. "Now I've got to go. Don't worry if I'm not back till late."

"Good-bye, dearie, and thanks for the daffy-dills. It was mighty sweet of you to think of me."

I made a sign, CLOSED TODAY, and hung it on my office door so that I would not be interrupted. Then I typed away at Mr. Partridge's third story with a vengeance. The bright sun shining through my window and my fierce concentration helped to keep the dark content of what I was typing at bay.

Wrists aching, I stopped just before sundown. I had completed about two thirds of the manuscript, which was most satisfactory. I locked both handwritten and typed copies in the file drawer, feeling much better. I had never been able to understand how procrastinators can live with themselves!

Before leaving the office, I checked back through my desk calendar. I thought I could remember—one doesn't forget the date one begins one's lifework—but I wanted to be sure. Yes, there it was: Mr. Partridge had come to me on March 13, 1905. Considering his gloomy personality, it might have been more fitting had he appeared on the fifteenth: *Beware the ides of March!* But the thirteenth it had been, and so one month would fall on the thirteenth of April, which would be this Thursday. I would have his typed manuscript ready for him, and I did not doubt for a minute that he would soon find a publisher. In these times, with Spiritualism all the rage, his creepy supernatural tales were just the kind of thing people loved to curl up with on a quiet evening and scare themselves to death.

I cast a last longing glance at the telephone as I donned my cape. I had never heard from Justin on a Saturday, but he did sometimes call, and I had halfway hoped . . . Never mind. I *was* a little lonely. I had no real friends yet in San Francisco, except for Justin, so it was only natural . . . *Never mind!* Just stop it, Fremont!

Sunday loomed rather large and empty, though; I thought I would stop in the bookstore and buy a novel to occupy my thoughts and my time. Something exciting that would keep me reading, preferably a mystery, but *not* supernatural. The idea buoyed me for about half a minute, until I found that the bookstore was closed. I made a mental note of their hours, which were posted on the door: nine to seven on the weekdays; ten to three on Saturdays; closed Sunday. I would remember that; and I would also make an effort to be friendly with the owners, a youngish couple whose name escaped me at the moment. I would never make friends with whom I could go places and do things if I didn't try.

Sunday it rained, and I was restless. In the early afternoon I decided to go to the Public Library. The streetcars did not run on Sundays but the cable cars did, so I would not have too long a walk.

San Francisco's Public Library, being considerably newer, was not as large or extensive in its holdings as the one in Boston, which had always been one of my favorite places. Nevertheless, I love a library and browsed happily among its shelves. As I was passing through the ranks of tables in the Reading Room after checking out my choices, I saw the back of a closely cropped dark head.

Yes, the head belonged to Michael Archer. He wore gold-rimmed half-spectacles for reading, which reinforced my initial impression that he was older than I, but not as old as Mrs. O'Leary. I placed him in his forties. He seemed to sense that someone was looking at him, because he turned his head and saw me. Immediately, his shapely lips curved in a smile. I nodded, and would have passed on by. I had observed that he was surrounded by books and papers, and I did not wish to interrupt his scholarly pursuit. But he rose when I neared his table, and beckoned to me.

"You have found me out," he said in the low voice that libraries require. His eyes glittered with amusement, as they had when we'd played our verbal game two nights before.

"Aha!" I whispered, "so this is where you go!"

He rubbed the sides of his beard and raised his eyebrows. "Not very mysterious, is it? At any rate, you are here too, Fremont. How nice to see you again."

I inclined my head, smiling, wondering if he really was or had been a spy.

"I see by the burden you carry," he observed, "that you are a lover of books."

"Very good, Watson," I replied. Whispering like this, I felt like a co-conspirator.

Michael Archer leaned closer. "If you will wait for me to gather up my things, I'll take you to tea. It is about that time, I believe."

So we walked in the rain, each carrying our own books, and we both got wet because neither of us had a free hand for an umbrella. It was lovely. We had tea in the Garden Court at the Fairmont Hotel, a real High Tea with dozens of delicious things to choose from—not like Augusta with her pretensions when all she had served was cucumber sandwiches. I felt terribly civilized for the first time since leaving Boston. I told Michael—forbearing to mention Mrs. O. as my source —that I had identified his faint accent as Russian. He admitted that I was correct, and told me of his family who had been in the Russian fur trade and spoke only that language at home.

I had a delightful time. It was pleasant to make our way back home together, and amusing to see the expression on our landlady's face when we came through the front door. I felt as if I had learned a great deal about Michael Archer that afternoon.

But I realized later that this was an illusion. In reality, the man had given me only the outlines and edges of his life. He had told me, for instance, that he had changed his name to reflect his American citizenship, taking Michael Archer from his first two Russian names, Mikhail Arkady. But he had not revealed his Russian surname. He had not said *where* he had lived with his parents. He had told me very little of substance at all.

Mid-morning on Monday I went down to the bookstore and reintroduced myself to its owners, Ted and Krista Sorenson. They were both tall and blond and big-boned and looked so much alike that they might have been brother and sister rather than husband and wife. I thanked them for allowing me to post my handbill, and said how many customers I had received as a result. They both nodded seriously but made no reply. At that point they had customers of their own to take care of, so I turned away to browse.

Soon I located a copy of *Collier's Weekly,* which contained the latest of Sir Arthur Conan Doyle's mysteries about Mr. Sherlock Holmes. I hid behind the magazine, turning its pages while I pondered a completely new kind of problem: How does a woman on her own, without the sheltering guidance of family, go about making friends? The Sorensons were both so taciturn that they gave none of the little social clues one might pick up on, so I had to rely on instinct. Extending an invitation to them did not feel like the right thing to do. So I contented myself with paying for the magazine and saying that I hoped we would see more of each other in the future. Ted Sorenson said, "We get the *Collier's* every week." Which of course had nothing to do with what *I* meant at all.

Perhaps, I thought as I climbed the stairs once more to my office, if I made a habit of stopping in every so often, they might extend an invitation. Or perhaps not, in which case it might be no great loss. If they were as sober and hardworking and deadly earnest (translation: without a sense of humor) as I was beginning to suspect, I would probably be uncomfortable with them anyway.

I stopped at the top of the stairs, feeling as if I'd been hit in the head with a revelation: This life change of mine was not just about having my own business and avoiding betrothal to the widow Augusta's nephew. It was, even more than that, a whole new social experience. I could *choose* whom I spent time with! I could make my own friends how and where I pleased, no longer bound by my own family's definition of who was "right," what families were "good." That kind of freedom was revolutionary, and well worth some awkwardness and loneliness, and the few mistakes I was bound to make.

Just before noon the bell on the door jingled and a possible mistake walked in.

"Hello, Justin," I said, looking up. I felt cautious. A week and a half is a long time to go without seeing or hearing from someone you were in the habit of seeing every day. Even a short-standing, as opposed to long-standing, habit.

"Happy Monday, Fremont," he said, flourishing a nosegay of violets from behind his back.

I felt absolutely perverse. I love violets, but I didn't take them, nor did I refuse them. I stayed at my typewriter and asked, "Are we celebrating Mondays now?"

"Sure. Why not?" Seeing that I made no move to accept the nosegay, he laid it carefully on my desk, straightening out its two purple streamers in my direction. "I got these from your favorite vendor. You don't even have to put them in water, they're in a little glass vial but you can't see it, it's all wrapped up in green tape."

"Thank you." I gave in enough to wheel over to the desk. This man was hard to resist; his face was as bright and innocent as a puppy's. I touched one of the ribbons and said, "I haven't seen you in a long time."

"I know. I was in court for a week, and before that I was getting ready. I'm taking you out to lunch, Fremont, to any restaurant you choose. I'm flush, I won a case!"

"Congratulations," I said sincerely. But I wasn't quite through being perverse. "I can't have lunch with you, though."

"You can't? Why?" His face, which seemed such a perfect mirror of his emotions, fell.

"Because I brought my lunch, and I don't want it to go to waste. If you'd like to ask me to lunch later in the week—"

"My heart's set on today. You can feed your sack lunch to the pigeons, Fremont. We have to celebrate! Not only did I win the case, I got a new client out of it. This is it, now; I'm on my way!"

How could I say no after that? I did not feed my lunch to the pigeons because I doubted they would like dill pickles and egg salad sandwiches, but I did carry the nosegay of violets, and the day *was* beautiful, so warm I did not even need my cape. I asked Justin to choose the restaurant and he took me to a place that practically fell into the Bay from its perch on the side of Telegraph Hill. We came and went by horse-drawn cab—an extravagance that I myself had indulged in only once before, upon my arrival, when I'd had bags and a trunk to transport. I forgot all about perversity, and rejoiced with him over his new client, and winning his case, and being "on his way."

We celebrated longer than either of us had intended, and it was after two when I again climbed the stairs to my office. I'd told Justin not to be silly, to let the cab take him on up the street; he most certainly did not need to accompany me to my office door!

FREMONT JONES, TYPEWRITING SERVICES. If the day ever came when I was tired of seeing that sign, I should quit. I smiled; I did not think such a thing could ever happen. I unlocked the door, the bell jingled, I went inside. And stepped on a large, cream-colored envelope that had been shoved under the door in my absence.

"Oh, dear," I murmured, bending down to pick it up. I had missed a customer. I supposed I might miss other customers whenever I left the office, but I felt a pang, anyway. The envelope was so thick, and of such fine quality paper, that I could not open it without a letter opener. I proceeded to the desk, put down my nosegay, and took up the instrument.

Inside the envelope was a brief note:

41

My dear Miss Jones, Circumstances have conspired against me so that I will be unable to come to your establishment at the appointed time. I shall endeavor to appear at the earliest opportunity thereafter which may present itself to me. I entreat you to guard well the matter left in your care.
Yr. Obt. Svt., E.A.P.

E.A.P. Edgar Allan Partridge, no doubt. The note sounded like him: "Circumstances have conspired against me . . ." And yet, and yet . . . Something was wrong. At first I could not think what it was. I sat at my desk and tried to assess my own inner processes, which were certainly going awry. I should have been glad of the extra time to work on his manuscript, yet I was not. What was it? I felt the way one feels as a child when playing that game, Heavy, Heavy Hangs Over Thy Head, in which one must either correctly guess the object or have it dropped upon the noggin. What was it?

I read the note through again. Perhaps it was the charge in the last sentence: "Guard well the matter left in your care." But that was nothing new, just typical Partridge paranoia, no different from writing that circumstances conspired against him.

I sighed. Damn the man anyway! Edgar Allan Partridge was nothing but a passel of trouble! I closed my eyes and rubbed my temples and forced my insides to calm down. Yes, he was a passel of trouble; yes, he was disturbed, but was he not to be pitied rather than blamed for that? He was also talented, as his stories proved—not a great talent, but there are not many great talents in the world. I myself could not have written the first page of "The Man in the Glass Tower." And if that third story, which was by far the best, were as he claimed *true . . .*

I unlocked and opened the file drawer and took out my typed copy. It was then, in a flash, that I realized what had bothered me so much about the note: the handwriting! I knew Mr. Partridge's script so well, I had transcribed so many pages of it . . . !

Hastily I got out the handwritten manuscript and compared the note to the first page. I must not overreact, even though that was difficult where Partridge, the world's champion overreactor, was concerned. His usual hand was small, neat, and extremely legible. Line after line, page after page, lay so straight and even upon the paper that he might have used a ruler. In the note, the hand was large, almost scrawling, and all on a downward slope. Squinting in concentration, I endeavored to make a letter-by-letter comparison. I wished I had a magnifying glass. But even without one the comparison was revealing.

I concluded that Mr. Partridge *had* written the note, but either in extreme haste or in some kind of emotional or physical distress.

Drugs, I thought. Yes, that had to be it, he must take drugs. Hashish or opium or cocaine. What did I know about the effects of these drugs? Not very much. The great detective Mr. Holmes (it was hard not to think of him as a real person) took cocaine, one presumed because it sharpened the mental processes. Hashish was said to be relaxing, and opium to induce visions or vivid, fantastical dreams . . .

I reined in my mind, which has a way of going off on various tangents, and tried to think sensibly. Perhaps Mr. Partridge was a drug addict, which would explain why he behaved so peculiarly, and why he could write a note that looked the way this one did. No doubt the circumstances that conspired against him were not sinister in the least; it could be something so simple as his mother (surely even he would have a mother?) requiring him to accompany her on holiday. Or he had a toothache and the dentist could only see him on Thursday. It would no doubt prove to be something of that sort.

On my part, I would surely feel much better about everything if I kept to my original schedule and had all Mr. Partridge's typing completed by Thursday morning, as I'd intended before getting the blasted note! With that in mind, I scrolled a pristine sheet of paper into the typewriter, located the place where I'd left off in the manuscript, and began to type.

My fingers slowed in their dance above the keys, the rhythm faltered. I couldn't help it, I was reading again. I didn't want that. I took a break, got up from the typewriter, went to the window, and looked out at the street. There were people on the sidewalks, and carts and carriages and horses passing. My eyes saw them but my mind was with the boy in that third story.

The third story was called "Damned to Darkness." More than anything else, it was a kind of black fairy tale. It had all the elements of the sinister, darker variety of those tales that are supposed to be for children. But this one rang true. It was written with a passion that felt horribly real. In essence, the basic story line was almost trite: A child is raised to maturity in a huge, forbidding and foreboding house, kept a virtual prisoner there by a witch of a mother, tortured in mind rather than body. The witch-mother is a very powerful figure, larger than life —which in the early part of the story seems to be because we are always seeing her through the small boy's eyes. Yet the older the narrator gets, the more he understands, the more awful and powerful she becomes.

I forced myself back to the typewriter. Gritting my teeth, I began slowly, resigned to the certainty that I would now read as I typed. From "Damned to Darkness," page 102:

> In my thirteenth year I devised a plan, in the hope that Mother would no longer confine me to the Black Room. I went to her and said, "Mother, I know that you are a Great Sorceress, skilled in the Black Arts." I felt ridiculous saying this, because she was sitting in the drawing room having her tea at the time. Nevertheless, as it had been some months since she had last confined me—although of course I was still not allowed to leave the house—and therefore I knew that she would soon confine me again, I felt I must act. If I made myself her ally and her pupil, then might she not love me at long last? Or at least might she no longer subject me to the horrors of the Black Room, of which I had no doubt she was the author?
>
> Mother said, "And how do you know this, Peregrine?"
>
> I clasped my hands behind my back to keep them still, standing in the pose that one stands in for bravely facing dangers, as I had been taught by her servants, with the legs braced apart. I said, "In my dreams I have seen you conjure."
>
> She laughed, a wild shrill sound such as I imagine banshees might make when amused, throwing back her head so that I could see

her lovely teeth like so many pearls and the soft pinkness of her tongue. She left the tea table and came near to where I was standing, bent down and said, "And what, dear boy, did I conjure in your dreams?"

My knees began to tremble; I locked them to hold them fast. Beads of moisture gathered on my forehead and I feign would wipe them away, but I kept my hands clasped behind my back because I knew I must keep the pose. I said, "First, you made the wind come, and it billowed the curtains all out."

Mother turned her head toward the window and raised her chin so that I saw the long, swan-like line of her throat. She looked at me from the corner of her dark eye, and asked, "Like this?" And with that she raised her arm, in a slow, majestic sweep, murmuring an incantation whose words I could not understand. I heard the sound of the wind rising, and the curtains began to billow out exactly as they had in my dream.

All the tiny hairs upon my body stood on end. I said, "Yes."

"And what else did I do, Perry dear?"

I made a sound that was a squeak but then I found my voice, "You made a fire to flame up in the fireplace, where there had been no fire before."

Mother turned in a half circle, gracefully but quickly, her slender body in its red dress seeming to leave a scarlet arc in the air as she moved. As she faced the empty fireplace—it was summer, there were not even logs in it—she swept both arms up, her fingers spread wide apart and hooking downward like claws. She uttered a sharp command from deep in her throat that was no word I had ever heard, and flames leapt up in the empty fireplace. She looked at me over her shoulder, saying, "Like this?"

"Yes, Mother," I replied, blinking, the moisture now pouring down my face like a river. Surely I was not crying, surely the moisture was not tears!

She half-turned back to me. "And then, Peregrine, did I do something else?"

"Y-yes, Mother. Then you conjured a small black toad, all slick and wet and glistening, with red eyes, from out the fire."

"What a marvelous dream you had, my son," she said kindly, coming to me and caressing my face.

I began to relax. She will not do it, I thought, she will not bring the horrible toad.

But Mother's hand left its stroking of my neck beneath my chin, and she reached out her arm toward the fireplace. Her fingers curled in a beckoning gesture, and she began to hum. She hummed a song as her fingers moved, conjuring, calling, and from out the fire came the small black toad, horribly hopping, slick and wet and glistening, with eyes that were more red than the flames of the fire, as red as my mother's dress.

Mother bent down and scooped up the toad. She brought it to me and held it in front of my face. She said, "Perry, open your mouth . . ."

5.

Shaking the Foundations

—◦◦◦—

ON MAY DAY I experienced my first earthquake. It was rather startling, but not nearly so frightening as one's unfettered imagination would lead one to believe.

The event occurred at twenty-five minutes after seven o'clock in the morning. I had just arisen from a sound night's sleep, and as I am not one of those persons who spring cheerily out of bed, instantly wide awake, I was not quite sure at first what was happening. In fact, I was not sure that anything untoward was happening at all; I thought I had merely swayed on my feet. But then there was a definite jolt, which caused me to sit down hard upon the bed, and as I sat there I felt the house sway. The electric light in its chandelier swung from side to side, like a pendulum; the mirror on the wall went askew; windows rattled in their frames.

Before I had time to become concerned, it was all over. Far from being alarmed, I was excited to realize that I had experienced one of San Francisco's earthquakes. Why, an earthquake is no big thing, I thought. (Of course, by this time the following year I would know how wrong I had been!)

I could not resist stopping to chat about the excitement with Mrs. O'Leary on my way out to work. To my surprise, Michael Archer was already there. The pocket door that led into Mrs. O.'s parlor was open, and they stood talking on that very subject.

"Come in, Fremont," my landlady called, motioning to me, "we was just talking about earthquakes."

"Good morning," said Michael as I entered. "I hope you were not frightened by the experience."

"On the contrary," I said, "I found it interesting."

"You don't have anything like our quakes where you come from," said Mrs. O'Leary, "or so I'm thinking."

"If there has ever been an earthquake in Boston I haven't heard of it. I trust there was no damage to the house?"

"A number of my books fell off the shelves—" Michael began, and Mrs. O. interrupted.

"Made a big racket, they did, right over my head!"

"But that was the worst of it," he continued. "I thought I had best come down and let our landlady know that it must have sounded worse than it was. I am cognizant of my floors being adjacent to her ceilings."

I'm sure you are, I thought, quite enjoying this conversation. I made a contribution: "I hadn't heard very much about San Francisco before coming here, but I had heard about the earthquakes. Now that I've been through one, I can't see what all the fuss is about."

"Oh," said Mrs. O., clasping her hands under her apron and rocking back on her heels—she too was enjoying the talk, "this was just a little bump and shake. Now I remember back in '85— Was you here then, Mr. Archer?"

"I don't believe so," he said evasively.

Mrs. O'Leary didn't notice his evasiveness; she directed herself to me. "In '85 we had us a doozie. A big roller, it was, you could look out the windas and see all them hills just a-rollin' up and down. But even that didn't do no damage to speak of. Made a crack in that wall over there"—she pointed—"but we fixed it and papered over it, and that was that."

Michael Archer rubbed his bearded chin. "It's a mistake to take the forces of nature too lightly, Mrs. O'Leary. In some parts of the world, Japan for instance, earthquakes do a great deal of damage. The same could happen here one day."

"And what would you be knowin' of the Japans, Mr. Archer?" asked my landlady with a gleam in her eye.

"I read a lot," he countered with an amused, meaningful glance at me, "and speaking of reading, I have more books to restore to their proper places. If you will excuse me."

"I must go too," I said. "After such an exciting beginning, I hope you will both have a pleasant day."

"And you, Fremont," said Michael, gesturing for me to precede him into the hall.

He went up the stairs and I, out of the front door. But I had scarcely reached the bottom of the steps before Mrs. O'Leary was at the top of them, hissing at me to wait.

I turned around and she lumbered down, her white apron flapping in a stiff breeze that also made my cape billow out around me. My eyes questioned her delaying me.

"Reads a lot, he says. Humph!" Mrs. O. cut her eyes up to the windows of the second floor.

"I believe he does read a good deal. I have seen Mr. Archer several times in the reading room of the Public Library. And of course, he has so many books of his own."

"That's as may be. But he's been to the Japans, I'd bet my eyeteeth on it!"

I regarded my landlady affectionately. "I declare, your imagination is almost as good as mine. Perhaps I should tell you what my mother, rest her soul, was always telling me: Curiosity killed the cat."

"Why, Fremont"—Mrs. O. put her large, work-roughened hand over mine—"I didn't know you was an orphan."

"I'm not." On taking her flat I had told my landlady nothing of my past, only that I was an independent woman. "I have a father who is very much alive. In fact, he is now married to a woman I don't much like."

"A stepmother, eh, dearie?"

I nodded.

"And so you ran away from home?"

"Not exactly. I came, as so many others have come to San Francisco, to make my fortune. Not that it will be very much of a fortune —especially if I don't get to the office soon! Mrs. O'Leary, I know it isn't fitting for someone of my age to give advice to her elders, but I think you'd do well to leave off your imaginings about Michael Archer."

She narrowed her eyes. "Telling me to leave well enough alone, is that it?"

"I know what you do is none of my business. Please forgive me if I spoke out of turn."

Mrs. O. looked over her shoulder at her house, her eyes moving up to the second floor. She chewed on her lip. "The Captain—my husband—he used to say as how I had a naturally suspicious mind. The thing is, Fremont, when I get a bee in my bonnet about somebody, I'm usually right. I'm gonna keep on watching that Mr. Archer real close. Long as he don't know what I'm doin', I won't come to no harm." She looked back at me. "And you watch yerself around him, too. We don't want you to come to no harm, neither."

"Don't worry, I won't," I assured her with a smile. I wondered as I walked away downhill, careful of my footing on the steep slope, if I had given away my landlady's game to Michael Archer. I concluded that it didn't matter if I had, since both those individuals were harmless; and I dismissed the matter from my mind.

I delayed my own work that morning in order to help the Sorensons put their bookstore back to rights. In my office upstairs not a thing was out of place, but their books were scattered helter-skelter. My assistance earned me two nearly identical smiles—I was glad to see that they *could* smile—and a word of thanks. But no invitation. No "as you have been so helpful, allow us to provide you lunch one day," or tea, or coffee. The Sorensons simply were not very friendly people.

I had several short pieces waiting for me to type, and I got to them mid-morning. Once the fog had burned off, the day was bright and sunny and so I had opened the window before beginning to work. I liked the fresh air, and having the various street noises to keep me company.

The rumbling of a passing cart must have drowned out the small bell on my office door, because the first sign that I was no longer alone was a sensation of being watched. As this had often happened to me while typing Mr. Partridge's creepy manuscript (which I had finished some two weeks earlier), I almost ignored the feeling in favor of keeping up my typing speed. But curiosity won out, and I stopped and turned my head.

A Chinaman stood politely waiting just inside the door.

"Come in," I said. "I'm sorry I didn't hear the bell."

He bowed, and advanced silently nearer the desk. I was fascinated —I had never seen one of his race close up, though of course I had often seen them in the streets. I was not in the least nervous to be alone with him, though many San Franciscans—Mrs. O'Leary for one —are suspicious and even fearful of the Chinese.

This was an ancient gentleman, dressed all in shiny black from head to foot. His arms he had folded with hands hidden in the sleeves. He was taller than many of his race and thin as a pole, his thinness emphasized by the straight lines of the black robe that hung to an inch or two above his ankles. He wore a round cap, also black, and had a narrow, drooping mustache. I knew, though I could not see, that he would have hanging down his back the queue that all Chinese men wore—and in his case, due to his age, it would probably be very long.

Wheeling over to the desk, I asked, "How may I help you?"

"This humble person," he said, inclining his head, "has heard that Missee Jones writes on her machine for those who cannot write the language of this country. This humble person has also heard that Missee Jones is most honorable, and can be trusted."

"Why . . . how nice." I was dying to know from whom he had heard these things, but was unsure quite how to ask. "Will you have a seat, Mr.—?"

"Li Wong prefers to stand. Li Wong has money with which to pay." He took his hands out of his sleeves and held up a money pouch to demonstrate.

"We will discuss payment later, Mr. Li Wong," I said, wondering if the Chinese language had no pronoun for "I," or some prohibition against referring to oneself in the first person. This man's words were self-effacing but his manner was not—he bore himself nobly, and his English was excellent. I guessed that he would command respect among his own people.

He inclined his head again, returning his hands to his sleeves. "Please advise how to proceed," he said.

"Give me a moment to put a fresh sheet of paper in the typewriter, and then we can begin."

Li Wong had the gift of being able to move without producing a single sound. He glided near to my typewriter, where he stood waiting with folded arms, not moving a muscle. I could feel his keen interest in both me and my machine.

I smiled up at him when I was ready. "Now. It's really very simple. You tell me what you want to say, and I will type the words onto the paper."

Li Wong nodded his understanding. "I begin: In the event of my untimely death, I wish the following to be known to concerned persons . . ."

It is my habit, when typing for the various people who dictate, not to pay too close attention to the content of their words. I feel that they are entitled to as much privacy as I can give them. In Mr. Wong's case— Or was it Mr. Li? I recalled that the usual order of names is reversed by the Chinese. Anyway, in his case I could not help sensing that the information he dictated was of importance. How could something that began with the mention of death not be important? He spoke of some kind of business matter, elaborate arrangements and names of companies that meant nothing to me. And in any event, I would make myself forget them as soon as I finished typing.

I had filled most of the page when he concluded, "These things I, Li Wong, have caused to be recorded on the first day of May in the year one thousand nine hundred and five of the Western calendar, in the city of San Francisco, the state of California, of the United States of America. That is all, Missee Jones."

Very thorough, I thought, pulling the paper from the typewriter. "Do you wish to sign it? You may use my desk, if you like."

"Not sign here. Pay now, yes?"

"That will be ten cents, Mr. Li Wong," I said. "Would you like an envelope?"

He handed me two coins from his pouch. As he did so, I noticed his fingers, long and slender, the color of old parchment and, like that material, crisscrossed by tiny lines, as was his face. He took the page in hand and scrutinized it, saying, "Envelope not necessary."

"Envelope" was the first English word that had given him trouble —it came out with too many L's. Nodding his head as if pleased by the typewriting, he rolled the paper like a scroll and from within his sleeve produced a red ribbon—the first bit of color I'd seen about him —which he began to tie around it. The bell on my door rang and the door opened as he was doing this. At the sound, Mr. Li Wong's hands began to shake.

I would have needed an extra pair of eyes to see exactly what happened next. I stood up and went rapidly around my desk, instinctively wanting to shield the old Chinese gentleman with his suddenly shaking hands. "Hello, Justin," I said, "I'll be with you in just a minute."

Justin was glaring at Li Wong—I had never seen such a hostile expression on my friend's face before. Li Wong, who had stood so straight and tall and dignified before me, now hunched himself over in a servile posture, dipping and bobbing the upper half of his body; saying in a high-pitched voice quite unlike himself, "Thankee, Missee, thankee, Missee," over and over again as he made a wide wobbling circle around Justin and finally backed out the door. The bell rang again as he closed it behind him, somewhat like a silver exclamation point.

"What was *he* doing here?" Justin demanded, and simultaneously I said, "I think you frightened the poor man."

"Well, what *was* he doing here?"

"You sound as if you know him," I observed, going back to my desk. A bit of color caught the corner of my eye. I looked, and saw to my surprise that Mr. Li Wong had left the red ribbon on my desk, and his typewritten statement, as well!

"It's hard to tell." Justin looked at the closed office door, as if its blank surface might hold an impression his eyes could develop, like a photographic negative.

While Justin's head was turned I picked up the one page of Li Wong's statement and placed on top of it the letter I'd left off typing when he came in. "The Chinese gentleman had something for me to type," I said, my hands resting on top of both sheets of paper. I reached out and took up the red ribbon and began idly (to all appearances, my mind being not in the least idle) winding it around my finger.

"I don't like it," said Justin pugnaciously, thrusting his hands in his pockets and his chin out. On a face like his the expression would have been comical except for the tone of his voice.

"That's obvious," said I, unwinding the ribbon and winding it up again, "but I haven't yet figured out exactly what it is you don't like."

"I don't like you being in here all alone with a *Chinee!*"

"If you know something about that particular Chinese gentleman, Justin, I would be glad to hear it."

"What's his name?"

"I thought you recognized him?" The nature of Li Wong's statement, and the fact that he had left it behind, made me cautious. Even with Justin, whom I trusted.

"No, they all look alike to me, and you shouldn't have anything to do with any of them, Fremont. The Chinese are dirty and devious and thieving and, and immoral!"

"You surprise me, sir," I said mildly. But my tone of voice was deceptive. I do not care for prejudice in any form. In my opinion, we women have been subjected to so much of it that I cannot see how anyone of my sex could fail to identify with those similarly oppressed. Of course Justin was not of my sex, and his intentions were doubtless honorable. I should not judge him prematurely.

"Yes," he said. "Well, you surprise me too, Fremont. Having a dirty Chinaman in this office!" He narrowed his eyes. "And what would somebody like that have that was worth typing in the first place? Who was that Chinee, and what did you type for him?"

I looked Justin in the eye, my ability to withhold judgment fading fast. "I can't tell you that. My clients and their business have just as much right to confidentiality as yours do, Justin."

"Hogwash! I'm a lawyer, and you're just a, just a—"

"Just a woman who types things for people?" I opened the center drawer of my desk and dropped the red ribbon inside. Closing the drawer with an audible snap, I looked Justin in the eye again. "And how would you like it, Mr. Lawyer, if I were to tell anyone who might happen to inquire, that you are my client, and the content of what I type for you?"

Justin colored and looked uncomfortable, which I was glad to see. He conceded, "Your point is well-taken. But still, there's a difference—"

"You came to join me for lunch, I assume, since you have yours in that sack you are crushing beneath your elbow?"

"Yes, I did. And you're avoiding the issue, Fremont."

I took out a folder and put the two sheets of paper inside. Later I would retrieve the letter that I had yet to finish typing and label the folder for Mr. Li Wong's statement. Taking my keys from the pocket of my skirt, I locked the folder in the file drawer.

I said, "What I'm avoiding is an argument. But since you're being so persistent, I'll say this, Justin. My clients are as important to me as yours are to you. My work is as deserving of respect as yours is, regardless which of us is the more highly paid. I take each person who comes through that office door on face value, just as I did you, the first time you came here. I will gladly type for a Chinese just as I would for an Italian, or a Swede, or a Negro, or a German, or an American. Now. Are you still interested in us eating our lunch together? Because if you are not, I will be perfectly content to eat alone!"

Subsequently, Justin did leave me alone, saying that he thought I needed time "to smooth my ruffled feathers." He had the monumental ego to act as if his departure were his own idea, when very clearly I had dismissed him. Men! They are all perverse, and one's occasional desire for their company is the most perverse of all.

I had hoped that Mr. Li Wong might have been waiting around the corner or down in the bookstore for Justin to leave, and would then return for his papers, but he did not. Fortunately, other clients came to take my mind off the matter, and I did not think of Mr. Li Wong—or Justin—again until I was covering my typewriter and preparing to depart at the end of the day. Then I recalled that I had never finished typing the letter I'd used to cover the Chinese gentleman's statement from Justin's potentially prying eyes.

I unlocked the file drawer. The preponderance of material within was Mr. Edgar Allan Partridge's collection of stories, which I had divided among three folders because there were too many pages to fit in one. I wished he would come and collect them; he was overdue, even by his revised schedule. I took out the unlabeled folder I sought and closed the drawer—out of sight, out of mind was the best way I knew to deal with E.A.P.

With a sigh—I was really more than ready to be done with this workday—I uncovered the typewriter and finished the letter. I put it in with other work to be paid for when it was claimed, and labeled the folder where it had inadvertently spent the day "L.W." for Li Wong. I placed everything in the file drawer and locked it. *Now,* at last, I could leave.

Yet, with my hand on the doorknob, I lingered. Had I forgotten anything? I frowned, my eyes making a rapid check. Then I closed them for a moment and rubbed the frown away. I had forgotten nothing; I was just disturbed. The truth was, I was still disturbed about that episode with Justin.

I couldn't shake it off. The things I usually found refreshing after a day's work—a leisurely bath in the deep tub, a simple meal (my talents do not greatly extend to cooking) eaten sitting in the window seat of my living room as I watched the fog creep in to fill the streets—did not dispel my inner disturbance. At last, I put down the novel I was trying without success to read and faced myself.

I might have been unfair to Justin Cameron; he had lived in San Francisco all his life, and perhaps his attitude toward the Chinese people had some justification. Yet, I was right to feel the way I did about my customers and my work. This sort of dilemma was all too familiar to me. One of my professors at Wellesley used to say, "Caroline, it is possible to be right *and* keep your opinion to yourself. Sometimes that is the wiser course."

Would I never learn? Probably not; probably I would always go on wanting to be accepted and liked for all of who I am, not just a part; probably I would always feel that if I kept my mouth shut as much as society dictated for a "lady" (how I detested that term, with its false ring of aristocracy!) of my upbringing, I was being hypocritical. And I do loathe a hypocrite. Therefore, I doubtless would continue to offend men such as Justin, with whom I might want to have some sort of an amorous liaison.

That made me smile: realizing that I did want an amorous liaison with Justin. There was the source of my disturbance—I was afraid my habit of speaking my mind had robbed me of the chance. The realization in itself made me feel better.

I got up from my chair, put the book on the table beneath the lamp, and went into the kitchen to make a cup of tea. While I waited for the kettle to boil, I heard Michael Archer moving about in his own kitchen below me. I had an idea. I thought, Why not?

I hastily removed my dressing gown and put on the first dress that came to hand—it happened to be one of my more feminine garments, cream-colored cotton with rosebuds sprigged all over it—and coiled my hair on top of my head. As I was about to go downstairs I recalled the tea kettle, and went back to turn it off. The delay caused me to lose some of my nerve. What if Michael thought me too brazen, seeking out his company uninvited at such a late hour? It was nearly nine o'clock.

But, I assured myself, Michael Archer was different, as different in his own way as I was in mine; he was not likely to be disturbed by a lack of convention. Nor, being a good twenty years older than I, would he be likely to read more into my visit than its stated purpose.

Fortunately (I do not think my ego could have withstood two rejections in the same day) I was right. When I called out from the landing of the stair, Michael came from his library and said, "Fremont! To what do I owe the pleasure?"

"I was hoping, if you will excuse the interruption, that you might help me with something. It won't take long—I'm aware that it's rather late in the evening to be calling."

He came near enough that I could see in his eyes the amusement with which he so often regarded me. Michael's eyes changed from blue to gray according to some pattern I had not yet figured out; tonight they were blue. He said, "If it doesn't require great physical strength, or more than a minimum of manual dexterity, I will be glad to help."

"This requires only mental effort, and a fund of knowledge I am certain you possess."

"You intrigue me. Come in. I have just finished supper and am drinking coffee. Would you like some?"

"Yes, I would. Thank you."

He left me in the library while he went to get another cup, and I had an opportunity to scrutinize the shelves. Here there was evidence of an orderly mind: The books were arranged by category. But not too orderly: Within their categories they were not alphabetical by author. Immediately before me was a section on archaeology. To the left, history beginning with the Greeks and Romans. Or was that mythology? And . . .

He returned, and at his gesture I sat on the other end of the couch he had been occupying. There was a large, low drum table in front of it on which sat his cup and the coffeepot, along with a happy jumble of books and papers. He looked cozy in a thick-knit sweater the dark red shade of burgundy wine.

"Something rather disturbing happened to me today," I began, and then faltered; I wished I had started in some other fashion.

"I am sorry to hear it."

"I, ah, I had a disagreement with a friend, and it is possible that I was wrong. If I knew more about San Francisco and its inhabitants, I might not have behaved quite as I did. To the point: It would be helpful for me to learn about the Chinese people, and their character in general. I thought perhaps you might enlighten me?"

I could almost see the wheels of thought turning in Michael's head, as he sorted through the various things he might say. I was not surprised when, with his keen mind, he came out with a correct assumption. "You have had an encounter, in your business I presume, with a Chinese. And this led somehow to your disagreement with your friend."

"Precisely."

"I can give you a few relevant facts. You must feel free to question me or suggest a new direction if I am not being helpful."

"Thank you, I will."

"The Chinese came to this country for one reason only: to make money. And they are willing to work very hard for it. The first Chinese came to San Francisco about fifty years ago, in the gold rush days. Then more were brought over, and many more came on their own, to work on the railroads, laying track through the Sierra Nevada. The West could not have been opened up as quickly as it was without their labor. When the transcontinental rail linkage was established, there were thousands of Chinese out of work and without enough money to return to China. A large proportion of them came here, where there was already a Chinatown."

"We segregate them," I said, "as the Jews used to be forced into ghettos in Europe. It's medieval."

"You are too hard on America, Fremont. The Chinese segregate themselves. Their culture is very different, and because most of them intended to return to China when they had earned enough money to have a better life there, they did not learn our language. Certainly they have been discriminated against right here in San Francisco, particularly in the last decade with the edict that led to the tong wars—"

"Tong wars?"

"Ah. You do not know about the tongs?"

I shook my head.

"Chinatown is really a village within the city. A village with its own unwritten laws and customs, its own hierarchical structure that is difficult for a Westerner to understand. In fact, much of it they keep secret. The tongs are like—well, the closest analogy I can think of is the Scottish clans. And they are also like fraternal organizations, the Masons for instance, with codes and symbols whose meanings are known only to an initiate, a member of the tong. Tong leaders are greatly respected—again, think of the laird in Scotland—and for that respect they give a lot in return to their members: a feeling of belonging, security, a sense of identity. And more: the tongs negotiate in business on behalf of their members, and provide insurance.

"That's what caused the wars. In response to that edict I mentioned, the tong leaders misjudged. The new law wasn't all that horribly unfair, just a requirement that all Chinese carry identity papers in order to work. The tong leaders advised their members to resist, not carry the papers; but the law was strictly enforced and Chinese lost their jobs by the hundreds. The tongs' insurance function was overwhelmed and the tong leaders lost respect, people no longer had faith in them. But they had relied on the structure of the tongs and needed them emotionally, which caused ordinary Chinese folk to become vulnerable to any unscrupulous strong leader who might move in. That's exactly what happened: The criminal element—which is always present in abundance in this town—moved into the vacuum. Violence was the result. But that is over now. All has been relatively quiet in Chinatown for the past two or three years. I presume, but do not know for certain, that the tongs are reorganizing."

I had a strong hunch that Li Wong was a tong leader. Perhaps he had laid low during the wars, and had been gathering his group back together. I could make up many interesting scenarios with the information Michael had given me, but for now I had another question to ask: "So you would not judge that, in general, the Chinese are of bad character?"

"Of course not. They are like us, like people all over the world: within their own ranks they have good and bad, no more and no less than we do. The tong wars are still fresh in everyone's mind and have given our Chinese a bad reputation, which they will have to live down. That is all."

"Thank you." I rose to go. "What you've told me has been very helpful."

Michael Archer rose and took my hand. "You've scarcely touched your coffee. Let me give you another cup, warm from the pot."

"No, thank you."

"At least tell me one thing before you go."

I raised my eyebrows inquiringly.

"The friend with whom you had the disagreement: Is this friend female, or male?"

"Male," I said, and no more. But how interesting that he should ask!

To my relief, Mr. Li Wong was waiting at my door when I got to the office the next morning. He said in his quaint way, "This humble

60

person found it necessary to depart in haste yesterday and has come to claim his paper."

I gave it to him, and the red ribbon, and he tied it up and put it in his sleeve and departed. I would have liked to ask him to sit down and tell me all about himself, but he was far too dignified for me to make such an approach. I hoped he would come again, or send others of his tong. I wanted to get to know Mr. Li Wong.

However, I would never get to know him. It seemed that the Chinese gentleman's apparent fear of an "untimely death" had been well-founded. For in less than a week I read in the *Chronicle* that there had been a shooting in Chinatown. The name of the person killed was Li Wong.

6.

Mission

(of One Kind or Another)

———❦———

I HAD BOUGHT the issue of the *Chronicle* that reported Li Wong's death at the bookstore to read while I ate my lunch, because it was raining and I did not intend to go out. I am not sure how long I sat there, staring out my window and watching the rain. Like tears it was, sliding down and down the glass, which bore the name of my business: SENOJ TNOMERF, SECIVRES GNITIRWEPYT. Like the sign seen from the inside of the window, I felt turned completely around by the bad news.

I wished I could remember the exact contents of the statement I'd typed for Mr. Li Wong. I would have written it down and taken it to the police. But the bits and pieces that I seemed to recall were jumbled and confusing. I wanted to help find Li Wong's murderer, but I couldn't. I knew I should leave it at that.

I did an odd thing when I left the office that day: I took E.A.P.'s handwritten manuscript home with me. The nicely typed version I left locked in the file drawer. I did this on impulse, without stopping —perhaps without allowing myself—to think why.

I became downcast and stayed that way for several days, to the extent that I could not even work up a proper enthusiasm when Justin called on the office telephone to inquire about the state of my feathers. I said they were quite smooth, thank you. He remarked that I sounded peculiar, and I said I had a bit of catarrh—which was true. It is per-verse how one always seems to come down with some bothersome physical problem when one's spirits are already out of sorts.

Justin was not the least out of sorts. He had won another case, acquired another important client. I felt I was supposed to remark on his absence for the past two weeks, but I did not. This time, he proposed that we celebrate not with violets and lunch, but by spending Saturday afternoon together. He said he would take me to that Victo-rian extravaganza at the beach called Sutro's Baths, and afterward we would dine at the Cliff House.

"As long as I am not expected to bathe in Mr. Sutro's bath, I will be glad to come," I said. I found that my spirits had lifted somewhat when I hung up the telephone. Saturday was two whole days away; surely I would feel the proper enthusiasm by then. I had not been to that part of San Francisco before, and had heard that the view from the Cliff House was spectacular.

Later, at home, I sat in my window seat drinking hot tea with lemon and honey to nurse my sniffles. I heard a voice calling my name: Michael Archer's voice. I looked down with regret at what I was wearing—my oldest, wooliest, warmest robe, a garment so un-fashionable in appearance that it could not even be called a dressing gown. To be proper, I should have called out that I was not appropri-ately attired, but the robe had a voluminous collar I had turned up around my ears, and it hung past my ankles to my toes. To refuse his company for modesty's sake seemed silly—my modesty was well-cov-ered.

So I went to the door and called down to him, "I'm here. If you won't be shocked out of your senses by a woman in a certain state of *déshabillé,* you may come up."

"I hope I have never yet been shocked by *déshabillé,"* he said as he paused with his hand on the newel post at the top of the stairs, and his eyes swept over me critically, "although I must say that you have given that word a new definition in my experience. What color would you say that robe is, Fremont?"

I sniffled; I couldn't help it. "It was once viridian, if you must know, but that was a long time ago. Come into the living room,

Michael. I was sitting by the window and watching the fog cover the city."

"You seem to have the sniffles. Are you sure you should be sitting by a window?" He went to the window himself, whereas I paused by one of the two comfortable chairs with which my living room was furnished. Looking out, he said, "You have a good view from here, better than mine. I would not have thought that being only one floor higher would make such a difference."

I joined him. "I never get tired of looking at it," I said. "I think I am in love with the fog." I sensed that Michael looked down at me but I did not look up to meet his eyes. In truth, I was standing too close to him, but if I had not, I could not have seen out of the window.

"Some day, Fremont, I will take you across the Bay to Sausalito. There is a place I know there, high up, much higher than here. If you go at sundown you can watch the fog roll in through the narrow passage of the Golden Gate. It looks so solid you feel as if you could walk right down the hillside and step onto it, except that it rolls and billows and curls over on itself like an ocean wave. And as the sun sets, its rays turn the fog to gold and peach and pink and finally the deepest rose."

"How lovely that must be."

"Yes. I promise, I will take you there someday."

For many moments longer we continued to look out at our fog, which was like a moving blanket of palest gray. Finally I broke the silence by reaching out for my mug of tea, which I had left on the window seat.

"Would you like some tea, Michael?"

"What?" He came back from his reverie. "Oh, no, thank you. You sound as if what you really need is a shot of brandy, Fremont, for medicinal purposes. I have some, if you would allow me to get it."

"Brandy strangles me. I'm not sick, really, I'll be fine." I went over and sat in my usual chair, and Michael took the other.

"I came up to tell you that I'll be away for a week or so. I wouldn't want to spoil Mrs. O'Leary's fun by telling her, but I wanted you to know."

"That was kind of you. I hope you have a pleasant trip."

His eyes sparkled. "You aren't going to ask where I'm going?"

"That," I sniffled, "would be impolite."

Michael tipped his head to one side, examining my face. "You seem rather unlike your usual self. If you're not sick, then is there something else wrong?"

I took up the end of my robe's sash and began to roll it—I habitually do pointless things with my hands when I am otherwise unsure what to say or do. Michael was good at waiting me out. I said tentatively, "I'm just mopish."

"Ah. The friend with whom you had the disagreement, would he be the cause of your mopishness?"

I looked up, surprised. I had forgotten he knew about that. "Not in the least. In fact, he has invited me to spend the afternoon with him on Saturday."

"I suppose that is cause for rejoicing."

I scarcely heard him; rolling and unrolling the sash, I was busy making a decision. Finally, I did. "I have been upset by something I read in the newspaper last week. Perhaps you read the same thing, about a murder in Chinatown."

Michael's handsome face grew somber. "Li Wong. Yes, I read it."

"You remember me asking you about the Chinese . . . Well, a Mr. Li Wong was the cause of my questions. I presume he was that murdered man of the same name. He made a tremendous impression on me and I wanted very much to get to know him, especially after you told me about the tongs. I was sure that Mr. Li Wong must be a tong leader and that he would be a fascinating person to know. And then, then—" I opened my hands in a gesture of helplessness.

"Li Wong came to you for your typewriting services? He brought you something to be typed?"

"Not exactly." I turned my head away, still torn, but soon turned back again. "Michael, I usually keep my customers and whatever they bring me in confidence, but—"

Michael leaned forward in his chair, his forearms resting upon his thighs. "You may be sure that I will keep whatever you tell me to myself."

66

I sighed, and the sigh turned into a sniffle. I really wanted badly to talk about this. "I suppose, since he is dead, it can't matter. Very well. Some of my customers, or clients, sometimes I call them one thing and sometimes the other—anyway, some of them come because they cannot write. Can't write a legible hand, or can't write in English, or just never learned to read and write. These people tell me what they want to say, and I type it for them as they speak. Letters, mostly. Li Wong had somehow heard about this aspect of my work. He came to me, I suppose, because he wanted to dictate something. He can't write in English, although I'm sure that in Chinese he is, or was, very learned."

"You are correct about that."

Now I, too, leaned forward. "What's bothering me so much is that, from what he told me to type, I'm sure he knew his life was in danger. He wasn't just paranoid"—I shuddered, thinking of E.A.P., who doubtless was—"he was putting his life in order. Or something like that."

Michael wrinkled his brow. "He dictated a will?"

"No. It was a statement that he wanted written down in case something happened to him. I don't know what he did with the paper I typed after he took it away. I keep expecting to read in the *Chronicle* that the police have found clues as to why he was killed, or who did it, but there has been nothing. Someone must have Li Wong's statement, Michael. Someone knows why he was murdered!"

Grimly Michael asked, "Do *you* know, Fremont?"

I shook my head and fell back in my chair. "I can't remember what's in that statement. I've tried and tried, and I just can't."

"That surprises me. I would have thought you'd have an exceptional memory."

"I do. You don't understand, Michael. When I type for people, I deliberately try not to pay attention to the content of whatever it is that I'm typing. Especially when I'm doing it for the people who dictate, because their things are always so personal. Apparently *not* remembering, once you have decided on it, is as easy for a strong-minded person to achieve as remembering. I do recall bits and pieces of what Li Wong said, but they're all muddled up. They don't make enough sense to go to the police with; it would be of no help to them."

Michael leaned back and stroked his beard, deep in thought. When he did look at me, his eyes had become as gray and as hard as steel. "Fremont, when we are done talking I want you to forget that you and I have had this conversation. I am going to tell you that you have made a correct assumption about Li Wong. He was an important man, perhaps the most important in all of the legitimate community of Chinatown. At the time of the tong wars, he disappeared. Many people assumed he had returned to China, since he was one of the few who could afford to do so. But he may have gone into hiding. The criminal element, both white and Chinese, stood to lose a great deal by Li Wong's reemergence. In recent months there have been rumors that he was back, but no one knew for certain. He would have assumed leadership of his tong once more, and he was popular. He'd have been working to reestablish certain business ties for his people, and putting together the elaborate, secret arrangements by which the tongs offer their insurance. And now, he is dead."

"I don't understand about the insurance. Obviously it's not the kind we have, where you buy a policy."

"Not at all. None of us Westerners really understand it. It has to do with honor and vengeance and complex ways of pulling strings to set those things in motion. That is irrelevant now. What is relevant, Fremont, is that you must never—I repeat, NEVER—tell anyone about Li Wong's coming to you. We must hope that the statement you typed has been read by whomever Li Wong intended to read it, and then destroyed. Because if it still exists, and the wrong people see it or hear about it and trace the typing of it back to you . . . well, they would never believe that you can't remember what Li Wong's statement said. In short, your life would be in danger."

I felt all the blood drain, drop by drop, out of my face as I absorbed this. I croaked, "Surely not."

"Believe me. It's a damn good thing you didn't go to the police!"

"B-but the police—"

"Are supposed to protect the people? Yes, but not all of them are honest, some are just as crooked as the most bent crooks in town. I wish to God I knew which kind Mrs. O'Leary's husband was, even if he is dead! I'd bet she still stays in touch . . ." He ran his hand over his close-cropped head in an exasperated gesture, then looked over at me. "I think you need that brandy now."

"I think you're right."

Michael brought the brandy and I half-strangled, as I always did, on the stuff. However, it was a popular medicinal remedy, which I had partaken of often enough to know that it worked wonders. When its warm glow had spread all through me and I had regained my normal manner of breathing, I said to Michael, "There is something more that bothers me a good deal, and I think I must mention it. Why did Li Wong want his statement typed in English?"

He reached out, as one might to a child, picked up a long strand of hair that had fallen over my shoulder, and tucked it behind my neck. His lips curved. "Oh, so you thought of that, did you?"

"Well, of course I did. I'm not an idiot!"

"No. You're altogether too bright and bold for your own good. If one knew the answer to that question, my dear Fremont, one would no doubt hold the central piece in an intricate puzzle. I will think about it. If I come up with anything, I will let you know. On your part, promise me that everything we have said tonight about Li Wong will remain exclusively between us."

"I promise."

"Good. And now, I must go." He kissed me on the forehead, in much the same manner he'd handled my hair, as if I were a child. Probably to him, I *was* a child. But as I watched Michael go down the stairs I rather wished he'd kissed me somewhere else—which aberrant desire I attributed to the influence of the brandy.

I thought Mr. Sutro's bathhouse, popularly called Sutro's Palace, was the most bizarre place I'd ever seen—but I did not say so to Justin. I was watching my tongue. I had dressed like a lady, even to the wearing of a hat (though not, of course, a corset), and was determined to act like one.

Many elements combined to make the place bizarre: for one thing, the building itself was enormous even from the street side. And once one entered, one could see that it extended downward many feet, being situated on the side of a cliff. The "palace" was constructed principally of glass, with domes and cupolas and various Victorian folderols. For another thing, aside from the baths, Mr. Sutro had filled the structure with objects and artifacts brought back from his travels; his taste indicated that he had much in common with President Teddy Roosevelt. Which is to say, his taste did not have much in common with mine. I do not particularly care for stuffed black bears standing on their hind legs and showing their ferocious teeth, or the purloined tusks and feet of elephants, or long strings of human heads shrunken by African pygmies. Justin's comment—"This is as good as a circus sideshow"—might have provoked from me the rejoinder "Or as bad," but being on my best behavior I only thought it.

The baths themselves, called "plunges," were bizarre for their excessive number—surely two or three would have been enough, but there were six. All were filled with sea water, piped in and heated to various temperatures. Supposedly the different degrees of heat produced different salutary effects for the bather. Perhaps they did, but the most visible effect produced was a great deal of steam. I did think, as Justin and I strolled around the balconies and watched the bathers, that it might be interesting to acquire a bathing suit and, as they say, "take the plunge." I wondered if they gave swimming lessons—I had always wanted to learn to swim.

When we had explored Sutro's Palace to Justin's satisfaction, we went outside and took the Cliff Walk, which is exactly that. There was also an overhead cable tram which one could take out to the Seal Rocks, but it was not running at the moment—a disappointment. Yet it was not possible to be too disappointed by my first good view of the Pacific coastline. Oh, it was spectacular! The sound of the surf crashing on the rocky cliffs mesmerized me; I loved the feel of its fine, wind-borne spray upon my face. My hat became more encumbrance than ornament, and I took it off and did not mind in the least that the wind unpinned my hair and whipped it about my head.

"This is wonderful!" I said to Justin. I could have stood there forever.

The day was clear and blue, and soon Justin turned tour guide, naming various points of the landscape. "This is Point Lobos," he said, "and there, to the north, is Point Reyes. Closer there's Land's End, and in a direct line from there out in the sea, there's Mile Rock. There's a lighthouse on Mile Rock. It's so clear today that you can see the Farallon Islands—look way, way out on the horizon, those dark spots. They're thirty miles out. There, do you see?"

"Yes, I see," I said. Something had begun to bother me, though, as Justin spoke. Some bit of darkness had insinuated itself into my enjoyment of this wild, beautiful place, although I couldn't put my finger on what it was.

I forgot all about it during our luncheon in the Cliff House. Justin was better company than ever before, and I simply enjoyed myself. After the meal, I browsed through the gift shop while waiting for Justin to come out of the Gents. I was tempted to buy a picture book of the coastline, but that was silly; I could come back here as often as I wanted. There were free brochures for tourists that also had pictures, so I availed myself of one.

It was later that evening, as I sat happily musing over the delightful time and reflecting how glad I was that I had come to San Francisco, that I again felt the intrusion of a piece of darkness. My brochure was at hand. I took it up and looked at the pictures and read the captions. *Point Lobos* . . . that rang a bell, suggested somehow a lighthouse. And yet the lighthouse was not on Point Lobos, but a mile out to sea, and why, why . . .

Suddenly my mind made the connection: the word for wolf in Spanish is lobo. Point Lobos, Wolves Point. And Mr. Edgar Allan Partridge had written of a lighthouse on the Point of the Wolf!

The truth was that E.A.P. had been tugging at the edges of my mind for several weeks, and only with a good deal of mental discipline had I kept him at bay. Now, I let him in. I sat there turning cold all over, and my imagination produced that ridiculous raven saying, "Nevermore."

Nevermore. Once I let loose my mind there is never any telling where it will go, except that it is quite likely to go where I least want it to. Sometimes my mind is perverse. Sometimes perversity is right upon the mark. Something—some perverse (in the darkest meaning of the word) circumstance?—had prevented Mr. Partridge from coming to claim the manuscript that meant so much to him.

My head filled with What Ifs. What if someone, as he'd thought, was really after him? What if they'd now got him? What if Partridge's danger was just as real as Li Wong's? And of course, there was the biggest What If of all: What if those strange stories were really true?

For three nights I did not sleep well, and it was not because of the catarrh—that had cleared up. It was because, having let Edgar Allan Partridge into my head, I now could not get him out. Whenever my mind was not occupied with some specific task, thoughts about his possible fate rushed in to take over. This prevented me from going to sleep in my usual prompt fashion once my head was laid upon the pillow. When I did sleep, I dreamed . . . and my dreams were filled with strange images that had their origin in his stories.

During a lull in my work at the office, I unlocked the file drawer and took out Partridge's typescript. The handwritten manuscript was still in my room at Mrs. O'Leary's. Long ago I had deposited his ninety-two dollars in the bank and made note of how much I was due to return to him. He had paid me, he had entrusted his work to my care: I felt I had an obligation to the man. I could do nothing for Li Wong, because I still had not remembered his statement in any reliable detail, and now believed I never would. But in the case of Mr. Partridge . . .

Led by instinct, I opened the folder that contained his third story, "Damned to Darkness." I looked at the first page, and read:

> I was a baby, lying in my crib. I know that some say we cannot have memories of the time we are so young, but I do; in fact I swear that I felt the forces of Darkness, and that I cried tears when I was yet in the womb. My entire existence has been marked by a strong conviction that I am never safe; marked, in fact, by terror under the barest restraint. You, dear reader, if you bear with me, shall come to understand.

As I said, I was a baby, lying in my crib—this is my first clear memory. A face appeared above me, a face that went with a smell that meant food. My tiny lips worked, suckling as yet on nothing. I was hungry. I reached out toward the face, and the face bent closer. Babe though I was, I could see it clearly, and as I looked upon that visage which would feed me, it began to change.

I had as yet no language, no concept of Mother; my concept was on the most primitive level. She was Life-Giver, Care-Giver. She whose skin was as white as the milk that flowed from her breasts for me, whose eyes sparkled like dark diamonds, whose hair held the smooth sheen of a raven's wing, she the giver of care and of life itself —was transformed into a Demon within my innocent sight. Her skin thickened and acquired a greenish glow. Her eyes turned red and hot, like fire. Her nostrils became gaping holes; her hair a nest of black, writhing worms.

Of course, beholding this horrible alteration, I began to cry. Later I would know that this was the worst possible thing I could do. Crying was a sign of weakness, and my mother abhorred weakness above all things. Therefore crying enraged her. But I was only a baby, first hungry and now frightened; how could I not cry? She shrieked at me, then picked me up and held me, not securely near her body, but high in the air.

And then she dropped me. Down and down and down I fell. I remember this with the unending, sickening fright that we all feel in dreams of falling. And there, falling and falling, my first memory ends.

I have asked myself since: Was the change I beheld in Mother a vision sent by some beneficent Agency to warn me? Or did Mother effect the transformation herself, either to teach me the first of many lessons or simply to see how I would react? This has ever been my dilemma: a desire to know my own true nature. Was I truly born of this woman, made of the same evil stuff as she? Who was my father? Indeed, why was I born into this world?

I believe that I now know the answers to these questions. And so shall you, dear reader, as my tale unfolds.

A horror story, yes. And yet within it a ring of universality. For who among us has not questioned our own true nature and wanted to know why we were born? I could not help but think that the haunted little man who had sat in this very office with me, casting nervous glances over his shoulder, might well have had a terrible experience such as this. *Something* had made him the way he was, just as surely as something had kept him from returning for his manuscript.

My sympathy was all for that baby who had received fear instead of food. And by extension, for the man that baby had grown to be. I assumed that Peregrine, the boy-narrator of the story, was in fact Edgar Allan Partridge. The very least I could do was to find him so that I might return the manuscript. Publication of these stories would give him a certain amount of fame, and perhaps that would help to make up for a life that had been, in Mr. Partridge's words, one of terror kept barely under restraint.

I got up from the desk and went to the window, pondering a dilemma I had just recognized. If Mr. Partridge was not paranoid, would the publication of his stories place him in more, or less danger? If I were to look for him, and find him, would I really be doing him a service?

I came to the only conclusion it was possible to reach: He who is lost must be found. I alone held the clues to Edgar Allan Partridge's tortured existence, and his whereabouts. Or *perhaps* I did, if I were to take him at his word and presume that his stories, however veiled in symbol and metaphor, were true. That was what I must first ascertain: the truth of the stories.

I would therefore begin with the simplest, most straightforward of the three: the second story, of the ghost who haunts the Mission Dolores. My search would begin with the Mission.

7.

They Come in Battalions

I TOOK ADVANTAGE of my earlier closing hour on Saturday to pay a late afternoon visit to the Mission Dolores. I rode a streetcar to the Mission District, and the driver was able to give me directions that, as it turned out, I did not need in the least. On a corner was a tall church in the Spanish style—this was the basilica, which proved to be adjacent to the Mission itself. One reached the Mission and its graveyard by going through a gate in a wall made of adobe bricks. The atmosphere within the enclosure was so markedly different that it gave me pause.

I felt a kind of heavy quiet that was neither portentous nor peaceful; it was—well, as fanciful as it may seem, it was sad. Sorrowful, as in full of sorrow. I thought about chickens and eggs, which came first. In other words, did the Spanish fathers who founded this Mission and named it *Nuestra Señora de los Dolores,* Our Lady of Sorrows, do so because the place already felt sad? Or did it take on an aura of sorrow because it was named Dolores? Who could ever know?

Having thus indulged my errant mind, I wandered through the small garden and into the graveyard. So far as I could see, I was alone here. Truly, I would not have minded a bit of company. I had a vague plan in mind—to look for the grave of the woman whose first name had been Elena.

I did not find it. There were a number of Spanish names, but Elena was not among them. I supposed I had best seek out the priest who went with the place, and so I retraced my steps through the graveyard and went into the Mission itself.

The building was made of the same adobe as the wall, and was surprisingly small—the reason, no doubt, why the church next door had been constructed in more recent years. Though I am not a Roman Catholic—indeed I am not religious in the conventional sense of that word—I liked being inside the Mission Dolores. Here were coolness and shadowy silence, a feeling of being safely away from the world. The sorrowful feeling was absent, apparently connected only to the garden and the graveyard . . . how curious! The Mission's walls and curved ceiling were painted with religious scenes, and of course there were statues which, being life-size, were a bit startling until one got used to them. But there was no priest.

I decided to seek out the stairs to the bell tower, where Elena was reputed by Mr. Partridge to do her haunting. In the back of the building I found a door that seemed likely to lead to them, but it was locked. Frustrated, I went out into the garden again. This time I was not alone. A nun walked across the enclosure in a purposeful way that made her black veil and skirt stream out behind her. I rushed after, and when I was near enough that I did not have to raise my voice by much, I said, "Please, stop! I'd like a word with you."

She turned, and I saw that she was very young—she looked like a healthy, red-cheeked child in a wimple. "Yes? How may I help you?" she asked in a breathless little voice.

What did one call a nun? I fished in my memory and caught it: "Sister, I'm looking for information. About, ah, old legends connected with this Mission. Perhaps you could help me, or direct me to someone who can."

From the expression in her eyes, it seemed as if she might be wrinkling her brow; however, it was impossible to tell since her forehead was covered by the white wimple. What remained of her face was as transparent of thought as Justin's. I could see the exact moment when she found her answer, as if a light had been turned on inside. She said, "I expect you had better try the library. Oh, not here, I mean the big library downtown. I don't know any legends. I've just been sent down from the Mother House, to teach at the school across the street. I haven't been here very long."

I could believe that; she could not have been anywhere very long.

76

Or perhaps she was years older than I, and her innocence preserved her. I felt positively jaded by comparison. In any event, I had already looked for a book of San Francisco ghost stories at the library and, to my dismay, found none. I said, "Perhaps the priest might know?"

"Oh!" She bobbed her head agreeably. "Certainly you could ask him. But not this afternoon. He's in the big church, hearing confessions. If you will excuse me, I'm on an errand to the rectory and I mustn't be late."

"Of course. I'm sorry to have detained you."

With a fleeting smile and a nod of her head, she turned and once more hurried along. I tapped my foot impatiently. I did not want to leave without talking to the priest. I had come this far and my curiosity was deeply aroused. I looked up at the bell tower and could not, from where I stood, even see its bells. If the ghost of the woman Elena were to appear before my eyes, that would solve my problem: I see the ghost myself, *ergo* the story must be true. Of course, no ghost appeared. I was under the impression, from what I had read of hauntings and such, that not everyone could see ghosts. Up to this time in my life I had never seen one, but that was no reason to conclude that they did not exist.

I stopped myself from getting into a vigorous but pointless internal debate over the existence of ghosts and whether or not I might prove to be one of those blessed, or cursed, with the ability to see them. Opening the plum-colored jacket that matched my skirt, I checked the watch pinned to my blouse. It was almost four-thirty. I had been here an hour. How long did priests hear those confessions? Well, he would have to stop sometime. I would go into the church and wait for him to appear.

The basilica, to give it the Latin name, intimidated me in a way that the Mission had not done. I felt like an awkward alien. However, I was not nearly about to give up now. When my eyes had adjusted to the lack of light, I saw a few people clustered in pews off to my left— the sinners awaiting their opportunity to be confessed, no doubt. I went and sat behind them and watched with interest as one after another came and went from a big wooden box against the wall. It had three doors, and looked a good deal like a wardrobe. From the fact that the center door stayed closed, I concluded that the priest must be in there.

While I waited, I fell under some kind of Catholic spell. I began to wish that I could make confession and be forgiven for all the things I had done wrong in my life. I got into a complete fug thinking about it. The fug became amplified by a creepy feeling that someone was watching me from behind. A very Partridgish sort of feeling. I turned around and scanned the few rows of pews behind me—I was already near the back of the church—and I didn't see anyone. However, I did notice when I turned around again that I was the only person left waiting outside the priest's box. This heartened me; I was sure he must come out soon.

Did the man intend to stay in there all night? After at least ten more minutes I lost patience with waiting. I was still the only person in my part of the church; the others had either gone up nearer the altar or left altogether. So I decided to go into that box myself and ask him to come out and talk to me.

I opened one of the narrow wooden doors, went in, and closed it behind me. Claustrophobic Catholics must have to die unshriven, I thought while I stood in the dark, cramped space. Soon I heard a sliding sound, as of a panel being drawn back. But nothing else.

Finally a male voice whispered, "Do you wish to confess, my child?"

It came from the vicinity of my middle, so I supposed I would have to kneel down; there was no help for it if I wished to be heard. I knelt, feeling decidedly odd, and also whispered. "I am not a Catholic, I have not come to confess. I wish to talk to you about a matter of some importance, and as there is no one else waiting—"

The voice interrupted gruffly, "I will stay here until half past five o'clock. If you wish to speak with me, you may wait in the Mission garden. Be off with you, now."

I felt as if I had committed yet another sin to be heaped upon my heathen head. With uncharacteristic meekness, I went and waited as he'd said.

I did not like waiting in the garden with its aura of sadness. The feeling that I was being watched became so strong that I actually got up from my bench and looked behind the bushes that separated the garden from the graveyard. That resting place of the dead, which had seemed rather interesting earlier (in general I like to prowl about old cemeteries and read their stone markers), now seemed ominous.

"Nonsense!" I declared aloud, and felt somewhat better. I checked my watch again, saw that I had not much longer to wait, and resumed my seat.

When at last the priest strode up, he took me by surprise. I had been watching the gate, but he came from the other direction, out of the Mission. I jumped at the sound of his voice, and my eyes went wide, presenting—I was sure—a picture not at all in keeping with my usual business-like self.

"You are she who came into the Confessional?"

"Yes," I nodded, trying to regain my composure.

"I did not mean to startle you."

"It's only that I expected you to come through the gate."

"There is a connecting door between the basilica and the Mission. I must say"—he looked me over thoroughly—"you are a very bold young woman to come after me in the way that you did, if you are indeed not Catholic."

His expression was disapproving, and as he had the stern visage of a bird of prey to begin with, I felt inclined to shrivel. I do not, however, shrivel easily. I stared back at him, noting that the long black garment he wore, which I believed was called a cassock, had a stain upon the chest where he must have spilled part of his lunch. I also noted, by the sprouts of graying hair that served him for eyebrows—his pate being quite bald—that he was not a young man. For my purposes, this was good.

"Indeed I am not, sir," I said.

"You should call me Father, no matter what you are," he said, sitting next to me on the bench. "Now, what is it you want with me?"

"I seek to verify the truth of a tale I have heard about the Mission Dolores."

"Tell it, then."

"I have heard that many years ago there was here a Spanish

79

woman called Elena, who fell in love with the priest of the Mission, and he with her. They, ah—"

"They had carnal knowledge of each other," the priest said nastily, as if it were the worst thing in the world, "and it ended as such things must end. Very badly for both."

"It's true, then," I said. My voice sounded strange to me, too breathy, I did not have full control of it. I had not known until that moment that I did not wish the story to be true—I did not wish *any* of Mr. Partridge's strange stories to be true.

The priest was looking at me with a severe expression in his small, beady eyes. "That tale is far from being general knowledge. In fact, it has been suppressed. It is an abomination to the sacred priesthood and a danger to the faithful!"

"What about Elena's ghost?" You can't suppress a ghost, I thought.

"The ghost was exorcised. She no longer haunts the bell tower. How did you come to know of this story?"

"An acquaintance of mine told me. I, ah, I'm very concerned about him, actually. He seems to be missing. Perhaps you've seen him, perhaps he came here before me to ask questions of you? A man of slight build, very white skin, as if he hardly ever goes out in the sun, a nervous manner, he habitually wears black . . . ?"

The priest did not immediately reply. He took his lower lip between thumb and forefinger and tugged at it—a rather distasteful nervous mannerism for a man of God, or a godly man, to have. It revealed yellowed teeth that were none too attractive. When he did speak, what he said made a chill run down my spine.

"Evil!" He spat the word.

"Do you refer to my acquaintance, sir?" I asked, forgetting to call him Father.

He leapt off the bench and began to wave his arms, crying, "Will I never be free? What else must I do, what else?"

I stood up, my heart beating too rapidly in my chest. "Please calm yourself, Father, and tell me what is wrong."

"I'm not going to talk about it, do you hear? And you shouldn't either, young woman, if you know what's good for you," he said. But then he went on to talk about it: "I did my duty. I believed the story. I even saw the ghost myself. That priest, who should have been my brother in Christ, was evil, he was possessed. He befouled the grave-yard by burying that woman there, a suicide. She was a witch, she bewitched him and turned him into a demon. I know it! I was just a young man when I came here, far too young to have to deal with true evil, but I did it. I found Elena's grave. I had her bones dug up. The bishop wouldn't let me have an exorcist, but I, I . . . I got one anyway. I—" Suddenly he clapped his hand over his mouth. His eyes were wild.

"Then you have not seen my acquaintance," I said calmly. Perhaps by being in control I could lend some measure of it to him. I went on: "It was not you who told him the story."

Hand still over his mouth, the priest shook his head back and forth. Slowly he pulled himself together. He held his chin up, put his shoulders back, and smoothed the stained front of his cassock. "I have not mentioned any of that for forty years. It has been forgotten, as it well should be. Believe me, you must put the whole thing out of your mind. My wish for you, my child, is that you will also forget the acquaintance who would tell you that evil tale. If he is gone, then it's good riddance. Those who are fascinated by evil all too easily fall prey to it themselves."

"Don't worry," I said, wanting to reassure him. I felt sorry for the man. Probably, under ordinary circumstances, he was quite a good priest and a nice person. "I will go now. I'm sorry that I have upset you."

"Wait, come back. I will give you my blessing."

I let the priest mumble Latin and make the sign of the cross in front of my face. His action did not have the desired effect on me. I did not feel blessed; what I felt was a great degree of unease.

I sought out Mrs. O'Leary's company that night because Michael Archer was still away and I did not want to be alone. The weather was perverse, having come up with a number of dark, ominous clouds at the very time I left the Mission Dolores and walked along the streetcar route, looking ever backward over my shoulder for one to come along.

To stand and wait had been more than I could bear; I had to keep moving. Swirling winds prevented my beloved fog from coming in. The ominousness continued for an almost unbearable length of time, the storm hovering, teasing, threatening, long after I had returned home to Vallejo Street. When, at around eight p.m., it finally did break, I would have expected to feel a release of tension. But that did not happen. Instead, the crashing, booming thunder and cracks of lightning positively unnerved me. Therefore, decently clad in my best dressing gown, I went down to the first floor and knocked on my landlady's door.

"This storm is making me nervous," I said. "I wonder if I might come in and sit with you a while."

"Why bless you, Fremont, I'da thought a herd of wild horses couldn't cause you to turn a hair! Of course you can come in. I'm always glad to have a bit o' company."

Her square-jawed, friendly face was a welcome sight. And I was glad to see that she too had removed her day clothes—she wore a robe that was quite as disreputable as my old woolly one. "Thank you," I said, "this is kind of you."

"Tch, tch," she clucked, ushering me into her parlor. She looked up at the ceiling as a tremendous crack of lightning sounded directly overhead, and all the electric lights blinked off and then on again. "Downright weird, that's what it is. We don't have many thunder and lightning storms in San Francisco, and I can't remember when was the last time we had one this time of year. Sit yerself down, Fremont. Do y' drink beer? I picked up the habit from my husband—he liked his pint—and I kept right on liking it m'self after he was gone."

"I'd like to try it. I haven't had much experience with beer." I sat on a curved and tufted Victorian love seat while she lumbered out to her kitchen. On a round marble-topped table near my elbow were a number of framed photographs. The O'Leary family, I presumed. The largest was of a man with enormous mustaches wearing a policeman's uniform with its row of prominent buttons down the front; his hat was off and stuffed in his armpit and he stood stiffly, posing for the camera. "Is this your husband?" I asked when Mrs. O. returned.

"That's himself," she nodded. She handed me a pint of beer in a thick glass mug, then took the picture in hand and regarded it fondly. "A fine-looking man he was, if I do say so."

I wanted to ask how he had died, but at the moment, with the storm and all, death was the last thing I wanted to talk about. So I merely said, "Yes," and sipped my beer. It had a bitter taste that would take some getting used to, but I liked the bubbles.

Mrs. O'Leary settled herself in an armless chair, her ample body overflowing its sides, and we fell to talking of nothing in particular. The lights blinked a few more times, but the storm was moving off. Its leaving, and the beer, calmed my nerves. Eventually I felt I could deal once more with the matter that was uppermost in my mind.

I deliberately chose a circuitous approach. "How long have you lived in San Francisco, Mrs. O.?"

"All my life, dearie, all my life. My parents come for the gold rush and like most folks who did that, they didn't find no gold. They left the mountains and come back to San Francisco and settled down and just about as soon as they got settled, I was born." She proceeded to give me a history of her life that was none too brief, but it was interesting. She concluded, "And then I married Seamus O'Leary. He was already on the police force. We didn't never have no children, more's the pity. It weren't for lack of trying, you can be sure!"

I smiled at the twinkle in her eye as she said that. When a decent interval had passed, I asked, "Do you know if there was ever a lighthouse on Point Lobos? Where the Cliff House is now?"

"No, never was. They built all the lighthouses within my memory, up and down the coast. That one out in the water off Land's End, that's the nearest to here. Always has been."

"Oh," I said, wondering what that meant to my line of inquiry. I took another tack. "If a number of young women had gone missing at some time within, say, the last fifty years, I suppose that you with your connection to the police would have heard of it."

"What would you be thinking, Fremont?" She eyed me critically. "Whatever it is, you hold that thought while I get us another pint. Don't say no, now, one more ain't gonna do you no harm."

While she was out of the room I tried to figure out what, exactly, I *was* thinking. Since Mr. Partridge's Mission Dolores story had proved to be right on the mark (I tried not to speculate as to how he would have known about it with the priest having suppressed it, probably twenty years before E.A.P. was born), then the one about the lighthouse must have some truth in it too, no matter how much it seemed to be the product of a twisted, even demented, imagination.

My landlady returned. "Now then, you tell me, Fremont, what made you ask about missing women?"

"I will tell you, but first, please, have you heard of such an occurrence?"

Mrs. O'Leary took a great swig of her beer, wiped her mouth with the back of her hand, and looked at me sideways. Slyly. I had never seen that expression on her face before. "Depends what kind of women you be talking about," she said.

I did not really want more beer. I set the mug aside. "Young, probably pretty. It needn't have happened in San Francisco, I suppose, but at least it must have been in the vicinity. Along the coast."

"Missing. Disappeared, like? Probably what you mean is murdered. Dead."

"Yes. But perhaps their bodies were never found."

"That's a real peculiar question, Fremont, coming from somebody like you. I dunno . . . unless they was prostitutes?"

"I doubt they would have been . . . that." As much as I prefer to call a spade a spade, I could not say the word.

"So, what put an idea like that in your head?"

"I read a story somewhere—I don't remember where exactly, you see I read a lot, it's my principal recreation—about a man who lived on the coast where there was a lighthouse. It seems he, ah, lost control of his senses and his actions and may have killed a number of young women. As well as I recall, the story was purported to be true. I can't get it out of my mind, and so I wondered if it really was the truth. I thought, with your connections to the police, that you might know. It's not important, really. More like idle curiosity."

She shook her head. There were spots of color on her cheeks. "Musta been a made-up story, and I'll tell you why. Because there ain't been all that many women to go around out here, if you know what I mean. Men'd go killing each other off but wouldn't kill no women. Oh, maybe once in a while, if it was a drunken brawl in a whorehouse, one would get herself shot, but a whole bunch of women killed? No siree."

She swigged beer, and continued: "Now if'n we were talkin' 'bout the Chinees, that's different."

My landlady launched into a lurid recounting of the way young Chinese women were brought from China to Chinatown and turned into virtual slaves. It was a shocking, sickening tale of female oppression that I began to think would go on and on forever. I perceived that Mrs. O. was getting drunk on her beer, and I did not like to see her that way. As soon as I could without giving offense, I took my leave.

I reflected, as I climbed the stairs to my own apartment, that my pursuit of the truth about Edgar Allan Partridge was leading me into the dark corners of human behavior. In only one day I had seen two decent people—Mrs. O'Leary, and the priest whose name I had not learned—turn rather ugly right before my eyes. I had learned truths I might rather not know. Perhaps I should stop my inquiry.

But even as I thought it, I knew I would not stop.

The next day, Sunday, Michael Archer returned from wherever he had been. I did not see him, but I heard him moving around below me.

And on Monday morning, when I got to my office, I had a horrible shock. Someone had broken in.

8.

Rolling Toward the Inexorable

I'd had no personal acquaintance with violence. The closest I'd ever in my life come to having my person or possessions violated was when I'd been tapped on the bottom by a nursemaid when I was seven, and Father had dismissed her for that. He was a devotee of Mr. Emerson and Monsieur Rousseau, and did not believe in corporal punishment; and Mother, though at times I'm sure she would have dearly loved to throttle me, never went against his wishes.

Therefore, nothing had prepared me for the way I felt: first, when I saw my office door standing ajar with gouge marks like wounds on the frame; then, when I entered into a veritable carnage of paper. As I stood just inside the door, a cold wave of something like fear began behind my eyes and passed down through my throat to my shoulders, my chest, and so on, until it reached my toes. As soon as the wave passed out of my body, outrage set in. This office was mine, *mine,* my sanctum, my holy of holies—how *dare* anyone do this to me?

I strode across the room, heedless of the fact that I was stepping on my own precious typing, to the desk. I seized the telephone, determined to call the police. I lifted the receiver to my ear and heard the operator's voice say, "Number, please" . . . and then I depressed the lever with my finger and hung up the receiver without saying a word. Somehow, through the anger, my brain had intervened with logic so cold that my head felt frozen. I should not call the police. They would come and ask questions, ask why anyone would break into my office. And I remembered what Michael had said: No one must know about the statement I had typed for Li Wong and not all the police could be trusted.

Not only that, but newspaper reporters had a way of following the police around. I knew this because I had become an avid reader of the *Chronicle* since Li Wong's death. A report of a break-in at Fremont Jones Typewriting Services would be bad for business.

I took off my jacket, rolled up my sleeves, and got to work picking up and sorting the scattered papers. I thought as I worked that perhaps this had nothing to do with Li Wong. Perhaps someone had a grudge against one of the several lawyers I typed for. I had no way of knowing who might be working on a controversial case. Even Justin—

As if he had been summoned by my thinking of him, Justin came through the door. "Egad, Fremont!" he declared at seeing me down on my knees in a sea of paper, "What happened here?"

"Take a look at the doorjamb," I said, continuing to pick up and sort. I regretted now my angry striding through these papers. Those that were dirtied were marked with my own footprints.

Justin had examined the doorjamb and now was crouched down looking at the lock. "I'd say whoever it was used a simple tool, something like a crowbar. Maybe a large screwdriver. Why in the world would anyone want to break in here? You don't keep cash about the place, do you?"

I shook my head.

"The bookstore would have been a more likely target. Say, did you ask if they'd had trouble too?"

I shook my head again. That had not occurred to me.

"Shall I pop down and see?"

Justin was half out the door when I called him back. "I'd rather you didn't, Justin. I have a feeling the Sorensons barely tolerate my presence in this building. They have not been very friendly. I expect, if they've had the same problem, I will hear about it from them eventually."

"Well . . . if you say so. But damn it all, Fremont, I don't like this a bit."

"I'm not too fond of it myself." I was discovering, though, that not much real damage had been done. The papers that had been in my "work completed" box on top of the desk were all accounted for, with only a page or two that had been wrinkled or dirtied by my own foot needing to be retyped. Nothing was missing. The vast preponderance of the mess came from the scattered pages of Mr. Partridge's manuscript.

"Hm," said Justin. "Who else is on this floor?"

"No one. There's an empty office next door—I have visions of being able to expand into it someday. The rest of the space is storage for the bookstore. I've never seen them come up here, though, so I don't know if they actually use it or not."

"I'll be back in a minute. Don't worry, I'm not going down there. I just want to check down the hall."

While Justin was gone I got up from the floor and went around behind my desk. The poor file drawer had been mutilated by someone in a frenzy to break its lock. One thing was obvious. Whatever the intruder had been after, it wasn't Partridge's manuscript, which had been tossed about as if in a fury that the drawer contained nothing else. It would take me hours to put all those pages back in order. But that would have to wait. First, I had to retype the ruined work that was due to be picked up today.

Including Justin's, I realized. That must be why he was here. I located a ten-page memorandum to a judge about something or other, and set about retyping one page of it. I was rolling a clean white sheet into the typewriter when he came back. "Did you find anything?" I asked.

"No."

"I didn't think you would." I had really grown remarkably calm and steady—my hands did not shake at all now.

"Looks like whoever did this picked exclusively on you, Fremont. You called the police, of course."

"No, I did not. You know how the reporters follow them around. I didn't want this to get in the papers. Bad publicity would ruin my business, just when things are going so well. Now if you'll excuse me . . ." I began to type.

"You didn't call them? But—Fremont, will you stop using that damn machine and talk to me?"

"This damn machine is in the process of completing the work you no doubt came to pick up, Justin. Please be quiet and let me concentrate or else I will make mistakes."

He paced to the table in front of the window and back, driving his fist into the palm of his hand. Muttering curses, no doubt, though I couldn't hear the words. I typed like an automaton and soon had completed the page. "There. Now I'll just slip it in where it belongs . . . Here you are, Justin. That will be one dollar."

"You're a peculiar woman, Fremont Jones."

"But a very good typist." I grinned. I liked it when Justin got exasperated with me because he always seemed all the more fond when his exasperation was over.

"Here's your dollar." And there was his sunny smile. He said, "I care about you, in case you don't know it. I don't like to think of anybody coming in here and tearing the place to pieces. What if you'd been here? You might have been hurt. Do you have any idea what the burglar, thief, whatever you want to call him, was looking for?"

I glanced down at my thoroughly destroyed file drawer. For a brief moment I entertained the idea of telling Justin the whole truth, that I thought word had somehow got out that I'd typed something for Li Wong. But though I trusted that Justin would defend me with his life if anyone attacked me in his presence, I did not trust him to keep his mouth shut. He was a person who talked first and thought later—how he managed to be a successful lawyer was beyond me.

So I said, "I expect it was as you at first suggested—a burglar looking for money. And of course there was none here, so he made a mess of the place instead."

"And you're determined not to call the police. You won't let me change your mind, won't let me do it for you?"

"No. I dread the publicity, Justin. And really, there was very little damage done. The intruder did not even touch my typewriter, and that's the most valuable thing I own. Now, as happy as I always am to see you, I'd like you to be on your way. I have a lot of work to do here."

"I see you do. I guess you're right." Yet he lingered. He came around to the side of my desk, bent his head, and swiftly kissed my cheek. "I would hate it, Fremont, if anything bad happened to you. I'll call you later in the week. I expect I'll have a surprise for you by the weekend. Good-bye for now."

"Good-bye, Justin."

I put my fingers to my cheek. He'd said he cared, that he didn't want anything bad to happen to me. He'd kissed my cheek. I wondered what the surprise might be. And I thought how resilient human nature is, that I should now feel so warm all over where previously I had been so cold.

Some three hours later, I sat at the table in front of the window, preparing to eat lunch. As I took a sandwich out of the paper sack, I thought that lunchtimes had been more fun before Justin's business picked up. He hardly ever had time to eat with me anymore. The next thing I knew, he'd be making so much money that he'd hire his own secretary, and then I wouldn't see him at all. Unless . . . No, I shouldn't think things like that.

One of the problems with a determination not to marry is that I have never figured out where falling in love fits into this scenario. In fact, when I was at Wellesley and my fellow students were going around enraptured and getting engagement rings slipped upon their fingers, I had failed to see the point of it. I'd felt a few brief flutterings of desire, I do not deny that, but men near my own age had not held my interest for long. I'd had an enduring, secret crush on one of my father's friends, but of course it had come to nothing and burned itself out in time. Now . . .

I knew I was falling in love with Justin. When he touched me, even if it were only my elbow to guide me across the street, I felt a delicious thrill. And of course, I wanted more. But if one is not to marry, then where are the delicious thrills to lead? I did not know. I did not like to think about it. And so I didn't anymore.

I opened the newspaper and began to scan for news of Chinatown, for anything that might shed light on the mystery of Li Wong's murder. Since I started reading the newspaper so assiduously, I had learned a good deal about my new home. Much of it, since reporters are so invariably attracted to the scandalous, had to do with the bribery and corruption that were rife in San Francisco's business world. I seldom had reason to go down into the business district, its sole attraction for me being the fact that it was the only part of town in which the streets were flat. Well, that wasn't quite true; the streets were reputed to be flat in North Beach also, but I had not been there at all. Anyway, the wonder was that there could be all this scandalous hoopla in the business district and down along the docks, while the rest of the city should be such a joyous place.

Today's big article was about a stock swindle. My father, who knew a good deal about stocks, might have been interested. I, who hoped never to have to understand anything about margins and shares and selling short and all that, was not. I munched on my sandwich and turned pages idly until, tucked away at the bottom of an inner page, a headline caught my eye: JAPAN INVADES KOREA—TSAR RUMORED DISPLEASED. All kinds of bells went off in my head—Michael Archer a.k.a. Mikhail Arkady Something, Japan, Tsar, Russia . . . I read avidly.

I gathered that Russia had been coveting the peninsula of Korea as an opening to the Pacific. Interesting. I hadn't realized that Russia, which as I recalled was mostly land-locked, had much of a navy. But this Tsar Nicholas II, who was apparently something of a sailing buff, had built up the navy, and had plans for Korea that Japan was now in the process of thwarting. The question was, would Russia go to war with Japan?

Most unprofitably, although Mrs. O'Leary would certainly have approved, I allowed my mind to have free rein over Michael's recent absence. His mention of Japan, as if he were familiar with that so very foreign country—more foreign to me and, I supposed, to most Americans than China. I could not help but think that maybe Mrs. O. was right. Maybe my friend Michael Archer was really a spy. If that were the case, my own hunch was that he would be a spy for our side, that he had knowledge of Russia through his family background, that he spoke the language and so could pass for a Russian. Might he have gone to gather information for the United States Government about the possible war between Russia and Japan?

No, he could hardly have done that. One cannot sail, not even on a steamship, to Japan and back in less than two weeks. Which was how long he had been gone. But he could have contacts with whom he might meet at some out-of-the-way place. Oh, how I wished that I could ask him, and that he would let me in on his secrets!

I mused over this for a while longer, and gave it up only when the telephone rang. The caller was one of my customers, wanting to make a referral. Did I have the time to type a book for a retired professor? Did I! A big job like that would pay my rent for weeks to come. All frivolous thinking was banished from my head as I went to work with a will to clear my desk before the promised professor, retired, might appear later in the afternoon.

The professor came as promised, and so did the locksmith I'd called to install a new lock on my office door. He was also able to repair the damage to the lock on my file drawer. I had a busy and most gratifying afternoon, and felt only the merest qualm as I locked the door and left at the end of my working day. I banished the qualm by reasoning that the burglar, or whatever one wanted to call him, had discovered that what he sought was not there, and so would have no need to come back.

Imagine my happy surprise to find a blooming gloxinia in a pot, sitting on my hall table! There was a card:

> *As the flowers you gave me brought such enjoyment, I seek to return the favor. I am back, as you see, and hope that you have recovered from your sniffles in my absence.*
> *With warmest regards, Michael.*

"How nice!" I exclaimed aloud. The flowers were lovely, with large petals that were white at their frilly edges and grew ever pinker toward the center, where they plunged into a glowing throat of deep magenta. Their velvety texture made me want to touch them. I carried the pot into my living room and placed it in the deep windowsill —to one side, as I so often sat in this window.

It should have come as no surprise to me that, not long after, I nearly drowned myself by falling asleep in the bathtub. Of course, I had good reason to be exhausted—it had been an exhausting day.

Thanking Michael for the gloxinia would have to wait until another time.

The next morning I wrote him a note of thanks while I drank my second cup of coffee. (Until after the first cup I cannot possibly do anything at all civil. A great advantage to living alone is that I no longer have to be polite at the breakfast table.) On my way out of the house, I left the note on *his* hall table, where he would surely find it.

The fine mist of dissipating fog was refreshing upon my face, and the cable car ride as exhilarating as always. I had got to know the people I encountered in my daily routine—the driver of the cable car, the newsboy on the corner of Van Ness and Sacramento streets from whom I bought the *Chronicle* every morning. I felt quite satisfied to have so settled in. Someday I would receive a letter from my father— less irate than the only one I had received thus far—saying that he forgave me for leaving Boston. Augusta had the talent for being a thorn in one's side, even from a great distance. She wrote regularly, short little letters full of curlicues (even her handwriting had pretensions) and words designed to instill guilt. I scanned them and consigned them to the trash where, in my opinion, guilt belongs. If Father, with or without the concurrence of his new wife, could have been happy with me and my accomplishments, my own happiness would have been complete.

I began my morning's work by typing a brief, brisk, newsy response to Augusta's latest. It was always a relief to have that out of the way. The retired professor's book—memoirs of his extensive travels, now in the form of several thick notebooks—waited on the corner of my desk. I had at the moment no small jobs waiting. However, before beginning on the professor's book, I thought I had best retype the pages of Mr. Partridge's manuscript that had been ruined in the break-in. There was always the chance that the poor man might still return for his stories. On my part, I was not at all sure how to proceed with finding out what had happened to him.

As I was reassembling the manuscript, inserting the pages I had retyped, "Damned to Darkness" once more drew me in. I gave in to temptation. I would read a little of Peregrine's story, beginning with page 32:

94

I was three years old when first I was introduced to the Black Room. Hubert, the manservant, took me there. I went trustingly, because Hubert had always been kind to me. I liked him. Hubert was tall, almost as tall as the trees in the conservatory, which were the only trees I had ever seen, as I was not allowed to go out of the house. He had pale yellow hair, like a prince in a picture book, though his face was not quite as handsome.

With my little hand tucked in Hubert's, I trotted along into a part of the house where I had never been before. We went down a hall behind the green door, turned a corner, and began to climb some narrow stairs. "Where are we going?" I asked, naturally enough.

"You will see," was the reply.

The stairs were so steep that my short legs had a hard time of them, and Hubert continually pulled upward on my arm in a way that was unpleasant. But I did not complain, because of my liking for him. It seemed to me that we went up and up, the stairs always turning, for a very long time. This must mean that we were going to the top of the house. I became excited. There was a room up there that I liked very much, all its walls were glass, from which I could look out and pretend I was the king and this was my kingdom.

But we did not go to that room. When at last we came out of the narrow, cramped stairway, we were in a place I did not remember at all. I felt uncomfortable, and inclined to lag behind. Hubert pulled on my arm, and I needs must go with him.

He opened a door upon a room that was quite small, larger than a closet, but like a closet it had no windows. Not a single one. The walls were all dark wood, so dark they were almost black. I remembered a word from the fairy stories I liked so much even though they frightened me: ebony. Walls as black as ebony. The room was not the shape of other rooms. When I was older I knew that it was in the shape of a hexagon, but at three I knew only that it was different. The ceiling went up to a point high overhead. There was no rug on the floor. Both ceiling and floor were of the same dark wood as the walls. There was not a stick of furniture, not a toy nor a book nor anything.

"You will stay here for a while, Master Peregrine."

Being three years old, of course I asked, "Why?" I was always asking why, even though I knew it irritated people, especially my mother, whose irritation was a thing to be avoided.

"It is a part of your education," Hubert said. "In this room you will learn to be strong, and not to feel fear."

I felt my lower lip begin to tremble. I said, correctly, "I must not cry."

"That is right. You must stand," Hubert demonstrated, "like this."

I was always an obedient child. In imitation of the only male person I had ever known, I clasped my hands behind my back and set my legs apart. Hubert came over and touched my bare knee—I wore short pants and knee-high stockings—and said, "Make your knees stiff, Master Peregrine." I did so. "That is very good," said Hubert. He straightened up to all of his great height and looked down at me.

"Now I will leave you here. It will be dark when I close the door. No matter what happens, you must continue to stand in that pose, you must not move a muscle. You must not call out, and you must not cry. Remember, you are learning to be strong and not to feel fear. When the time is right, I will come for you. Do you understand?"

"I don't want to stay here," I said.

"You must," said Hubert firmly, and closed the door.

The instant darkness was absolute: soul-devouring black. My ears roared with silence. I heard a whimper, and knew that I had made it. I held on to my own hands tighter, locked my knees so hard I felt as if they might break. I could not bear to look into the blackness, so I closed my eyes, but that was worse. I opened them again. My eyelashes were sticky, my face was wet—already I had failed. I was crying, but silently. I wanted to wipe my cheeks but to do that I would have to break the pose.

You might wonder, dear reader, why this stupid child did not do as he pleased, since he was quite alone and there was no one to see. Ah, you shall learn the horrid truth of it.

Moments passed, an eternity, who could tell? Just when I had reached the limit of my endurance, I felt a wind spring up—there in that enclosed room, where no wind should be. Wind came through windows when they were open, I knew, and there were no windows. At first the wind was welcome because it dried my tear-stained face.

But then I heard—or perhaps I only felt—a vibration, Boom, Boom, Boom, Boom, *like a huge, beating heart. Not my own heart, which I felt fluttering in my chest like the canary in its cage when the cat teased it.*

BOOM, BOOM, BOOM. Still I could see nothing, but I knew. The door had not opened, there was no place in this room to hide, but I knew. I knew that in the awful darkness I was no longer alone. My knees buckled and I was falling, falling, falling. Falling into Blackness.

I remember nothing after that, until Hubert gathered me in his arms and lifted me up and I opened my eyes. I said in the small voice of a three-year-old child, "I failed." Failure was a concept with which I was already, alas, quite familiar.

Hubert said, "That was only the first trial, Master Peregrine. There will be others."

The plight of that little boy moved me to my own tears. I would not give up my attempt to find out the fate of Mr. Edgar Allan Partridge. I could not.

Where, how, and most of all *when* I was to continue my investigations—those were good questions. My days were full, and by midweek the balance of my Saturday was full also. Justin called, and said I must accompany him as soon as I closed the office that day. He wanted to show me something very exciting, a big surprise.

9.

Vulnerability Discovered

"WHERE ARE WE going?" I asked, peering out the window of the hansom cab Justin had rented for our outing. We were still on Sacramento Street and had just crossed Van Ness, heading west.

"You'll see," he said.

"Is our destination a part of this big surprise?"

"Could be." He raised one eyebrow, trying, I thought, to look mysterious. The effect was ruined somewhat by the corners of his mouth twitching.

"Give me a hint," I teased.

"No hints. No more questions. I ought to make you close your eyes. On second thought, I ought to have brought a blindfold, because even if I made you promise to keep your eyes closed, Fremont, I'm sure you'd peek. Your insatiable curiosity would get the better of you. Since I didn't bring a blindfold, the very least you can do is let the suspense build in silence."

"Um-hm," I responded, and then obligingly kept silent. Of course, I had speculated for days as to the nature of this "surprise." I had rather hoped it would be a trip across the Bay to meet Justin's parents. They lived, as I recalled from one of our earliest conversations, in Berkeley, where his father was a professor at the University of California. I should like to have visited there, with or without meeting the senior Camerons. But we were going in the opposite direction. In fact, we were climbing yet another hill in the direction of the old Presidio.

Short of that district, however, the driver turned onto another street whose name I missed for studying the interesting Victorian facades of the houses we passed. We went several blocks and turned again, onto Pacific Avenue, and shortly the cab stopped.

"We get out here," said Justin, suiting his actions to his words and handing me out behind him. He paid the cabbie and I stood waiting on the sidewalk, wondering if I had dressed appropriately for whatever lay in store. I wore the plum-colored suit, which was more elegant than my usual workday garb, but not by much.

"Now turn around," said Justin touching my shoulder, "and regard the house in front of you."

I did so. It was no mansion—the mansions being principally on Nob Hill on the other side of Van Ness Avenue—but it was quite a nice house, painted light gray with white trim. Somewhat narrower than the houses on either side, it was distinguished by a darker gray mansard roof, and an elegant treatment of its front door—two slim columns on either side of a shallow portico with a dentiled cornice at the top.

I guessed, "The surprise is in this house?"

In answer, Justin took my hand and began to pull me up the steps. I protested, hanging back, "Really, Justin, you might have warned me if you were taking me to meet friends of yours. What sort of occasion—"

Justin stopped me by turning and laying his index finger upon my lips. From his pocket he produced a key, held it up with a dramatic flourish, like a magician, then turned and inserted it into the door lock. *"Voilà!"* he proclaimed, flinging open the front door.

Clearly, he meant for me to enter; just as clearly, I was not so sure I should. Though I am certainly not a timid person, I hope I am not foolhardy, and I had no idea what waited on the other side of that door. Yet Justin's innocent face was wreathed in smiles, and his eyes were practically dancing out of his head in anticipation. I did not want to disappoint him. I stepped across the threshold.

Nothing leapt out at me. Instead, I was engulfed by that kind of watchful silence that empty houses always seem to exude. I heard Justin's step behind me and his closing of the door. I turned to him, saying, "What—" and once more he placed his finger upon my lips.

"Come, Fremont," he said softly, "I want to show you something beautiful."

He led me down a narrow, uncarpeted hall. Glancing to either side, I saw empty rooms through open doors. Near the back of the house, through an open arch on our right, was a large room, which we entered, and Justin dropped my hand. This was furnished, but I had scarce time to observe the furnishings. A large, many-paned bow window took up most of the rear wall. My heart, and my breath, caught in my throat. Through the window I saw the blue waters of San Francisco Bay dotted with boats, tiny from this distance, and the green and brown hills of Marin beyond. "Oh, yes!" I exclaimed, hastening right up to the glass. "What a splendid view!"

Justin followed, put his arm around my shoulder, and pulled me close to his side. "As I said, beautiful. This is my surprise. This house is mine, Fremont. I bought it just this week, and you are my first guest. I wanted you to be the first to share all this with me."

"I'm honored. And impressed." I glanced up at him. He was not looking at the view, but down at me. My heart pounded. The polite, rather shy man I'd begun to know so well was gone; he had been replaced by one with hungry blue eyes and a passionate curve to his mouth.

He touched my cheek; with the tips of his fingers he stroked the line of my jaw, and the hunger in his eyes deepened and flared like the blaze of light in a star sapphire. "I'm going to be successful, Fremont. Very, very successful," he said, as if the promise of his success gave him courage, and license for what he was about to do.

He needed no license—I wanted his kiss. I liked the change in him, liked the strength in his hand as he gripped my chin and brought his mouth down over mine. My lips were parted; I had been about to say, "Congratulations," but I did not get the chance. Justin's tongue took advantage of my parted lips.

It was our first real kiss, and unlike any other kiss—first or otherwise—I'd ever joined in. His tongue set me on fire. Instantly! I wanted to drink him in.

Together we were all heat, all flames, without time or regard for tenderness, and in truth I could not say how my jacket came unbuttoned, and my blouse, whether by my own hand or his. But it was Justin who loosed the ribbons of my camisole, and eased the jacket and blouse from my shoulders so that they fell to the floor. Justin who knelt before me and freed my breasts from the camisole and took their throbbing tips into his mouth, one after the other. I thought I would die of it.

I moaned. I sounded like some tormented creature, a wild thing. I tangled my hands in the hair of his head, pressing him closer, and closed my eyes. My mind struggled to surface through all the exquisite sensations. His hand went beneath my skirt, and I thought, *I should stop him*. I meant to say, "No more," and perhaps I did; but he did not stop. And I did not really want him to.

My body felt as if all my bones had dissolved, melted in the heat we generated. Indeed I *was* melting, I felt my own juices flowing in a way that should have been shameful, but that somehow was natural and right, and that served to increase my own surprising ardor. Justin's mouth was again on mine, and his hands—strong and masterful—laid me down upon the rug in front of that wonderful wide window. It was such a relief not to have to stand on my boneless legs. Again I heard the moaning that came from me.

Justin's tongue, that bringer of fire, darted along my skin. I burned, I burned! His fingers touched me; beneath my skirt I was naked except for my stockings. When had that happened? I had no time to think of it, for Justin's fingers were doing things to me there where no one had ever touched!

I gasped. My eyes flew open. I saw Justin's face inches above me and opened my mouth to speak, but his mouth came over mine again, and once more I drank him in. This time I drowned. Gladly.

"You were a virgin," Justin said.

He lay beside me, fully clothed from the waist up—though his tie was loosened—and naked from the waist down. His member, which had seemed huge only a few moments ago, was now limp in a little nest of golden hair that was darker than the hair upon his head. I wanted to touch that changeable, magical shaft but did not dare, which was odd, considering what he had done to me.

"Did that surprise you?" I asked. I was a bit unsure whether I had enjoyed the whole experience or not. There had been pain, but not much. On reflection, I rather wanted to do it again. Now that I knew what it was all about, I would probably enjoy the concluding part more.

"Well, yes. I hope I didn't hurt you. And I didn't think about the blood. This is a new rug."

He looked so dismayed that I laughed. Then I sat up and took stock of myself. "You need not worry," I said, "as I was not hurt and there is not all that much blood, and what there is, is on my petticoat. I shall have to take it off." But later, I thought, as I rearranged my skirts to cover myself, and I lay back down. I was exhausted.

Now, for the first time, Justin grew tender. He leaned up on one elbow and stroked my hair back from my face. He bent his head and kissed my cheek. Softly he inquired, "Did you like it?"

"Up until the last. I did not expect that to happen," I answered honestly.

"But you were so, so—"

"Passionate? Yes, I was. And so were you. I was only responding in kind."

Justin took up my hand and laced his fingers through mine. "You're such an unusual woman. I never know what to expect from you. I've been planning this for weeks, ever since I realized that I might be able to buy a house like this. I couldn't take you where I lived before, you see, it was a worse hole in the wall than my office. But as soon as I saw this big window I thought: Here. This is where I will make love to Fremont for the first time. Only, I didn't know it really would be your first time."

I turned my head and looked out of the window. It would have been nice, I thought, if the sun were setting and turning the sky lovely shades of rose and gold. But it was not; the sky was still quite blue. What Justin and I had done had not taken very long at all. Somehow that made me feel sad.

"Your surprise," I whispered involuntarily. Then I realized what I had said. Yes, it had been a surprise all right. But was I sorry I had let it happen? I really didn't know. In that moment I felt strange, empty and alone, though Justin was beside me, and only a short while ago he had filled me literally. I did not understand why I should feel this way.

Justin had sat up and was pulling on his trousers. He said, "Come on, let me show you the rest of the house. I'll tell you what I have planned for all the rooms."

"I think you had better show me the bathroom first," I observed. "I shall have to put myself back together."

That night I started a diary. I had always scorned the keeping of a journal as something of little value that ladies are taught to do, like embroidery. But I had to tell my thoughts to someone, and there was no one else to tell. Nor was there anyone to ask any of the questions that pounded inside my head. Does everyone feel like that the first time, excited, yet somehow unfulfilled? Would it have been different if I had waited until marriage? I *couldn't* wait until marriage; I was never going to marry. And I was in love with Justin. I'd thought I was. Of course I was!

The diary accepted everything, and gave nothing in return. Not even guilt. The guilt was coming from inside me. I didn't believe in guilt, yet there it was.

Sunday was always a quiet day, with no work to go to and Mrs. O'Leary at church the whole morning long, and sometimes into the afternoon. Her social life revolved around her church. I sat in my window, not reading the book in my hand, and thought perhaps I had lost something in being brought up without traditional religion. A church gave one a ready-made place to form friendships, an automatic common bond with other people. Religion gave one a framework on which to hang the kind of guilt that I continued to feel. Muscles I had never used before were sore, and every movement was a reminder.

Nonsense! I said to myself, getting down from the window seat. I should dress, go out, do something. And be firm in putting guilt aside. Hadn't I always thought it the greatest waste of time and energy in the world?

I went into my bedroom, shed my dressing gown, and draped it across the foot of the bed where it would be handy later. On my way to the wardrobe, already puzzling over what to wear, I caught a glimpse of my pale body in the long mirror on the wall. I went and stood before it and looked at myself—an occupation I am not often given to.

Actually, I thought, I have quite a nice body. Not voluptuous or even sensual—I was far too lean for that. But my breasts were big enough to please (I touched them lightly and thought of Justin's mouth, touching not lightly at all), my waist nipped in as it should, and my legs were long and rather shapely. Had I pleased him?

If only . . . if only . . . What? In the mirror I saw my eyes widen as I suddenly knew the answer to that partially formed question. If only he had made love to me a second time, more slowly, more tenderly, perhaps upstairs in his new house where he did have a bed. I had seen it. I now realized that I had wanted to take him by the hand and lead him to that bed and say, "Again. Make love to me again. And let me touch you in all the ways that you have touched me." Tears came into my eyes, and I hated those tears, hated my confusion and my remorse. For the tiniest of moments I even hated myself, for the first time in my life.

The moment passed, I made it pass, and I padded over to the wardrobe and pulled out my most feminine daytime dress: cream-colored cotton with a sheer, high-collared yoke trimmed in lace and a lace edging along the sleeves. The skirt was full, and in the new, shorter length that stopped an inch above the ankles. This dress had stockings and shoes to match, and I put them on too, and piled my hair up on top of my head. All dressed up and no place, really, to go.

I met Michael Archer on the stairs. To be precise, he was on his way down before me, heard me behind him, and waited for me to catch up.

"Thank you again for the gloxinia," I said as his eyes swept over me and his lips shaped a smile of approval. "I trust you found my note."

"I did, and you are quite welcome. I see you are on your way out."

105

"As you also appear to be." Suddenly I remembered the newspaper article about Russia and Japan, and wondered if I could somehow lure him into telling me his secrets. Pausing halfway down the last flight of steps, I said tentatively, "I suppose you have some particular destination planned."

"Yes, I do," he said, regarding me with interest, his head a little to one side. "But no particular company. May I inquire what your own plans are for this lovely Sunday afternoon?"

"I'm just going for a walk. You're right, it is too lovely a day to stay indoors."

Michael went down two steps, turned back, and looked me over from head to foot. He said, "I wonder . . . But you are so elegantly dressed . . ."

"Well, it *is* Sunday," I said, as if I needed an excuse.

"Indeed. I was wondering if you might care to join me. I'm taking my boat out into the Bay. Do you sail, Fremont?"

"I have. Not often, but I don't get seasick. I should like very much to join you."

He reached up his hand, I gave him mine, and he ushered me down the remaining steps. "We'll just have to be careful that you don't fall into the water and ruin your dress."

"Would you like me to change? I could do it quickly."

"No. You're even lovelier than the weather, my dear Fremont. Don't worry, I'll take good care of you."

Michael's boat was small and swift, with sails fore and aft rigged to a single mast, and the name *Katya* painted upon the stern. When I asked who was the *Katya* he'd named the boat after, Michael said enigmatically, "She is no longer living," in a way that precluded further inquiry.

Michael proved quite skilled at handling the boat himself, so I gathered that he often sailed alone. I could be of no help in the setting of the sails, but I did hold the wheel and keep us on course while he made occasional adjustments.

Almost as interesting as the sailing itself was my first foray into the world of San Francisco's waterfront. In getting to the pier where the smaller vessels were docked, we had passed large ships being loaded or unloaded by a number of bustling men, most of them Chinese. I'd found the level of activity surprising for a Sunday, and remarked upon it. Michael said that because the Chinese had no religious concept of a "day of rest," the shipping companies exploited their labor by requiring them to work seven days a week.

I had watched the hardworking Chinese with interest, reminded of something that lay at the back of my mind, but I could not call it forth. I did not think about it anymore until we were well out on the Bay. Michael was at the wheel and I sat in the stern enjoying the feeling of motion and the fresh, stiff breeze that polished my cheeks. Suddenly for no reason, as sometimes happens when one has fruitlessly tried and failed to recall a piece of information, it popped into my head: *Trans-Hawaiian Trading Company*. I could hear Li Wong saying the words, with a sideways slash of his finger to indicate the hyphen, and see myself typing them onto the paper!

I got up carefully from my seat and made my way to Michael. He turned his head and smiled over his shoulder, saying, "Enjoying yourself?"

"Yes!" We spoke in raised voices in order to hear each other over the wind in the sails and the water rushing beneath the hull. I planted my feet wide apart for balance and leaned toward him. "Michael, I've just remembered something about Li Wong."

The expression on his face changed from pleasant to wary in an instant. "Tell me."

"It's not much." A gust of wind tore a strand of my hair loose and whipped it across my eyes; at the same moment the deck lurched a little and upset my balance. He reached out a hand to steady me, keeping the other on the wheel. When I'd recovered and wiped the hair from my eyes I said, "It's just a name he mentioned: Trans-Hawaiian Trading Company."

"Can you remember the context?"

"Not really. I have a general idea that Li Wong was in the midst of working out some sort of agreement with them, with this trading company, and he wanted it set down in writing so that what he'd done would not be lost. In case something happened to him—which, of course, it did. Are you familiar with that company, Michael?"

He scowled, and nodded curtly.

"Well?" I asked, fighting another piece of hair out of my eyes.

"Let me think about it. For now, you'd best sit down again, Fremont, or else hold onto the rail. Your shoes don't provide much traction on the deck."

He was right about that. Watching my head as I passed under the boom, I went up into the prow, where I held on with both hands. The wind had made a mess of my topknot, so I took it down and let my hair stream freely back from my face. That was much better!

We had passed by Alcatraz Island and were on the far side of the Bay now, sailing in the direction of the Golden Gate. I left off my concern for Li Wong as I grasped a new idea, and soon was making my way back to Michael once more.

He looked at me, amused, as I gingerly stepped and sometimes slid my way to him. "You don't stay put for very long, do you? Or your hair, either, I see."

This time I did not trust my feet alone to keep me upright. I came alongside of Michael and grasped the small rail behind his back where he stood at the wheel, much in the way a symphony orchestra conductor stands with a railing around his podium. This put me quite close to him, but I felt more stable. "I have a request," I said over his shoulder.

"Which is?" He did not turn his head.

"Could we sail to Mile Rock? I'd like to see the lighthouse."

"I can try it." Michael craned his neck, as if listening to something I could not hear. "The water is relatively calm today, but we'll have to pass through the straits at the Golden Gate and the current can be treacherous there, no matter how calm the waters may appear. I'd intended to stay within the Bay."

"Please. I really want to see it."

"All right, but things might get a little rough."

"I don't mind."

Turning the boat southward when we had passed through the Golden Gate proved quite exciting. I held the wheel while Michael manipulated the sails, and I wished I knew better what I was doing. The boat felt like a live creature under my inexpert hands, pulsing and heaving and shuddering, then darting forward all in a rush. Our new direction achieved, I surrendered the wheel to Michael and once more went into the prow, where I could get the best view.

We passed near Mile Rock and I looked up at the towering lighthouse, thinking of E.A.P.'s strange story about the Lens that ate light. True to its name, Mile Rock was one single huge rock, upon which the sea crashed relentlessly. There must have been a lighthouse keeper, but how anyone could live in such a place I could not imagine. At any rate, scrutinizing it as best I could with the wind and the spray in my face, I did not think this was the site about which Mr. Partridge had constructed his tale. The details did not fit. But there were other lighthouses, and perhaps on other days Michael Archer could be persuaded to take me to them. Ah, there was food for thought!

My thoughts, however, having (as it so often seemed) a will of their own, were soon going in a quite different direction. Over the wind Michael called my name: "Fremont!" and I made my way back to him. He directed me to sit in the stern and hold on tight. He intended to lash the wheel while he reset the sails to turn us back toward Land's End, and thence into the Bay once more. He expected we would have a rough turning, and we did. As I watched him work, my errant mind presented me with a new vision of Michael Archer. A most disquieting vision.

This man, who on land was an elegant, bookish gentleman with fine clothes and a precisely trimmed, gray-shot beard, was another person entirely as he pitted himself and his boat against the heaving, resistant sea. I had not realized before how physically strong Michael was, but now every reach of his arms, every brace of his well-muscled legs, drove his strength home to me. The very set of his head against the wind declared that here was a man in his element; and though he might be some twenty years older than I, he was still in the prime of his life.

So, on the surface of the sea Michael was in his element, and I was completely out of mine. I sat where he had placed me, able to do nothing but cling to the railings on either side. I felt more helpless than I had ever felt in my adult life. I admired Michael, but now I began to fear him, too.

The deck pitched sharply as the boat lurched into its turn. Her seams creaked and groaned, protesting like a creature reluctantly obedient to her master. Michael returned from the rigging to unlash the wheel, and the light caught his eyes, gleaming; his expression was one of exultant, primitive enjoyment. I could see that against an enemy he would be ruthless, wild, and, more than likely, victorious.

I felt a fool. I did not really know this man, as Mrs. O'Leary was always pointing out to me. Yet the moment I set foot upon his boat I had placed myself at his mercy. If he wanted to, he could pick me up bodily and pitch me into the sea, with no one ever the wiser. That certainly would be the end of me, for I could not swim. I would sink down, down, down, my only future to become a meal for the denizens of the deep!

10.

The Game Is
Well Afoot

MICHAEL DID NOT pitch me over the side. Instead, remarking that I looked chilled, he took off his corduroy jacket and gave it to me to wear. I was grateful for its warmth. When we were once more on a smooth course, he asked me to take the wheel while he rummaged about in the small hatch below deck. He came up with an old sweater, which he pulled over his head, and a bottle of some kind of liquor.

"Whiskey," he said, brandishing the bottle, "not the drink of choice for ladies, and I have no glasses, but would you like a swig, Fremont? To chase away the remainder of the chill?"

Hands still on the wheel, I glanced with distaste at the bottle and replied, "No, thank you." My fear of him had faded—a strange interlude that had played itself out—but I didn't relish the thought of his getting drunk on me!

Michael uncorked the bottle and took a lengthy swallow. "Ah!" he said with satisfaction, reinserting the cork and pounding it in smartly with the heel of his hand. "That was quite a ride we had!"

"Exhilarating," I said with some acerbity.

Michael laughed. After stashing the whiskey bottle in a coil of rope, he planted his fists on his hips and cocked his head to one side, observing my performance at the wheel. "You'd make a fine sailor if you'd a mind for it, Fremont."

I raised one eyebrow skeptically.

"You have a steady hand on the wheel, and more important than that, you possess a sailor's most important attribute."

"And, pray tell, what might that be?"

"Fearlessness," said Michael, coming over to claim the wheel once more.

"I was not entirely without fear," I said, stepping away and averting my eyes. I did not want to talk of fear.

"Then you kept it admirably under control."

"I should hope so."

"Would you like me to teach you the rudiments of sailing? Not today, of course, I'm sure we have both had enough of battling the waves for one day. But if you are interested, we could set a schedule for some sailing lessons."

I was greatly tempted. Haltingly I said, "First, I think I should learn to swim—"

"By all means!" Michael grimaced. "I forgot that most ladies are not taught that skill."

"After that, perhaps . . ." I could not finish. I turned my back to him and leaned against the starboard railing, watching the steep sides of San Francisco's hills slide by, dropping into the Bay. To trust or not to trust, that was my dilemma, and I was truly caught in it.

I felt a change in the boat's direction, and the tilt of the deck as she began to tack. Surprised, I jerked around; the wind whipped my hair across my face. "Where are you going?" I demanded, "I thought we were headed back to shore."

"We've an hour or more to spare before the fog comes in, and there's something I've been wanting to talk to you about. I have just realized that we will never have more privacy than we do on this boat."

How well I knew that!

"So, I intend to anchor for a short while in the lee of Alcatraz. That way we can talk without having to yell over the wind."

I wanted to get back, but I was also curious to know what Michael wanted to talk about. As usual, curiosity won. I did not protest as he maneuvered us into relative shelter and dropped anchor. When he had secured the sails, he joined me in the stern—the only real seating on the boat.

"I am all ears," I said.

"No, you are not," Michael said playfully. The afternoon's outing had put him in high spirits, and high color. His eyes, the exact blue-gray of the Bay's waters, danced with light; his cheeks glowed ruddy with windburn. "You are, at the moment, mostly hair, Fremont. And a jacket several sizes too large for you!"

"The jacket is warm, the hair can be fixed." I was determined not to be beguiled by Michael's jaunty charm. "Whereas my curiosity cries out to be satisfied! Please, what is it that you wanted to talk about in all this privacy?"

"Li Wong."

"Have you learned something new?"

"I was wondering if you had recalled any more of what he said about the Trans-Hawaiian Trading Company."

"No. Just that he mentioned the name, and I think one other company name. But exactly what he said . . . that's still a mystery to me."

Michael looked me so hard in the eyes that I felt he did not believe me. I stared stonily back at him.

"We have played somewhat, you and I," he said, "at being Holmes and Watson. Is that not so?"

I nodded, wondering where he was going with this line of thinking.

"Your Holmes to my Watson," he persisted.

"Though doubtless it should be the other way around."

"Oh, I think not. I am quite content to play Watson to you, Fremont. Except for one thing."

"Which is?"

"Partners—like Watson and Holmes—must have complete trust in each other, and you have not given me your trust."

I was astonished—and something more. "How do you come to that conclusion, Michael?"

"I can sense it. I am experienced in these matters. I know that you have not told me everything."

113

Now the something more exploded: anger. "How can you have the audacity to say that I do not trust you when this very afternoon I have placed my life in your hands? We could have capsized, you could have tossed me overboard, and I cannot swim!"

"Ssh. Easy!"

"I will not be gentled by you as if I were a horse!" My emotions were running quite out of control, and I did not care. The fact that he was right had nothing to do with it. "And just who are you to talk of trust? You haven't told me lots and lots of things. I don't even know who you really are. How can you sit there and demand that I trust you?"

Michael asked quietly, "What would you like to know?"

This simple question, so gently put, penetrated my anger like a shot to the brain. I took a deep breath and plunged. "Michael Archer, are you some kind of spy?"

He did not move a muscle, did not even blink, but he did react. The ruddiness of his cheeks lessened by a barely perceptible degree, and behind the pupils of his eyes an opaqueness descended, like a shade drawn behind a window. "An interesting question," he said. "I wonder what provoked it."

"That is not an answer."

"Our inquisitive and gossip-mongering landlady has no doubt been putting ideas into your head."

"Perhaps, but do give me credit for having a mind of my own."

"Oh, I give you more than enough credit for that. I am a great admirer of your mind, Fremont Jones. But I fear I have interrupted you. Please continue."

"Very well. I concluded that the idea, which I admit was suggested by Mrs. O'Leary, had merit for several reasons. You are young to have retired, unless you were exceptionally wealthy, which you do not appear to be. This in itself suggests some form of government service, to which one might be recalled. You no doubt speak Russian like a native, as you would have learned it from your parents in your own home while growing up. When we were discussing the recent earthquake, you spoke of Japan with an air of certainty, as if you had considerable knowledge of that faraway place. And your most recent absence coincides with the business I have read a little about, of Russia and Japan possibly going to war over Korea. So I ask you again: Are you a spy, Michael?"

Michael relaxed. He leaned back, rubbing his hands on his thighs. His eyes cleared, and he chuckled. "Oh, well done! The great Holmes himself could not have done better. Now tell me, *my* Holmes, have you shared any of your deductions with Mrs. O'Leary?"

"No, I have not." I shook my head impatiently.

"Good. I implore you to keep it that way."

"We still have our dilemma," I pointed out.

"Ah, yes. The matter of trust. You admit, then, that you have not told me everything you know about the Li Wong matter?"

"There is something I am holding back," I acknowledged. I did not say that I had done so simply because he had not been there to tell. As it turned out, that which I had by chance withheld was proving a useful tool for the unraveling of Michael's secrets.

His eyes probed deep, deep into me, as if he wished to penetrate my soul. He rubbed at the sides of his beard. Finally, he moistened his lips thoughtfully with his tongue, and spoke. "I cannot answer your question directly. But I may do so by indirection. I will tell you about Katya."

Katya! I felt my eyes widen, but maintained an anticipatory silence.

"Katya would have been my wife if she had lived. This was nearly twenty years ago; we were both very young. I met her in Russia. I was there on business. I could not tell her the exact nature of my business. Do you understand, Fremont?"

I nodded, gravely. Spies are sworn not to reveal themselves, even to those closest to them. How could I have been so naive—or perhaps so arrogant—as to think that Michael would reveal such a thing to me?

He was continuing his story, looking not at me now but out across the water. And I doubted that he saw the water; what he was seeing was a memory. "I loved Katya, and I was the cause of her death."

Such sorrow, such longing on his face and in his voice! I reached out and placed my hand over Michael's, where it rested on his thigh. I wanted to comfort him, though I supposed it was not really possible to do so.

"Because of her proximity to me, Katya learned something about a dangerous matter. She did not realize how dangerous it was, and I did not tell her, because in order to do so I would have had to reveal the true nature of my business in Russia. My Katya was murdered for that knowledge." Now Michael noticed my hand on his. He turned his palm upward and grasped my fingers as he turned to face me. "No one in this country knows about Katya, Fremont. I did not even tell my parents when I returned here."

"I'm so sorry," I said. Michael's fingers gripped mine so tightly that it hurt.

"It's over. It was a long time ago."

"But you still love her. I can see—and feel—that."

"Yes." With one last squeeze of my fingers, Michael let go of my hand and placed his own hands over his face. He rubbed at his eyes, and his cheeks, and finally smoothed his beard to its point. As he did these things, he released a long, heavy breath, as if he were letting go of pain. "Now, we must deal with our own situation. You must believe me when I tell you that I am concerned for your own safety, Fremont. The murder of Li Wong is a serious business. I implore you to trust me, and tell me what you have been holding back."

Thus disarmed, I told Michael about the break-in at my office, including my decision not to go to the police. He made no comment as I related the incident, and asked only one question at the conclusion: "Does anyone besides yourself know of this?"

"Only Justin. He happened to come to the office while I was still picking up papers off the floor."

"Who is Justin?"

I felt myself blush before I could think how to phrase my answer. Of course, Michael noticed.

"Aha," he said, "the young man, no doubt, with whom you had the disagreement and subsequently spent a Saturday. And more Saturdays since, I would guess. Am I right?"

"Yes. On all counts. You needn't be concerned about Justin. He's about my own age, just starting out in a law practice. He's on my side. He understood completely when I told him that I didn't want anyone to know, not even the police, because it would be bad for my business."

"Mm-hm. And you are quite fond of him."

I blushed again. "You might say that. Yes."

Michael turned his head away. He ran his hand through his hair, though it was so closely cropped that no wind could possibly disarrange it. At length he said, "Well, two things are clear to me about your break-in. No, make that three. One: It was done by an amateur, and might possibly have had nothing to do with Li Wong. A professional would not have made such a mess of your office, and would have been able to open the locks without breaking them. Two: If it did have to do with Li Wong, then someone has learned of the statement but does not know what was in it. Three: Therefore, the statement has not yet been found, nor did it ever reach those for whom it was intended. Perhaps Li Wong changed his mind and destroyed it before his death. In any event, Fremont, I think that break-in was a blessing in disguise for you. Whoever did it, assuming that Li Wong's statement was what they were looking for, knows now that you do not have it."

"All but the first I had already concluded myself," I said. "And I take it that you, Michael, have not learned any more about Li Wong than what you knew when you went away?"

"Not yet. But I'll stay on it." He stood up, stretched, and pointed. "Look toward the Golden Gate. We have a race with the fog ahead of us."

The race was exhilarating. The white bank of fog loomed in the distance like some amorphous beast that advanced by slow degrees. The *Katya,* under Michael's expert guidance, leapt to life and won the race. But only by a hair. Or perhaps one might more appropriately say, by a wisp.

I went to bed that night thinking about Michael and Katya. Such a sad story, and in a way it was romantic to think that he still loved her. That no doubt he had remained unmarried in order to be faithful to her memory. I thought too that Michael had all but acknowledged he

117

was a spy. I should feel deeply satisfied that he had trusted me enough to tell me of the love he had shared with no one else.

I squirmed against my pillows. There was only one problem: I was *not* satisfied. I told myself that this dissatisfaction was perverse. I sat up and punched the pillows crossly. What was there about Michael Archer that made me so reluctant to trust him?

I did not know the answer to that question. I fell asleep still turning it over and over in my mind, and had bad dreams the whole night long.

By the time I saw Justin again, I'd had the opportunity to write in my diary a considerable dialogue on the subject of myself and Justin Cameron. Midweek he showed up with a sack of lunch in his hand, as of old, and the same old cheerful smile on his face. I was ridiculously glad to see him, and wanted immediately to rush into his arms. I did not, however. I waited to see what he would do. My intention was to take my cues from him. Up to a point.

I said, "It's good to see you, Justin."

"I should have called you, I know." He dropped his sack on my desk, came around it, and pulled me up into his arms. "This will make up for it, I hope." He kissed me, long and well.

My body, which had already learned a great deal from him, responded with delicious ardor. However, I was able—helped by the fact that we were in my office—to keep my head. When I pulled away I laughed a little and said, "A kiss like that could make up for a good many things."

"Can you take a long lunch? Two hours? I thought we might hop on a streetcar and take our sandwiches to Golden Gate Park. Have you been there yet?"

"I have not." I made a quick decision: If I stayed an hour later at the end of the day, I could do it. "Yes, that sounds very nice. Just give me time to make a sign for the door saying at what hour I will be back."

I hung up my sign and we left. We sat on the grass in the park and Justin talked of how glorious it would be when finished. Already one could see its possibilities. For a minute or two I missed the Boston

Common and the Public Garden, and the ducks, and the swanboats. I told Justin about them, and a little bit about my childhood and my mother and my father.

"I am surprised you would leave a situation like that," he remarked.

"I wanted my independence, and to start my own business, as I've told you before." I did not care much for his tone. "And how are your parents, Justin?"

"My parents?" His eyebrows climbed up his high forehead. "What do you know about my parents, Fremont?"

"Only what you said the first time we went out together, remember? By way of introducing yourself, you told me about your father being a professor, living in Berkeley, and so on."

"Oh. Now I remember. Well, the truth is, I don't see much of them these days. We don't exactly get along. They, er, they didn't approve of my choice of profession."

"I should think they would be proud to have a lawyer in the family. Especially since you're doing so well! Surely you've told them about your new house? Your mother, at least, would be pleased about that. Mine would be. If she were still living and within a hundred-mile radius she'd be all over me with advice and pieces of furniture and plants and doilies and birdcages, most of which I wouldn't want a bit!"

"I don't want to tell them yet. About furniture and all that, I was hoping *you* might help me. What do you say? On Saturday, don't go to your office. Come with me instead. We'll shop. Not too much, though. I can only afford to furnish one room at the time."

"I don't know—"

"I'm sure you know more about such things than I, and I'd really like your advice. Come on, say you'll do it."

I was tempted, but I remembered my dialogue with the diary, and I shook my head. "No. Furnishing your house is something you really must do yourself. And besides, I have far too much work to do. I can barely get through it all in the time I have scheduled at the office. I can't afford to close, not even for one Saturday."

Justin pouted, but his face could not hold that expression for long. I offered him half of the orange I'd just peeled, and he took it absently, gazing off into the distance, occupied with his own thoughts. I was content to be sitting with him in the warm sun, with the incomparable fragrance of oranges on my fingers and their sweetness in my mouth. I thought: How good it is to have a friend. A lover. Idly, as if it were quite natural for me to touch him, I stroked the back of Justin's hand there in the grass, where he leaned his weight upon it.

He turned to me, smiled. I smiled too. I felt so happy.

"Look!" Justin exclaimed, "an ice cream vendor! Come on, Fremont, I'll buy us cones." Hand in hand we ran across the grass, laughing like children.

When the time came, it was going to be hard to keep the resolution I'd reached at the end of the dialogue in my diary.

"Psst!" Mrs. O'Leary stuck her head out of her door and caught me as I was leaving for work the next day. "In here, Fremont. I got some news for ya."

"Yes?" Her whispering and closing of the door behind me made me very curious.

"Y' remember what ya asked, about them women might have got killed somewheres along the coast near a lighthouse?"

"I certainly do."

"Well, I asked around some. Provoked an interestin' reaction or two, I did." She folded her hands under the broad shelf of her breasts and rocked back on her heels, looking as if she'd definitely enjoyed provoking those reactions. "And here's what I found out: Was two, three young girls went missin' up toward Bodega Head a couple years back. Never found. What's more, the search was give up too quick-like. The Captain woulda never approved, if it hadda been his territory."

How interesting! "Where is this Bodega Head, and does it have a lighthouse?"

"It's north of here, not too far. The lighthouse is on Point Reyes, but it's all of a piece, Fremont. Not far from the one place to the other. How'dya say you got put onto this, again?"

"I read about it somewhere, and I just couldn't forget it."

Mrs. O'Leary looked at me suspiciously. "That's mighty peculiar, seein' as how I had the devil's own time trying to get anybody to open up about it to me. I says to myself, That's a cover-up, that's what it is. And things as has been covered up don't go gettin' writ about."

This was becoming more interesting all the time! I said hastily, "Nevertheless, somebody did write about it. How else would I have learned of it? I wasn't even here two years ago."

"Humpf!" She rocked back and forth some more, still seeming suspicious. "I'll tell ya what I think, Miss Fremont Jones. I think that Mr. Archer is the one what put you up to this, and ya just don't wanna admit it."

"Michael?" I exclaimed.

"Oh, so it's Michael now, is it? Well, why should I be surprised— I seen as how you two was gettin' thick as thieves."

"Mrs. O'Leary, please. Michael Archer has occasionally been kind to me, that's all. We are definitely not close. I'd be much obliged if you would tell me why you think he might know about these disappearances that, as you yourself said, seem to have been covered up?"

"Because Bodega Head is about halfway between Point Reyes and Fort Ross, and Fort Ross is where all them Russians is from. Originally, anyways. Hasta be familiar territory to him, Fremont. Hasta."

"I didn't know that." My mind was spinning. I needed to get to my office where it was quiet and I could think. Impulsively I grabbed my landlady's hands and squeezed them. "Thank you! Thank you so much for taking the trouble to look into the matter for me. It's always very gratifying to have one's curiosity satisfied. Now, I must be on my way!"

"You watch yerself, Fremont," she said kindly, patting me on the shoulder. Apparently my supposed closeness to Michael Archer had been forgiven. "Don't ya go gettin' yerself into any trouble!"

I gave her my brightest smile in answer. And wondered, as I hurried not to miss the cable car, just how much trouble I would be getting into. Or, possibly, was already in.

When I reached my office and sat at the desk, I leaned down and patted the outside of the locked file drawer. I said quietly, "I haven't forgotten you, Edgar Allan Partridge. In fact, I think I'm really getting somewhere!"

How to proceed now, that was the question. I kept it at the back of my mind all morning as I typed at the professor's memoirs. Unfortunately for him, but fortunately for me, they were exceedingly boring and therefore easy to type. My fingers flew while my mind was completely elsewhere.

It simply could not be possible that there was any connection between Michael Archer and Edgar Allan Partridge. That would be too great a coincidence. Still, it was probably best that I not follow my first instinct, which had been to ask Michael to take me up to Bodega Head on his boat.

The first thing I needed was a better understanding of the geography of the Northern California coastline. Exactly how far was Bodega Head from San Francisco? And Point Reyes? How would I get there, if not by boat? And once there, would I be allowed to go into the lighthouse? I was simply seething with questions, and nothing would have pleased me more than to declare a holiday from work, close the office, and dash right up there!

But I could not do that. I scrolled a finished sheet of paper out of the typewriter and inserted a new one. The telephone rang. I answered it. Oddly, there was no one on the line. After saying hello several times and straining my ears in case the connection was poor, I hung up. The interruption had slowed down my galloping mind— probably a good thing. "Act in haste, repent at leisure," my father always quoted to me, his hasty, headstrong daughter.

I should proceed in a well-organized manner. First, to the library, to look at maps. While I was there, I could seek out back issues of the newspapers from two or three years ago. Mrs. O'Leary might be wrong about the cover-up; she did, after all, have a suspicious mind. I might find something. I could close up the office half an hour early today. It remained light until well after seven o'clock now, so I would have plenty of time.

I could hardly wait!

But the rest of the day did not go well. I believe there must be a special species of gremlins, invisible to the naked eye, that somehow know when one is anxious to accomplish something and thrive on setting obstacles in one's path. All afternoon I had a steady stream of customers in my office, including three little old ladies who arrived together, each of them wanting to dictate letters to relatives. So time-consuming! I wanted to turn them away but did not have the heart.

So it happened that not only was I unable to leave half an hour early, I was actually half an hour later than usual in locking up my office for the night. As I turned my key in the lock, I thought I saw someone from the corner of my eye. Oh no, not another customer this late! But when I looked around, there was no one there. Rather strange, but anyway a relief.

More gremlins, I thought as I was going down the stairs, the same ones that had caused my telephone to give me no less than two more of those calls with no voice at the other end of the line. The pesky little creatures had outdone themselves today!

I had good luck at the library and found a detailed map of the Northern California coast. Mrs. O'Leary was absolutely right: Bodega Head and Bodega Bay were not far from Fort Ross to the north; while to the south Bodega was close enough to Point Reyes that it could easily fall into the territory of a roaming, moon-crazed lighthouse keeper.

I could see, however, that if I were to go there, it would have to be by boat. The best road was too far inland, making it necessary to cross over a mountain range to get to the Bodegas on the coast. A trip by land looked perilous, not to mention time-consuming. Of course, not being a sailor, I had no idea how long it would take to go by water, either. But it could be done; I would find a way . . . *if* I decided to go.

As I sat at a table perusing the map and making notes, I had a persistent feeling of being watched from behind. I tried to shrug it off, but to no avail. Finally I turned around abruptly, thinking to catch someone in the act of staring. I might, just possibly, have seen a dark figure retreating behind a shelf of books. But it might just as well have been my imagination. I shrugged, made a sketch of the map between the Golden Gate and Fort Ross, and returned the map to its case on the shelf.

The reference librarian was helpful with back issues of newspa-

123

pers. She suggested that I look not at the San Francisco papers, but at the weekly *Fort Ross Register* for news of the region that interested me. Therefore, I was seated in the Periodical Room with three years' worth of the *Register* on the table in front of me, when once again I had that eerie feeling of someone behind. I ignored it for as long as I could, then whipped around. And there was no one. I was alone in the Periodical Room.

I made up a silent chant—"E.A.P, stop haunting me." It was silly and childish, but it made me feel better. Surely working on his concerns had brought forth some sort of sympathetic paranoia, purely imaginary!

The newspapers soon absorbed me completely. Alternately scanning and reading, at last I found an article in a paper dated September 10, 1902. Miss Ethel Faragon, age eighteen, was missing and presumed drowned. There was no accompanying photograph. Miss Faragon had taken her little catboat for a routine trip up the coast from Bodega Bay to Fort Ross, for the purposes of doing her weekly errands, and had failed to return at her usual time. Her boat was later found, broken up on the rocks at Point Reyes. The names of her mother and father, brothers and sisters, were listed, along with an appeal in case anyone had seen her alive, and mention was made of a small reward for information.

Aha! I thought. If Mrs. O. were right about a cover-up, it had not begun until after Miss Faragon's disappearance. Using that issue of the *Register* as a starting point, I worked my way forward in time, scanning and scanning, running the tip of my finger down the columns as my eyes began to tire.

There was never another article about a missing young woman. What there was, however, was a tiny paid advertisement down at the bottom of the back page of a January 1904 issue of the *Register*. The ad said: TEN DOLLARS REWARD FOR KNOWLEDGE OF THE WHEREABOUTS OF MISS JENNIE WEBSTER. CONTACT J. O. WEBSTER, MARSHALL. Marshall did not mean that J. O. Webster was a lawman, it was the name of a town I'd seen on the map. I consulted my notes. Yes, there it was, even closer to Point Reyes than Bodega. Aha, aha!

Oh, merciful heavens! Through the windows of the Periodical

Room there was not a scrap of sky to be seen, only the gray-white of nighttime fog. I grasped the watch pinned to my blouse and tilted up its face. Eight-thirty. I had completely lost track of the time, and now I would have to make my way back to Vallejo Street in murky darkness. Not a pleasant prospect!

At the mere thought of it, all my Partridgish paranoia returned full force.

11.

Through the Lens Darkly

——◦◦◦◦◦——

STANDING AT THE top of the library steps, trying and failing to see into the fog, which was as thick as cotton wool, I regretted my relative poverty. Had I still been in my father's house in Boston, I would not have hesitated to summon a cab. I shivered, not from cold but from the damp, and put up the hood of my cape.

BUT, I thought (trying to cheer myself), if I were in Boston, Augusta and her creepy nephew (I was sure he would be creepy) would be waiting in the parlor to pounce on me as soon as I got in the front door. This thought made me feel better about setting off into the fog for the streetcar stop, a mere half block away.

Paranoia can be so wearing! There seemed to be footsteps all around me, yet I was alone in an all-obscuring curtain of mist. Waiting has never been my strong point; I do not enjoy it even in optimum circumstances. Now I stood at the streetcar sign, shifting my weight from one foot to the other, and drowned out the sound of following footsteps by repeating the childish chant in my head.

I wished I had a weapon of some sort—even an umbrella would be better than nothing. The lady's weapon of choice, a hat pin, did not appeal to me at all; probably because I am not overfond of hats. I could not help thinking how easy it would be for someone to sneak up, using the fog for concealment, and commit some dastardly deed upon my person!

After what seemed like half an hour but was probably only five minutes, the streetcar arrived and I got on with a grateful sigh. I

127

indulged my paranoia to the extent that I watched to see if anyone got on after me, but no one did. I was safe, and lapsed into thinking about the information I'd gleaned in the library.

I went early to my office the next morning, so early that fog still filled the streets, but it was less menacing by day. The heavy mist was pierced by light to a pearly sheen, and it felt refreshingly cool upon my face. Though I had slept little, I felt alert and full of energy, eager to get on with the plans I'd made when I should have been sleeping.

My ultimate goal was simply to locate Edgar Allan Partridge so that I could give him the typed manuscript of his stories. This other compelling desire of mine, to find out the truth behind his strange tales, was in some part selfish, tainted by my own curiosity. At times during the long night, I'd told myself I should give up the latter. Yet I was irrationally convinced that something dire had happened to the man, and that his stories held the clue not only to the dire happening, but also, ultimately, to his whereabouts. Around and around I had gone with these thoughts, like a cat chasing her tail.

To stop the tail-chasing, around the hour of two a.m., I had made a logical listing of the steps through which I would proceed, Holmes-like, to my goal. But I would do this without Watson; Michael Archer was not to be involved. It would be a long time—if ever—before I could shake off the vestiges of that strange interlude on his boat, when I had feared him.

So, arriving in my office a good hour before my usual time (having noted that the Sorensons were nowhere about their bookstore and that I was, therefore, alone in the building), I locked the door upon myself and went to my desk. I took my list out of my handbag, sat down, and pulled the telephone to me. Item #1: After consulting today's paper for the number, I called the San Francisco *Chronicle*.

"Good morning," I said, "I would like to speak to the person in charge of the newsroom." When he came on the line, I explained that I was trying to locate a man who had worked as a reporter, possibly for them, within the last several years: "A Mr. Edgar Allan Partridge. He is relatively young and slight of build, with protruding eyes and a narrow face, black hair and very white skin."

No, they had never heard of him. No one by that name or physical description had been a reporter for the *Chronicle*. Next I tried the evening paper, with the same result. If Mr. Partridge had been telling the truth when he'd said, "I used to be a reporter," he had done his reporting somewhere other than San Francisco.

I crossed off Item #1 and proceeded to #2: the telephone directory, which I had removed from a desk drawer. How foolish I was going to feel if I found an address and telephone number for Edgar Allan Partridge in the book! I flipped pages until I was in the P's . . . but there was not a single Partridge. Of course, that did not mean there were no Partridges in the City; in San Francisco, as in Boston, only a small percentage of the population had telephone instruments in their homes. I closed the book and pulled out the drawer to put it away.

It was at this moment that I first realized Edgar Allan Partridge was probably not the man's real name. I wondered if it might really be Peregrine, like the boy in "Damned to Darkness"; went from that to thinking that a peregrine is a kind of falcon, and a falcon is a bird and so is a partridge . . . and the next thing I knew I was paging through the F's, looking for Falcons. There were none of those, either; and no Falcones, no Falconers. All right, then, how about that close relative, the Hawk? I pounced upon the H's: Ha, Han, Hau, Hav—no Hawks. But two Hawkinsons! I had actually lifted the receiver from its hook when I stopped myself. "You are getting carried away, Fremont Jones!" I said aloud, relieved that I had stopped myself in time. I would have felt very foolish indeed explaining to the poor Hawkinsons how I had come about calling their number!

I crossed off Item #2.

Item #3 read: Ascertain if San Francisco publishes a City Directory. This would have to wait until the Public Library opened. I busied myself with typing for an hour, at the end of which I learned from the reference librarian that there was no house-by-house directory for the City of San Francisco. Well, so much for the simple means of locating Mr. Partridge. I was not altogether sorry, for now I felt justified in satisfying my curiosity. The trip up the coast was now definite.

I paused long enough to go and unlock my office door, and then proceeded to Item #4, which was a question: How to hire a boat? Michael would have taken me on his boat, of course, but that was out. I would have to ask Justin's advice, and to do that I would have to lie to him. He was too protective of me; if I told him the truth of what I was doing he would want to take on the task himself, and I did not want that. I had already lied to Justin once this week. He'd invited me to his house for dinner on Friday night and I'd told him I could not come, as I had agreed to go with Mrs. O'Leary to her church supper. I was not yet ready to be alone with Justin again, not sure I could hold to the resolution I'd arrived at so laboriously through the long dialogue with my diary.

I reached for the telephone but pulled back my hand. Getting up from the desk instead, I went to the window. Delaying. The fog had burned off, so I opened the window and watched and listened to the bustle below. All my life I'd hated to lie, and in truth, I'd never been very good at even the small social prevarications one is taught to tell for the sake of politeness. I dithered, tracing the backward letters of my name on the glass with a finger.

The visit to the Mission Dolores had been nothing compared to what I was about to do. In the clear light of day, I asked myself once more the question I had asked the night before: Did I really want to continue this investigation into the dark, mad world of Edgar Allan Partridge? Did I want it enough to be devious and deceitful as I would have to be with people who seemed to care about me—Michael, Mrs. O'Leary, Justin? "Last chance," I muttered. Once committed I could not turn back, not even if I myself became mad as a hatter. Then I turned from the window and went on to Item #4.

I gave Justin Cameron's office telephone number to the operator, heard it ring. He answered himself, in an official tone of voice he had never used with me. He sounded almost like another person, a high-toned lawyer, and I was properly impressed.

"This is a business call, Justin," I said in my own version of officialness. "I have a client who is new to the area and has asked for advice that I am unable to give. I thought you might help me out."

"If I can," he said cautiously.

"It's not a legal matter. He wants to know of a trustworthy person with a boat for hire, who might take him up the coast as far as Fort Ross and back again."

"Hmm," said Justin thoughtfully, "is there a particular reason why this person wants to go by boat? I dare say most people would take the train. It's far simpler."

Why had I not thought of that? I felt a complete dolt as I said hastily, "Just a minute, please, Justin. I'll ask," and covered the mouthpiece with my hand as if I were talking to my mythical client. I counted to ten before continuing: "He says he is much obliged to you for mentioning it; he had assumed that the train service did not go north of here. And I myself was woefully ignorant on the subject. Thank you for allowing me to take your time."

"For you, Fremont, I am happy to take time. However, I *am* rather busy at the moment—"

"Of course. Good-bye, Justin." I hung up quickly and reached again for the telephone directory, in which I looked up the number of the Southern Pacific Railway. I soon learned that there were indeed trains that ran along the coast both to the north and to the south of San Francisco, with a ferry connection to the northbound line beginning at Sausalito. I had only to go to the railway station for a schedule and a round-trip ticket. I was relieved that I would not have to hire a boat; and even if I'd been rather stupid not to think of a train myself, I thought I'd carried off my bit of deception with Justin quite well. This gave me an odd kind of pleasure that I refused to dwell upon.

At the noon hour I set out on what proved to be a rather long walk, as the railway station was located south of Market Street in a district to which I had never been before. (The train I had taken from Boston some months earlier had its terminus in Oakland, from which point one took a ferry across the Bay.) Once I had crossed Market, I found myself in an area somewhat rougher than any I had heretofore encountered in the City. This was, apparently, where many of the unemployed hung about, and I did not care for the way they looked at me. I walked swiftly, purposefully, looking neither right nor left. I was conservatively dressed, yet some of the men made lewd remarks as I passed. I was tempted to toss a lewd word or two back at them, but held my tongue. At least they had enlarged my vocabulary!

At last I reached my destination. The ticket agent was most helpful in planning my trip, although he did raise his eyebrows as high as they would go above his round eyeglasses when I told him the stops I intended to make. In every case, with the exception of Fort Ross, he said, I would have to hire a conveyance to take me from the train to my destination. With a falsely confident smile, I assured him that I was prepared to do so. Actually, I was not prepared for anything about this trip; until I'd looked at the train schedule I had not even realized that I would have to stay overnight somewhere along the way. Undaunted, I paid for the ticket and shoved it, along with the train schedule, deep into my capacious handbag.

Outside the train station stood a slapdash vending stall whose wares caught my attention: umbrellas, walking sticks, canes, and among them the cold, hard gleam of metal. I stopped to look more closely, and I thought: Oh, yes! Just the very thing!

"Let me see that one, right there." I pointed. The merchant was a Chinese woman whose wide smile revealed teeth sadly broken and stained. Bowing, she presented to me an elegant walking stick of black wood. It had a silver knob on top, carved in the shape of a closed peony blossom. I knew, from the identical one on display, that the walking stick would come apart to reveal a long, thin blade, something between a knife and a rapier. But I could not get it to come apart. "Show me how it works, please."

She smiled, bowed again, and demonstrated. I had to ask her to show me twice, because the tiny release button was so cleverly carved into the peony blossom that it was invisible to the eye. But once one knew how, the button was easy to locate by feel. The secret weapon was also nicely balanced for use as a walking stick, and the right height for me. "I'll take it," I said. "How much?"

I knew one was supposed to bargain with street vendors, but because this woman had been brave enough to smile so much in spite of her teeth, I paid the price she asked. I was highly satisfied. Walking along with my elegant new weapon, I no longer felt so vulnerable. Though I did hope that I would never have to stab anybody!

From that moment on, I never went anywhere without my walking stick. At night in my apartment, I practiced unsheathing the knife until I could do it in the blink of an eye. I even practiced lunging and stabbing. Sometimes I felt a bit foolish, but on the whole I was glad to have the means to defend myself.

My cover story was that I was going to visit a friend of the family who lived in San Jose, leaving early on Saturday morning and returning sometime on Sunday. The fictional friend (by the name of Ruth Livingston—I'd written it and a few invented facts about her on a piece of paper and carried it in my pocket until I had it all memorized) was sending her own carriage and driver to transport me both ways. Of course, I had arranged for the carriage myself, and on the Saturday morning stood waiting nervously for it to arrive. The balance of Mr. Partridge's ninety-two dollars was paying for this, as well as for the rest of my trip.

The carriage arrived in due time and conveyed me to the dock from which the ferry would take me and the other train passengers across to Sausalito. It was a fine, clear day, and once underway, I felt my nervousness replaced by excitement and anticipation. I had my walking stick and a well-packed carpetbag; my plans were as complete as I could make them. I had, after all, traveled alone by train before— across the entire country. What could go wrong?

The "conveyance" I hired at Point Reyes Station proved far more costly and far less sturdy than one might have hoped. It was a ramshackle cart pulled by a mule and driven by one of the most disreputable-looking male persons it had ever been my misfortune to behold.

"You want to go to the lighthouse?" he had asked with his head cocked to one side, perhaps the better to see me with his one walleye. The other eye was three quarters obscured by a drooping lid; his face was covered with dirt, and so were his hands. His clothing was beyond description.

133

I tried not to wrinkle my nose in distaste. "Yes, I do. I am quite determined to see it. But if you don't care to make the trip, perhaps there is someone else—"

"Ain't nobody else, lady," said the disreputable creature. "Don't know what you'd want to go all the way out there fer anyways, 'specially on a day like this!" He rolled his head back and looked up at the sky, which was indeed roiling with steely gray clouds so low that we seemed to be standing among them. The wind was cold and stiff and scented with the sea.

"Lighthouses are a great interest of mine," I said staunchly, "and since I am here, I do want to see the Point Reyes Light. If you will kindly name your price?"

He did, and after ascertaining that for this exorbitant amount he would wait and return me to the train station, I'd paid it. Now we bumped along a mere track down the center of a long, narrow promontory that grew increasingly wild and bleak. Grudgingly I admitted to myself that I could understand both the man's reluctance to come out here and the high price he charged. Never in my life had I seen a place more isolated.

The wind gusted and tried to snatch up my aubergine cape. Not achieving that, it shrieked and moaned in my ears in a most unpleasant way. I shivered as I wrapped the cape more securely about my body, and not just from the cold. On such a dark day as this the man in Mr. Partridge's story would have had to feed the Great Lens. I felt an urge to howl myself, to drown out the wind; no wonder the poor man had gone mad. If he had ever existed in reality. My experiences so far on this trip had been discouraging, and I was beginning to think I had wasted Edgar Allan Partridge's money.

I had arrived at Fort Ross in the late morning of the previous day. The train ride had been completely uneventful. The scenery was interesting, though I was too keyed-up to enjoy it, and the train was precisely on schedule. I proceeded on foot to the offices of the *Register*, having asked directions from a porter as I disembarked. I had written ahead so that the editor expected me; nevertheless, my interview with him was a near-total waste of time.

He had never seen nor heard of, and certainly (he said emphatically) had not employed, Edgar Allan Partridge or anyone matching that description. He claimed to know no more of Ethel Faragon's disappearance than had been reported in his newspaper. She was still presumed to have drowned in a boating accident. No, he could not give me directions to her parents' house; they had come into a bit of money not long after Ethel's misfortune and had left the area. He did not know where they had gone.

No, he had not heard of a Miss Jennie Webster who had gone missing in Marshall; he had not seen the advertisement in his own paper; he couldn't be expected to read every single advertisement himself, could he? And why was I asking about other missing girls if I were what I claimed to be, an old acquaintance of Ethel Faragon? Was I a reporter myself, looking to dig up dirt in Fort Ross?

I assured the man that I was not a reporter and beat a hasty retreat. Feeling a complete failure and with my cheeks flaming, I walked the streets for some time before I calmed down enough to recall that Michael Archer had, most likely, once lived in Fort Ross—after which I began to look about me with interest. I observed that this was no longer the thriving town it had once been, and supposed a decline in the fur trade to be responsible. Eventually I found a hotel that looked respectable enough for me to enter, and ate my luncheon there. Then I returned to the station to await the train that would take me to my next destination.

It was late in the afternoon when I left the train in Tomales, some distance inland from the strait of water called Tomales Bay. At the train station, as the helpful ticket-seller in San Francisco had suggested, I found a carriage driver to convey me a few miles farther south, to Marshall, where I would have to spend the night. I directed the driver to take me to "the inn in Marshall," hoping as I said this that there would be one. There was; it was small but clean, and after depositing my carpetbag in my tiny room, I set off to find Mr. J. O. Webster before nightfall.

Finding him was not difficult. As I'd expected from the fact that Mr. Webster's newspaper advertisement had given no address for a response, the town was so small that everyone knew everyone else. I got directions from a newsboy hawking the evening paper on the street.

I quickly learned that Webster had found his Jennie. He introduced me to her in the back of the general store, which was the family's business. Jennie had an apple-cheeked toddler clinging to her skirts—the baby's unexpected (and, one understood, illegitimate) conception having been the reason she had run away from home. She'd come back on her own, her parents had forgiven her, and now Jennie was married to a man who loved the baby just as much as if it were his own.

I left before either Webster or his daughter thought to ask the reason for my interest in her brief disappearance. I didn't want to disturb their obvious happiness by asking, as I'd originally intended, about disappearances of other young women in the area.

Thereafter, I spent a restless night in a hard and narrow bed. If I slept at all, I certainly did not benefit from it, nor did the greasy breakfast provided by the inn sit well in my stomach. Capping it all off, I'd had difficulty finding a driver to take me back to Tomales, where I would make my train connection to Point Reyes Station. In the end, we'd gone recklessly hurtling through a thick fog to get me there in time.

The walleyed man, dirty, smelly, and sullen, was almost too much to take on top of all that. His cart lurched over a particularly nasty bump, and I grabbed the plank seat with both hands to steady myself. *Courage, Fremont!* I counseled myself. I tried to smile at my predicament, as that always makes one feel better, but my facial muscles would only stretch so far as a grimace.

This rocky spit of land along which we made our creaking progress was almost as narrow as a bridge. When I looked to left or right I could see nothing but gray clouds pushed by the wind into fantastic shapes. Seagulls, beating their wings furiously, rose up seemingly from out of nowhere, then, catching a downdraft, spread their wings wide and swooped into nothingness. The effect was disconcerting in the extreme. My mind told me that we must be very high up, but some deeper place inside me whispered the word "abyss."

136

I clutched the plank seat harder. Just as I felt a sick moment of panic, our track took a leftward turn and I saw that we had crested an imperceptible rise. The land—what there was of it—opened out like a round, flat tabletop. In its center, still some distance away, stood the Point Reyes Light.

I took heart. Through a lull in the wind I heard the crashing of the sea, and somehow that helped, acting as a point of reference. I sat up straight and tall, lifting my chin. This trip was not a total loss, after all. From my unpleasant encounter with the editor at the *Fort Ross Register,* I had at least learned that Mrs. O'Leary was probably right: If other young women in addition to Ethel Faragon had disappeared, someone had covered up all mention of it. And I did not yet know what I might find at the lighthouse . . .

"This is as fer as I go," said the driver, rolling his eye at me. He brought the mule to a halt at a distance of perhaps one hundred yards from the structure. Though I wondered why he would not take me right up, I was quite glad to alight from the uncomfortable vehicle and walk the rest of the way.

Leaving my carpetbag under the seat, I took my walking stick in hand and leapt down. "You will wait for me here," I stated firmly.

"Said I would," he agreed grudgingly.

I turned away, allowing myself a moment to appreciate the bleak beauty of the place. I took two steps, then stopped and called back. "I could be as long as half an hour!"

He grumbled something that I took to be reassurance—really, what other choice did I have?—and I strode onward. I looked up at the lighthouse. The closer I went the higher it loomed against the gray, disturbed sky. The top of it was all glass. Inside waited the Great Lens. Did it eat light?

I strode ahead, fingering the magic button in the top of my walking stick. I was ready to meet the lighthouse keeper, who might, on nights of the full moon, turn into a madman, a werewolf.

12.

Where, Oh Where
Can She Be?

THE LIGHTHOUSE WAS at work—because of the grayness of the day,
I supposed—its Great Lens turning and throwing out a wide beam of
light. To its landward side stood a one-story frame structure that had
once been painted white and had since achieved, through weathering,
a piebald leprousness. The home, no doubt, of the lighthouse keeper,
who had been too busy feeding the Lens to keep his dwelling smartly
painted.

I paused, testing the balance of the walking stick in my hand,
fingering its hidden button, knowing that I might have to release its
deadly secret blade before the hour was over. Where was the lighthouse keeper? Which building should I approach first?

As I hesitated, the front door of the shabby house opened. I almost
did not believe my eyes: A woman who was neither young nor particularly attractive stood in the doorway. She offered no greeting.

"Good morning," I said, approaching.

She was short, small-boned, and beady-eyed as a sparrow. "We
don't get many visitors out here," she said, cocking her head to one
side and looking me over.

"I can imagine. You are rather remote."

"Might say that," she nodded, pursing her mouth. "So who're
you, and what's your business?"

"I, ah . . ." I rubbed the back of my hand across my forehead, thinking fast, trusting an instinct not to give my real name. "I'm Caroline Freeman. Lighthouses are in a way my hobby, not my business. I'm traveling in this area, and I just wanted to see the Point Reyes Light up close."

The woman craned her neck and peered at something somewhere behind my right shoulder. "So *he* brung you, did he? Well, at least he knows to keep a distance."

"Um, ah, yes," I said lamely.

"Hobby? Humph. There's some of us don't have the time nor money for hobbies! Well, you seen it now, you've had your eyes full. You can go away." The remarkably unfriendly woman stepped back, about to close the door.

"Wait, please! Are you the lighthouse keeper?"

"I'm the lighthouse keeper's wife. He's in yonder," she jerked her head toward the tower.

"I wonder if I might speak with him? You know, ah, ask him a few questions about this particular light, the Lens, and so on?"

"Iffen he feels like it, I reckon he'd talk to you. Long as you're what you say you are, not somebody who come here to stir up trouble." She came out of the house, shut the door behind her, and stepped briskly across the bare, rocky ground.

"Has, ah, Mrs. . . . ?"

"Fuchs. Agatha Fuchs is the name. Husband's Henry."

"Mrs. Fuchs, has someone been out here trying to, how did you put it, stir up trouble?"

Agatha's dark beady eyes darted to me, and away. "Could be. You just ask Henry your questions. I'm not much of a talker." She paused with one hand on the tall, narrow door at the base of the lighthouse. "Course, Henry, he ain't much of a talker neither."

Having been thus warned, the only question I asked Henry Fuchs initially was if I might be allowed to go to the top of the lighthouse and see the light itself. He assented. There was no question of talking on the interminably twisting stairs; even the hills of San Francisco had not been enough preparation for such a climb.

From the glass enclosure at the top we climbed yet again, onto a platform that encircled the huge light. A Great Lens, indeed! It was an imposing presence, having countless mirrored facets that reflected and magnified the light produced in its center. Its slowly revolving brilliance was impossible to regard directly; like the sun, it would have blinded me. I felt a little catch of respect, like fear, in my breast as I paced full circle around.

Yes, one might make myth of such an awesome object. And if one were mad, or in a drug-induced state of fantasy, one might imagine this Great Lens a sentient Being, an eater as well as producer of light. I had not the slightest doubt that Edgar Allan Partridge had seen what I was now seeing, and set his morbid imagination to work upon it.

It was time, now, to ask more questions.

Henry Fuchs stood a half circle away from me, looking not at the light that was in his keeping but out in the other direction, to the cloudy sky and angry-looking sea. He was a tall, gaunt, gray-haired man, dressed in a faded plaid shirt and gray trousers. His appearance— for he was clearly not the Man in the story—gave me the first of my questions. I walked around to him.

"Mr. Fuchs, how long have you been keeper of the Point Reyes Light?"

He turned his head, but not his body. "Been here a couple of years. Why you asking?"

I held tightly to my walking stick. I felt a good deal of tension, which seemed to come from Fuchs, and it put me on guard. "I have a friend who is the reason for my interest in lighthouses. Recently, my friend has disappeared. I think he might have been here, and I wondered if you'd seen him. His name is Partridge, but he might not have used his real name. He's about a head shorter than you are, has dark hair—almost black—which he wears rather long, and a drooping mustache, and he's very thin."

Fuchs rubbed at gray stubble on his chin. "Ain't nobody like that been here. Mostly we don't have nobody come this way at all. That's the good thing about being a lighthouse keeper. People leave you alone." He stared at me pointedly.

I ignored his point, preferring to make one of my own. Mine was a stab in the dark, which I hoped a keeper of light would feel obliged

141

to illumine. "There are tales, perhaps only rumors, about a previous keeper of this light."

"Heard about that, didja?"

"I would like to know if what I heard was accurate."

Henry Fuchs studied me hard and long. Finally he said, "The man who was here before me and the wife, he lived alone. It's not good to be a keeper if you're not married. Too lonely. Can do things to a man's mind. That's what happened to him, he went clean out of his head, poor fella."

"W-what did he do?" I felt suddenly cold as ice.

"All I know is what I heard, probably same as you. That he'd go out on the edge of the cliff at night and howl at the moon. Poor soul kept trying to find a woman who'd stay out here with him; some say as how he took a couple of women against their will. I guess he was desperate. I can understand that, I surely can." Henry nodded sadly.

"Did he, ah, did he hurt the women he took?"

"Nah. If he'd hurt them he'd be in jail somewheres now, wouldn't he? Couldn't of kept that quiet, could they? Now you listen here, Miss— What did you say your name was?"

"Fre-Freeman." I caught my breath in sharply; I'd almost forgotten! "Caroline Freeman."

"Miss Freeman, you'd best just forget I talked to you about poor old Eubie. I been told not to talk none about him and what happened. Others has come asking, and I ain't talked." He shook a bony finger in my face. "I trusted you because you've got the look of a fine woman, and don't you go making me sorry I did that!"

"I won't," I hastened to assure Henry Fuchs. "My main concern is for my friend, and I know he had heard about this sad man who kept the lighthouse before you. This Eubie. That has to be a nickname —what was the man's real name?"

"I don't know. Alls I ever heard him called was Eubie. Never saw the fella myself, he was gone when me and the missus got here."

I didn't dare ask another question, so I said, "I wonder where he went. I hope to a hospital, somewhere people might help him."

Henry cocked his head, a mannerism he shared with his wife. "I

142

expect he had friends who helped him," he said slowly, consideringly, "same friends as fixed it about those women. Now, I'm not gonna say another word. You come on down out of here. I'm thinking you wasn't all that interested in this fine specimen of a light after all."

"Oh, but I am! It's so majestic, so awesome . . ." I raved on. My enthusiasm was so convincing that Henry launched into a detailed explanation of the workings of the Great Lens, and how one went about maintaining it. On this subject at least, he gave the lie to his wife's remark about his not being much of a talker. By the time I took my leave, Henry Fuchs and I had become quite congenial.

Old Walleye was not congenial in the least. " 'Bout time," he snorted, and scarcely gave me the opportunity to settle myself before clucking up his mule. We jounced off.

On the way back to Point Reyes Station, I kept turning the name Eubie over and over in my head. Eubie, Eubie, Eubie. That name reminded me of something, but I could not put my mental finger upon it. However, the attempt so occupied me that I did not notice the roughness of the ride, and when rain began to fall from the brooding sky it came as a surprise.

Had it not been for my aubergine cape, I would have been soaked through. As it was, my skirt and jacket were only damp; but my head was wet and I was altogether thoroughly chilled by the time the train arrived. It was not crowded, and I spread the wet cape over the seat next to me in the probably vain hope that it might dry a little.

Suddenly I felt exhausted. I put my head back. All on their own my eyes closed . . . and inexplicably my mind became filled with: Justin! I saw his dear face with its high forehead, the pale hair so inclined to fall down over one eye, the quirky smile and innocent expression so often in his eyes. I missed him, with an ache in my heart that soon spread throughout my body.

I should not have been thinking of Justin, it served no purpose, I had more serious things to which I should attend. But though I tried, I could not. A vision of Justin's face above mine, and the sweet remembered feel of his arms, persisted.

This would not do! I opened my eyes with an effort and sat up quite straight, shaking my head to clear it. Yet with my eyes open, I still saw that face. Not only that, I positively yearned for him!

I do not think myself a sentimental woman. I have never, for example, been known to fall in a swoon. Personally, I have always suspected that swooning is caused more by tight corsets than by tender emotions, which may be why I have not had the problem; nevertheless, I refuse to be ruled by my own emotions. So imagine my humiliation when, not only was I unable to stop yearning for my dear friend Justin, but tears came into my eyes! I turned my face to the window and dashed them away with the back of my hand. Then I began to reason with myself, to make the wheel of my mind turn with the same steady rhythm as the train's wheels upon their track.

That rumbling clackety-clack, spreading throughout my body, felt a comfort in itself. I realized that these two days had been more difficult than ever I had thought they would be. My small store of courage was quite used up, and I was physically very tired, as well. I was also—though loathe to admit it—simply lonely.

Fremont Jones, lonely? Perish the thought! Yet I was, no good would come from denial. I could not help wishing for a companion in my quest—and thus my mind had produced the equation "Justin equals companion," and presented me with his face and the accompanying feelings.

Aha! With this bit of illumination, my loneliness vanished. I have often thought that if one can understand oneself, then one can do virtually anything.

I felt quite refreshed. Moments later the train pulled into Sausalito, and I was occupied with the business of getting myself and my various possessions transferred to the waiting ferry. Here the rain was no more than a heavy mist. The sight of my City across the Bay cheered me, so that I scarcely minded my damp state.

Leaning upon the ferry's railing, I fell to musing over the reason for my trip: Edgar Allan Partridge. I thought not about Partridge the man, but Partridge the writer. A writer of some skill, who veiled elements of truth in the conventions of gothic fiction. Why had he chosen that means of expressing himself, rather than some other? Was

144

it simply because one day he had looked into a mirror and seen a resemblance to Edgar Allan Poe? Or did the admiration for Poe come first, causing him to imitate both his idol's physical appearance and his style of writing? Did Mr. Partridge admire Mr. Poe because they shared a morbid turn of mind, or did Partridge's morbidity develop as a result of reading Poe's stories? Why, with a whole bright world out there, would one choose to be so strangely, darkly, gothic?

The gothic was a part of the Romantic Movement, a reaction to the long (and dry!) predominance of rationalism throughout the seventeenth and eighteenth centuries. I allowed a parade of gothic writers to pass through my mind. In my own meandering way, I was getting somewhere with this line of thought.

With eyes closed, I lifted my face to the wind. Licking my lips, I tasted salt. And certainty: Edgar Allan Partridge, whatever his real name might be, *was* Peregrine. I felt sure of it. He had been, and likely still was, trapped in a life that was intolerable to him. His stories were his way out, his way of shocking, waking up the rest of the world to his plight.

And I was his godsend, his chosen helper. Yes! I wished mightily that I had his manuscript with me so that I might try, with my new knowledge, to tease apart the borders between reality and imagination. Had E.A.P. been among the friends who came to the lighthouse on Point Reyes to claim poor, insane Eubie? And if he was Peregrine, who, *really,* was that awful, powerful, sorceress of a mother?

I shuddered, having scared myself with this question. In my mind's eye, I saw Peregrine's mother in her scarlet dress, and her face blazed —*she* was the Great Lens, swallowing light. That image was not in the story; I had made the connection myself. It might or might not be valid.

Opening my eyes, I decided that I had best leave off thinking about Mr. Partridge's stories until I had them in front of me. In any event, the ferry had made considerable progress while I'd been so lost in thought. We were approaching the dock. Almost home!

Thinking of home made me think of Mrs. O'Leary. What if I confessed to her that my story of a visit to San Jose had been a ruse? What if I told her about the poor, mad keeper of the Point Reyes lighthouse—might she be able, through her contacts, to discover Eubie's real identity? And who his friends were? If I had those names, then surely Edgar Allan Partridge's real name would also be known to me! Surely Mrs. O. could be persuaded to help, and surely that would mean the plight of Edgar Allan Partridge was near a solution!

In the midst of all the *surelys,* through all my excitement, I heard a warning—in Michael Archer's voice. What if Mrs. O'Leary's husband had been the wrong sort of policeman? If he had been dishonest, would her contacts (doubtless her husband's old cronies in the police department) also be dishonest?

"No!" I said, "I don't believe it!"

"I beg your pardon?" said a man standing next to me.

I had been so lost in thought that I had not noticed him, nor had I realized I'd actually spoken. "Sorry," I apologized, "I was just thinking out loud."

"Don't mention it," he replied, with a somewhat too friendly smile I chose to ignore.

In any event, just then the ferry reached the dock with a bump. Seizing my carpetbag in one hand and holding firmly to my walking stick with the other, I hastened toward the gangway. My mind was made up: I would talk to Mrs. O'Leary the moment I arrived back at Vallejo Street. I had far more reason to trust her than I did Michael Archer. After all, he had practically admitted to me that he was a spy, which automatically made him untrustworthy. Didn't it?

Bursting through the front door, I called out, "Mrs. O'Leary!" No answer. Dropping my carpetbag at the foot of the stairs, I knocked on her closed parlor door and inquired more decorously, "Mrs. O'Leary?" I knocked again, and with my face near the panel said, "It's Fremont. I'm back, and I'd like very much to talk with you." Still she did not answer.

I stepped back from the door and listened to the house around me. Nothing. Not a sound. The house felt empty.

Sometimes I am more of an idiot than others. I should have re-membered: It was Sunday afternoon, a time my landlady often spent with her church friends. My eagerness would have to be restrained until later in the evening.

On the second-floor landing, I stopped and called Michael's name twice. I did not expect him to appear, because if he had been here he would have heard me yelling for Mrs. O'Leary and called down his own greeting. My expectation was correct: no Michael.

So I was alone in the house. Champing at the proverbial bit—I had been so ready to verbally engage my landlady—I rushed up the remaining stairs to my own apartment and into the bedroom, where I threw my carpetbag on the bed and hastily unpacked it. I began to undress, peering over my shoulder at the bed, which looked very tempting. The exhaustion I'd held so long at bay overcame me. In chemise and petticoat, I lay down and fell into a deep, dreamless sleep.

When I awoke, it was dusk. A glance through the open bedroom door showed that the hallway was dark, and no light shone from below. All around me the house was silent. Apparently, Mrs. O'Leary had not yet come home. Nor had Michael Archer.

I took a bath, put on a fresh dress, and tried to read a magazine while I ate my dinner. I was distracted, listening for the sound of someone's return. Where were they? Night had fallen, and the house was silent as a tomb!

Had I locked the front door behind me? For that matter, had it been locked when I got home? I couldn't remember, and decided I had best go down and check.

I did not care for this. Mrs. O'Leary had never been out so late, not even on a Sunday. My steps echoed hollowly on the stairs, and though I turned on lights as I went, still I was advancing into blackness.

A key (not mine, I'd put it in my pocket) was in the keyhole inside the front door, which was *not* locked. Feeling like seven kinds of fool, I grabbed the metal key and wrenched it home in the lock. To think! I had fallen asleep, been naked in my bath, any intruder might have walked right in and had his way with me, and it would have been my own fault for failing to lock the door behind me when I came in.

But, wait a minute . . . if I did not remove that key from the

147

inside of the lock, neither Mrs. O'Leary nor Michael would be able to insert their own from the outside. I reached out and extracted the key, placing it on the hall table. It did seem odd to me that Mrs. O'Leary would go out and leave her house unlocked for so many hours. I crossed my arms and rubbed at them, not liking the way I felt. My skin crawled; my stomach knotted. Something was not right here.

I left a lamp burning in the entry hall and went back up the stairs. There was an envelope on my own hall table—in my earlier haste I had not noticed it. I opened the envelope and read the note inside:

> *Dear Fremont, I've been called away. My sister is sick, and I have to go to her. I don't know how long I'll be gone, but don't worry. Hope you had a good time in San Jose. Take care of yourself.*
> *Best wishes, Maureen O'Leary.*

Maureen. Pretty name; I hadn't known it before. Well, there was my explanation for the empty house. Yet, as I folded the note back into its envelope and laid it on the table, I still felt uneasy. I took it up again and went to my window seat, where I read it through a second time.

She had never mentioned a sister. There was no indication here of where this sister lived. But that was not what was wrong. What was wrong was the quality of the evenly slanted script. It was quite legible, and Mrs. O'Leary had told me that her handwriting was very hard to read, which was why she'd had me type more than one letter for her. Letters to friends, but never to a sister. If she'd had a sister, wouldn't I have typed a letter to her by now? If Maureen O'Leary had written this note, would it be so handsomely done?

I thought not. Nor did I think Mrs. O'Leary would have gone away overnight and left her key in the inside of her front door. Yet, she must have; and she could have asked someone to write the note for her. Or, she could have perfectly good handwriting, asking me to type things as a kind little deception to help out my business. I had enough problems on my plate without inventing another. I had best take the note at face value, and be glad she'd left it for me.

I sighed, turned my head and looked out the window. A rare

fogless night lay like a drapery of black velvet upon the City, lights shining here and there like diamonds scattered upon its folds. Lovely, yes, but somehow not peaceful. Not tonight. I felt more alone than I had at any time since I'd come to San Francisco.

I might not have to be alone in the house for long, though. Michael could return at any time. But should his return be a comfort?

Eubie, Eubie . . . Eubie. At last, I had it: Hubert! Of course! Well, maybe not of course, but surely Eubie could be a nickname for Hubert? Hubert the manservant, whom the boy Peregrine loved and trusted in spite of the fact that Hubert was his mother's minion. Could the real Hubert have left that household and gone to be keeper of the lighthouse on Point Reyes . . . ?

I sat in my reading chair with Mr. Partridge's handwritten manuscript on my lap, grateful that I'd brought it home from my office. I flipped through the pages, looking for a section I vaguely remembered. And there it was, from "Damned to Darkness," beginning with page 115:

I could not get it out of me. I tried everything: vile-tasting concoctions, a feather to tickle the back of my throat, kneading my stomach with my own hands until both my hands and my stomach muscles were sore; I threw myself against the stair railing, which happened to be the exact height of my midsection, so hard that I heard my ribs crack. Nothing made it come out. Oh, I did vomit, and often. But I never brought up the horrid toad.

She'd made me swallow it, of course. She had held my nose until I'd had to open my mouth, and then popped the toad inside. The creature was cold and clammy and knew where it was supposed to go; it had begun on its own to climb down my throat. I could feel it moving on the back of my soft palate like a piece of gelid, viscous ice. I gagged. Mother clamped my mouth shut with both hands. My gagging was to no avail—farther, deeper crept the toad. And then I swallowed. I had to, it was a reflex that I could not prevent. Down and down my gullet went the toad, a lump of icy slime.

Mother's laughter was like the peal of bells; her eyes were obsid-

ian stars; she was very pleased. Of course she was: She had made me swallow a demon.

Days passed, and nothing happened except my frantic, secret attempts to vomit up the toad. I began to think the black, red-eyed creature had been only another of Mother's illusions, another test that I must pass. And I had passed it with flying colors, for I concealed my agony from her, desperate as I was for the kindness she now showed me. You are truly ours now, Perry, she crooned. And she was right, for I began to change.

I wondered if this was how she had changed Hubert, if she had made him too swallow a toad—

I heard a loud clatter and a voice, swearing: "Dad-rat it all! Fremont! Fremont, turn on the light, I know you're up here!"

Taking my time, I went into the hallway and turned on the light, surveying Michael Archer with a dispassionate eye. "I see my barrier has been effective," I commented. "If you had called up instead of coming, I would have told you not to bother, and you could have spared yourself the inconvenience."

I had strung a length of black yarn across the top of the stairs, the yarn in turn tied to my mopping bucket of galvanized tin, and this had crashed down from the chair on which I'd placed it, exactly as I'd intended. Michael was untangling yarn from his trouser legs.

"Do you mind telling me what the hell you're doing making a booby trap of your stairs?"

"I wanted to see if I could catch a booby, of course," said I, superciliously.

From the top step Michael looked up at me, unsure whether to be irritated or amused. "Well, may I come up, or not?"

"I would prefer that you do not. In case you are unaware of it, Mrs. O'Leary has gone out of town . . ."

"I figured something of the sort, that's what I came up for. To talk to you, find out why she's not at home at this hour. I thought something might be wrong."

"She did not leave a note for you, then?"

"If she had, would I be standing here?"

"You might. Very well . . . her note to me said that she has gone to stay with her sister, who is ill. And it occurred to me then that I would be alone and unchaperoned in a house with a man. Yourself. Therefore, I set up an alarm system to let me know if said man—or anyone—should venture into my area. It worked quite well, didn't it? But now I suppose I shall have to think of something new. This would not surprise you a second time . . ."

Michael, still standing on the top step, rubbed at his head in a perplexed manner. "Fremont, don't go all prudish on me. Surely you can't think that I—"

"What I think is that proprieties must be observed," I said in a rather nasty tone of voice, bringing my chin up sharply so that I looked down my nose at him. "I may be independent, Mr. Archer, but I am not without a sense of what is decent and what is not! As we must share a common stairway, and there is no door from the stair into the hall for me to lock, I feel I need some protection."

"You've lost your blooming mind!" Michael declared, backing down the stairs. "Don't worry, Miss Jones, I wouldn't come near you after that with a ten-foot pole!"

"Good!" I yelled after him.

I know that I can be quite rude—I was certainly told so often enough growing up—and I hoped I'd just been rude enough to keep Michael Archer at a distance for a while. Not that I was worried about whatever might be left of my virtue. Oh, no. I was worried about my safety. Perhaps even my life. And Mrs. O'Leary's.

13.

If Wishes Were Horses

———◦◦◦———

I SPENT THE night in an agony of ambivalence, with the result that I was no good for anything the next morning. I kept making mistakes in whatever I tried to type, including the retired professor's memoirs, which were what I usually worked on when my mind was mostly elsewhere. Finally I pushed away from the typewriter and sat at the desk with my face in my hands. This would never do!

I stuck a sign on my office door—BACK IN A MINUTE—and went downstairs to the bookstore, where I tried to have a diverting conversation with Krista Sorenson. This activity proved to be about as diverting as brushing one's teeth. As long as I was there, I bought the latest *Collier's,* even though the current issue had no further adventure of Sherlock Holmes, and took it back upstairs with me. Placing it on the table, I stood looking out the window and wondering how I might get a sample of Michael's handwriting.

I wished I'd kept the note he'd written when he gave me the gloxinia. He wrote a fine hand, I remembered that much; but not enough to know if it was or was not the same as had penned Mrs. O'Leary's missive. Oh, how I wished I'd kept it! *If wishes were horses, then beggars would ride.* Our helpful proverb for today.

Well, I couldn't go on like this. I should just have to go home to Vallejo Street during my lunch hour and snoop in Michael's apartment. That is, if he were not there. What did the man do all day? I really hadn't the slightest idea. Nor did I know if he locked his doors. As for myself, I had spent some unhappy wee small hours last night contemplating the wisdom of locking mine. I had concluded that it would do no good, that I would be far safer through continuing to act standoffish and prudish. As long as Michael did not know that I suspected him of having something to do with Mrs. O'Leary's absence, I should be in no danger of being likewise made absent.

It is a terrible thing to become suspicious of a person one has admired—and I did admire Michael Archer. He was witty and urbane and charming and intelligent, and handsome in his dark, exotic Russian way. Not to mention the fact that I had always found older men exceedingly attractive. *But* . . .

But he had practically admitted to me that he was a spy; and I (my God, how could I have been so foolish?) had told him that Mrs. O'Leary thought he was one. I did not like to think that Michael was a practiced liar, yet he must be. Spies are trained in deception; it is their very stock in trade. That touching story about Katya—could it have been invented to play upon my sympathy? Oh yes, it could have been. His seemingly kind concern for my welfare, his lighthearted insistence that we were Watson and Holmes *in re* Li Wong's murder, these could be deception too. All those times I had felt that someone was following me, the someone could have been Michael Archer. Spies are trained at following—I believed they called it surveillance.

If I could find one shred of evidence that Michael had made Mrs. O'Leary disappear, then the pendulum of my intolerable ambivalence would stop its swinging. I would go straight to the police. Finding that Michael's handwriting matched the note Mrs. O. had supposedly written would be proof enough for me!

I could picture her just inside the front door, her bulk taking up most of the hallway; she would say, "Wotcha doing home at this hour, Fremont?" But Mrs. O. wasn't there. The door had been locked, and I locked it behind me again when I entered. The second floor was quiet and rather gloomy.

"Michael, are you at home?" I called out. No reply.

I continued on to my own floor. My idea was that, in case of any interruptions, it should look as if I'd simply come home for lunch. I set that up, then went back to the stairway and stood listening for a few moments. Then, very stealthily, I crept down the stairs. I was definitely alone here.

None of Michael's doors was closed, much less locked. Very clever. No doubt he wanted it to appear as if his life were an open book. I went into the large double room where the walls were lined with books (closed, of course) because I thought I'd seen a desk there. Yes, there was a very large rolltop desk. What was more, the top was open and the writing surface covered with papers! I rushed over and began my inspection.

There were letters: *to* Michael, not *by* Michael. I did not take time to read them, only being careful not to get them out of their order in the pile. There were bills—of no use whatever. Surely the man must write notes to himself, keep some records in his own hand! In the cubbyholes at the back of the desk were more bills, more letters in envelopes, some postcards, old theater programs, stamps . . .

Ka-chunk! Oh lord, that was the sound of the front door closing. He was coming back! I hurried to the doorway, and as I reached it, I heard Michael's footsteps approaching the stair. Too late I realized there was no way I could get back to my own apartment without his seeing that I'd been in his. What I needed was a brazen lie, a reason for my presence—but I could not think of one fast enough. I had to hide! A glance over my shoulder confirmed what I'd thought: There was no place at all to hide in this sitting room *cum* library. The only item of furniture large enough to conceal a person was the sofa, and it was out in the middle of the room with a lamp table behind it. No concealment there.

Holding my breath, glad I did not wear the voluminous, rustling variety of petticoats, I ventured out into the hall. Through the banisters I could see the top of Michael's head as he came up the stairs. For one awful, heart-stopping second I froze, as a rabbit will under the gun. But then I moved, silently, up the hall to the front room.

Michael's bedroom. There were two possible hiding places: under the bed, or in the wardrobe. I crawled under the bed and lay there quivering, listening.

He came into the bedroom! I expected at any moment to hear, over the thundering of my own terrified heartbeat, Michael's voice

155

commanding, "Fremont, come out from under there!" But he was humming some tune—rather tunelessly, actually—and in the inch of space between the fringed hem of the bedspread and the floor I saw his black shoes; and then the bed creaked and sagged and I flattened myself as he sat on it and proceeded to remove those shoes. His socks were also black. The heel of one had a tiny hole that was going to need darning soon.

The bed creaked again. Oh dear God, I thought, he's going to take a nap and I'll be stuck under here for hours! But no sooner had I thought this than the black socks walked around the bed and I heard a click, followed by a faint wooden groan—Michael had opened the wardrobe—and I thanked my lucky stars that I had chosen the right hiding place!

He proceeded to change his clothes. Eventually he sat on the bed again and put his shoes back on, humming all the while, and then the shoes went away and the humming faded.

I lay there with my cheek against the cool hardwood floor. I had made an interesting discovery: One does not remain terrified forever. The pounding of blood in my ears had long since ceased. My hands were no longer the least bit cold or damp. And through it all, even when exposure had been only inches away, my mind worked like a clock. Of course, I was helped by my keen sense of hearing; I now heard Michael's steps departing down the stairs, and once more the distinctive *ka-chunk* of the front door closing. I let out a long breath, stretched out my arms, and slid out from under the bed.

Aha! As I dusted myself off I saw that I was to be rewarded for my ordeal—Michael had left his briefcase. It sat on the floor by the wardrobe, which remained with one door open, a shirt and a tie draped over it. Interesting to know that Michael Archer was not excessively neat; I would have thought he might be.

I was no longer concerned about interruptions, but there was the matter of time. I did have to get back to the office, so I did not try to make sense of the papers I found in Michael's briefcase. There were pages and pages in his own hand, which was not (alas, for all my trouble) the hand that had written Mrs. O'Leary's note. I had tucked it in the pocket of my skirt so that I would have it for comparison. My heart lightened just a tad at this discovery.

As I was about to replace the sheaf of papers in the briefcase, curiosity got the better of me. So much research—about what? The page I'd chosen at random to compare to my note had been something on mushrooms. Mushrooms? I sank down on the edge of the bed and quickly scanned a few more pages: oleander, rhododendron, monkshood . . . I blinked, reluctant to reach a somewhat obvious conclusion. All common plants, as mushrooms are the most common of fungi. Yet all—and there were more, on other pages—also poisonous. Michael Archer was doing research on how to poison people. How reassuring.

"You are the most welcome sight my eyes have seen lately!" I declared, none too demurely.

"I'm certainly glad to hear that," said Justin, standing in my office door. He closed it, the bell gave a merry jingle, and he crossed the room to my desk. "I've brought you something," he said, bringing his arm out from behind his back in a flourish.

"Flowers! How nice you are to always bring me flowers. Thank you, Justin." A cluster of tiny pink roses nestled in a circle of feathery green fern, backed by a matching pale pink ribbon.

"It's a corsage, you wear it."

"I know," I said happily, stroking the ribbon.

"I hope you'll wear it right now, and come with me. Surely you have finished work for the day?"

"It is five o'clock, I usually stop at this time. What did you have in mind?" I had thought I was tired, but suddenly I was not tired at all.

"I thought we might go to the Fairmont Hotel. In the Garden Court they have a woman who plays the harp at this hour. It's absolutely celestial!" Justin's blue eyes twinkled. I thought he looked rather like an angel himself—a decidedly male angel who was a temptation to human females. He went on tempting: "We could have sherry and listen to the harpist play. And afterward, a bite of supper."

I looked down at my pleated white shirtwaist and plain blue skirt, the same clothes I'd worn while hiding under Michael's bed. I still felt dusty, whether I looked it or not. "I'm not dressed for the Fairmont," I said.

"Nonsense! You look perfectly respectable. This is San Francisco, remember? People wear what they like here. And the corsage will dress up your outfit anyway." Justin leaned over the desk and cupped his fingers under my chin, lifting my face to his. His eyes, and his voice, softened. "Besides, Fremont, you look beautiful in anything. We haven't been out together in days. Please."

I succumbed. "All right. That would be lovely."

We took the cable car to the hotel, which was only a short distance away. As always, the touch of Justin's hand at my elbow when we crossed the street, at my waist when we boarded and descended from the cable car, brought a pleasurable thrill. I was glad we were to be together in a public place—once more I could postpone the inevitable.

Justin secured a table for us in a secluded corner, screened on two sides by giant ferns and a spiky palmetto. With the rippling harp music I felt indeed as if I had landed in a green patch of heaven. How lovely it was to let all my cares and suspicions dissolve.

We did not talk much while we sipped sherry and the harpist played. When Justin suggested that we stay at our table for a light meal, rather than have a more elaborate dinner in the dining room, I readily agreed.

"I have something to tell you," said Justin when the harpist was in her interval.

His serious tone intruded somewhat on my blissful mood. "By all means, do tell."

"I think you know that my practice is doing well."

"Yes, and I'm happy for you. My typewriting service is also doing well."

"Then perhaps what I'm about to tell you won't be bad news, Fremont."

I raised my eyebrows.

"I've hired a clerk. I won't need you to type for me anymore. Of course, I don't have one of your typewriting machines, but the clerk will prepare my papers the usual way, in longhand."

"I won't miss your business, and I'm glad you have a clerk. But I suppose this does mean that I will see you less often." I realized as I said this that I had not seen Justin as often as I was accustomed to for quite some time. "When did you hire your clerk?"

"A couple of weeks ago."

I nodded. "Your clerk is a man, of course." I wanted to bite my tongue but it was too late, I'd said it.

Justin grinned; his hair fell down toward one eye. "Of course. Law clerks are always men."

"A woman could do the work equally well," I said, but not belligerently. It was more a thoughtful observation.

Justin leaned back in his chair, scowling. "I declare, Fremont, you'll want to be practicing law yourself next! A woman law clerk? Nobody ever heard of such a thing." He tossed his head, sending his errant shock of hair back where it belonged.

I smiled. "Perhaps my remark was prompted by the tiniest shade of jealousy. I admit I would not entirely like for you to have a female law clerk, Justin. And I will miss seeing you as often as we saw one another when I first opened my business."

The waiter came to take away the plates and offer dessert, which I refused but Justin did not. In the silence while Justin was making his choice, I reflected that he seemed to have become unusually successful in a very short time. Of course, things were different in San Francisco. In Boston, young men did not start out practicing law on their own. They went into an established firm, always at the bottom, even if the firm happened to be their father's—as had been the case for a couple of my childhood friends.

Justin ordered coconut cake, which made me wish I had not refused dessert, coconut being a particular favorite of mine. I had asked for coffee only, and would have to be satisfied with that. When the waiter was gone again I said, "You will have to be moving to a larger office, now that you have a clerk. That place you have is scarcely big enough for two people."

"Oh, didn't I tell you? I can't believe I didn't. I have a new office. I moved last month."

"No"—I shook my head—"you didn't." And it was a good thing I hadn't decided to walk up Sacramento Street to see him. I would have been quite at a loss.

"Well," said Justin, zestily scattering coconut, "I've been so busy I just forgot. It's down on Montgomery Street. Makes it a bit harder to pop in on you."

"Um," I said noncommittally, sipping coffee. It was delicious, but I cast an envious eye at all that lovely coconut, and I wondered: How in the world had Justin been able to buy a house and rent a new office in the business district, both at the same time?

It was not good manners, but curiosity once again got the better of me. "Justin, hasn't the rise of your law career been rather meteoric? It wasn't all that long ago that you and I were sitting in the City of Paris, virtually counting pennies over the cost of a luncheon."

He blushed. His skin was so fair that he could not hide it, though he ducked his head. When he raised it again the flush was fading, and he looked like the cat that got the canary. "I told you, Fremont, I've been lucky. I got a really big corporate client. Now let's don't talk anymore about business. Let's talk about us."

Us! Ridiculous how a word of only two letters could sound so significant. "Us?"

"When are you coming to my house again?"

"I, ah, I thought we agreed," I hedged, "that you would do your own decorating. You were thinking of getting your mother over from Berkeley to help you, remember?" He hadn't exactly said that, but I sought to distract him.

"I never said any such thing. But anyway, I did two more rooms: the kitchen and breakfast room. Do you know how to cook, Fremont? Maybe you'll come and cook a meal for me sometime soon."

"I am not a good cook," I admitted, putting down my coffee cup.

"You surprise me." Justin winked and grinned. "I thought you did everything well, Fremont Jones."

"Where cooking is concerned, I only just get by. You see, we had a cook at home and I just never learned. Cooking is a skill I never thought of having to master."

Justin, wiping a last crumb of coconut from his mouth, leaned over the table and said in an intimate tone, "Then I'll bring the food in. Come soon, we'll eat in the breakfast room."

I knew that I could avoid the issue no longer. With a glance at the sheltering ferns and palmetto that gave at least an impression of some privacy, I too leaned forward and said quietly, "I believe I take your meaning. You have a fine house, Justin. But I cannot enjoy it with you in quite the way you want."

"Sure you can!" Smiling confidently, Justin reached out and placed his hand on mine. Too intimate a gesture for a public place.

I pulled my hand away. I had a hollow feeling inside, as if I were about to incur a great loss, and no one to blame for it but myself. My eyes felt too big for my face as I implored him, "Justin, can't we be just . . . *friends?*"

All of a sudden, Justin Cameron showed me his lawyer persona. He gathered it about himself, sitting very straight and tall. His chin jutted out. "Explain what you mean by just friends, if you please."

"I mean"—I swallowed hard, thinking of that lengthy and most difficult dialogue I'd had with my diary—"that I cannot be with you in quite the way we were before, in your house that day."

"You did not seem unwilling. You seemed to enjoy it."

"I did." I smiled, but my lips trembled. "But such . . . episodes can lead to consequences that one must think about."

"I believe it is the woman's responsibility to think about the consequences. And women have ways, you must have ways—"

"I *have* been thinking about the consequences," I interjected quickly, "and that is why I want us to have a simple friendship, Justin. I am very fond of you . . ." I faltered, for the truth was that I was more than fond of him.

"And I care about you, Fremont," said Justin, his eyes entreating, "I care a great deal." Remarkable, how the lawyer could vanish so quickly and the lover take his place.

If I did not push myself mercilessly onward, I would never be able to say what must be said. "Because I am so fond of you, I think you have a right to know that I have made a decision never to marry. I could not marry you, Justin, and that is why we must be no more than friends. Because the consequences of—of our being together in that other way—must logically lead to marriage, and I cannot do that."

Justin gave one short whoop of a laugh, and his lock of hair tumbled down again. He looked absurdly happy and relieved. "For God sakes, Fremont, if that's all that's worrying you, you can forget it! I don't want to get married either. We were made for each other, you and I!"

Justin insisted upon driving me home in a cab. When the horse clip-clopped to a stop in front of the house on Vallejo Street, I saw that the first and third floors were dark but lights showed in every window on the second floor.

"Wait here, cabbie, while I see the lady to the door," said Justin grandly as he handed me out.

We climbed the steps and at the top I tucked my walking stick under my arm so that I could retrieve the key from my purse. As I did so, a light came on and the front door swung open.

"Good evening, Fremont," said Michael Archer, very elegant in a burgundy silk smoking jacket with black velvet lapels.

I just looked at him with my mouth hanging open.

"This must be your friend, ah—"

"Justin," I said, recovering a degree of composure, "Justin Cameron, this is my neighbor, Michael Archer."

"How do you do," said Justin politely.

I turned my back on Michael. "Thank you for a lovely evening, Justin." I sounded, and felt, like a stiff schoolgirl delivered to her door.

"My pleasure entirely," Justin responded. With a swift glance over my shoulder, he bent his head and kissed my cheek. "I hope I will have a similar pleasure again soon," he said quite clearly enough for Michael to hear. "Now I'll say good night. Nice to have met you, Archer."

"Likewise," Michael responded.

"Good night, Justin." I waved as he stepped up into the cab, a

162

smile pasted on my face. Then I turned and stormed through the door, slamming it behind me. I gave it a jab with the tip of my walking stick for extra emphasis. I would far rather have jabbed Michael Archer!

"Handsome young fellow—" Michael began, but I had no intention of letting him finish.

"What in the world did you think you were doing, opening the door on us like that? You're not my father, to be waiting up for me when I'm out with a man!"

Michael backed away from me, holding both hands up with the palms out. "Easy, Fremont!"

I advanced on him, shaking my stick. "Even Mrs. O'Leary, nosy as she is, would at least have had the decency to wait in the hall before accosting me!"

"I didn't accost you. I was concerned when you did not come home, and wanted to be sure that you were all right."

"I don't have to account for my whereabouts to you, Michael. As I said, you are not my father, and I'll thank you to mind your own business and stay out of mine!" I flounced toward the stairs, pounding my stick with every step. I had seldom been more angry.

Michael stood in my way; he rubbed at his chin. "I suppose that I must seem old enough to be your father. But I assure you, my dear Fremont—"

"I am not your dear Fremont." I raised the walking stick and nudged his arm with it. "Now, if you will please get out of my way!"

In one strong movement, quick as a reflex, Michael grabbed the stick and jerked it from my hand. His eyes glittered as he examined it. "I've noticed that you've taken to carrying this handsome cane. I hope you haven't injured yourself? Turned an ankle, perhaps?"

"It's not a cane, and of course I haven't," I snapped. By the look on his face I knew he thought no such thing. "Give it back this instant."

"Fascinating!" said Michael. His clever fingers had found the secret button, and he slowly extracted the blade.

He knows, I thought, *he knows that I have been snooping in his apartment—what will he do to me?* My heart pounded, my former anger

163

evaporated; I only wanted my weapon in my own hands again. "That . . ." My voice came out in a squeak. I cleared my throat and tried again. "That is my property and I'll thank you to return it to me."

"Of course," said Michael smoothly. He slipped the blade into its scabbard and made a formal presentation of it, bowing and clicking his heels. The effect was spoiled somewhat by the fact that he wore carpet slippers.

"Thank you," I said, trying not to sigh in relief. My knees felt rather watery.

"I hope you know how to use it?"

"I have been practicing."

"Aha."

"Now, if you will please stand aside—"

He ignored the request. "That you have been practicing would indicate that you feel some need to protect yourself."

"You are astute tonight, Watson."

"You felt some need to protect yourself even before you placed the, ah, booby trap at the top of your stairs last night. I believe you have been carrying your stick for almost three weeks."

"Watson, you have scored two for two. Now, if you don't mind, I've had a long day, I'm tired, and I'd like to go up the stairs you're standing in front of!"

"Of course. I beg your pardon!" He moved aside, with an *after you* gesture.

Finally! I swept by him, but as I placed my foot on the bottom stair Michael grabbed my arm from behind and pulled me back against him. His beard touched my cheek, and he hissed into my ear, "Who are you afraid of, Fremont?"

I turned my head and looked into steely eyes only inches from mine. I determined that I, too, would be like steel. "I do not know," I said, "but whoever he is, he may be sure that I will defend myself."

Michael let me go. I heard him chuckle as I climbed the stairs. He said something under his breath. I thought he said, "An excellent woman!"

164

14.

Proverbially Speaking, Things Are Getting Hot

From the age of five I had a series of tutors. None of them stayed for very long; although I had been entirely isolated from the real world since birth, I somehow knew that the tutors' leaving was not my fault but was due rather to the extreme strangeness of our household. I was an intelligent child, and eager to learn, never happier than when I had a new book open before me.

There was only one thing I liked almost as well as books: to stand in the small glassed-in room at the very top of the house and look out at the world where I was not allowed to go.

"We do not go out," said Mother. "We cannot survive outside these walls."

"Why?" I asked. We had this conversation at least once a year, every year, and it was always the same, but I had to keep on asking.

"Because, Perry dear, we are different. Here, we are powerful; out there, we are weak. You are my son, my very own dear child, and you are like me. I stay in this house, and so shall you. Forever!"

Of course—for at least at first I was a far more normal child than she wanted to believe—this only made me desire all the more passionately to go outside.

From the small room at the top of the house, which I eventually learned was called a cupola, I could see for miles and miles around. I imagined myself to be a prince imprisoned in an enchanted tower, and this was my kingdom. An evil fairy-woman had snatched me away and kept me here, telling me that she was my true mother.

There was only one problem with this imagined scenario: As far as I could ascertain from looking around my kingdom, the evil fairy who said she was my mother must be a queen or a princess herself, because our house was like a castle. It had a wall of iron around it, and many angled roofs, and towers, and chimney pots. Certainly it seemed quite as large as any other house I could see, and larger than most. The other large houses were grand, like palaces, and like ours they were on the tops of the hills.

My true mother, I decided, lived in a kingdom across the water. She was a queen, good and beautiful, and my true father, the King, was also good and very powerful. The reason they did not come and take me back with them, even if they had to do battle with the evil fairy who said she was my mother, was that they did not know where I was. Some day, I would find a way out of this castle and its evil spell. I would go across the water.

Yet my mother's dire predictions about what would happen to me if I should venture outside did serve as a deterrent. There was also the fact that the servants were ordered to prevent me from leaving the house. However, the day finally came—I was nine years old—when my current tutor, who happened to be rather elderly, nodded off whilst I was writing an essay. And I escaped.

I knew enough not to run, for that would make too much noise. I had thought about this so often that I had planned an escape route, which I followed, exiting the house by a seldom-used side door. I breathed in the fresh air and waited for something dire to happen . . . But nothing did. Perhaps her evil spell did not work outside the walls of the house; perhaps that was why my mother would not allow me to go outside!

I was not yet, however, truly free. I had to make it through the gate in the iron wall, and then I would be free. It was just a gate. This was not really a castle, so there was no gate-keeper, but it would probably be locked all the same. The wall, and the gate, were topped with spiky points—could I climb over? Perhaps, but it would be ever so much easier to go out the gate.

The gate was locked and I could not climb the wall. There was nowhere to get a hand- or foot-hold, even if I were brave enough to risk going over those sharp spikes on the top. With forbidden tears running down my face I grasped the iron bars of the gate and looked out at the street. All that freedom, and no way to get to it, was too much to bear. For the first time in my life, I wanted to die.

At last I turned around, defeated, ready to go back. I thought I might at least get back to my schoolroom undetected—that was the best I could hope for now.

Here it is, I thought, finally: the description of Peregrine's house! I knew it was in here somewhere!

I raised my eyes to my mother's house, my prison. I had never before seen it from without. Now I received the full impact of that extraordinary, bizarre facade—

The tinkle of the bell on my office door made me look up from the pages of "Damned to Darkness." Really, this was an inopportune time for an interruption! And it was after five o'clock. I should have put the CLOSED sign on my door.

But when I saw the young woman who entered, I felt glad that I hadn't. I knew who she was even before she identified herself; her stature, so tall and slim for one of her race, and the striking angular bone structure of her face, marked her as a relation of Li Wong.

I stood up immediately and said in a pleasant way, in case she had glimpsed my initial displeasure, "I am Fremont Jones. How may I help you?"

"My name is Meiling Li," she said, inclining her head slightly. "I believe you were acquainted with my grandfather, Sun Wong Li."

"Yes, he came here twice. I knew him as Li Wong."

"Yes, so he was most often called. I will explain my presence. House of Li is now a house of women. Grandfather, father, brothers all are gone. Mother and Grandmother do not speak English, never leave Chinatown. They ask me to find Miss Fremont Jones."

I could not help being as impressed with the granddaughter as I had been with Li Wong. She told her sad story succinctly, in an attractively husky voice with only the slightest trace of an accent.

Meiling wore the plain black clothing favored by so many Chinese—in her case, a long tunic buttoned down the front but slit up the sides, over narrow black trousers. The effect was so attractive and looked so comfortable that I immediately wished I could have trousers too. She seemed about my own age and, I was happy to observe, did not affect a subservient demeanor. Her long, black hair was glossy with a blue sheen and she wore it the same way I usually wear mine, pulled back simply and clasped at the nape of the neck. I thought I sensed a kindred spirit in Meiling, and wished we might become friends.

"I admired your grandfather greatly," I said, "and was sorry to hear of his tragedy."

She inclined her head in acknowledgment, but not before I saw a shadow deepen the already dark shade of her eyes. "We have suffered a great loss," she said as she raised her head, "but my people are accustomed to losses."

"That does not make it right. Or any less painful."

"No, but your people seem to think my people are like cattle, that we have no feelings."

"I assure you that I think no such thing, and I will do anything I can to help. You said your mother and grandmother asked you to come here?"

"Yes. I am told to bring you to them. They wish to speak with you, through me as interpreter. And as I said, they do not leave Chinatown. You need not fear for your safety, Miss Jones. You will be safe as long as you are with me."

"Please call me Fremont. And I should like to call you Meiling, if I may."

"As you wish."

I was smiling to beat the band, but nothing I said or did brought any warmth to Meiling's features. Well, perhaps I could understand that; this was very serious business for the Li family.

She spoke again: "We go now, Miss, ah, Fremont."

"Certainly. Just give me a minute to put things away and close up the office."

I felt Meiling's watchful dark eyes upon me as I put Mr. Partridge's manuscript in the file drawer and locked it, covered the typewriter, gathered my purse and walking stick and slung my cape over my arm. I indicated by a gesture that she was to precede me out the door. While I was locking it Meiling said, not lightly, "I am trained in jujitsu."

I looked up; her tone implied that I might do something that required putting her jujitsu to use—on me! Nevertheless, I decided to accept this information casually. I smiled and said, "How excellent! That must be useful. I should very much like to learn jujitsu myself. You must tell me all about it. For example, is it common for Chinese girls to be taught jujitsu?" etc., etc.

All the way down the stairs and out onto Sacramento Street I plied Meiling with questions about that martial art. She was not very forthcoming, but I did learn that most girls were not given such lessons. She got hers because she insisted, and because she was Li Wong's granddaughter—we were as much kindred spirits as I'd suspected. I gathered it was out of the question that I might find anyone to give me jujitsu lessons, but I did fancy that she thawed a bit toward me.

Still talking of martial arts and the wisdom of being able to defend oneself—at least, *I* was talking about these things—Meiling and I walked over one block to California Street and caught a streetcar, which we rode to Stockton. There we disembarked and entered Chinatown.

Although I am seldom at a loss for words, words do fail me when it comes to a description of my first sight of Chinatown. Michael Archer, and others after him, had told me that Chinatown was like a separate village in the heart of San Francisco, but that did not begin to conjure up a mental picture that could have prepared me for what I now saw with my own eyes. Having grown up in New England, I have certain expectations associated with the word "village," and while I knew they would not apply in this instance, I had never imagined how vastly different another culture could be until I set foot in Chinatown that day.

The streets were darker and seemed narrower than those in the rest of the city. Though it was only about six o'clock in the evening, and it was the month of June, many brightly colored lamps and paper lanterns were already lit in doors and windows. The colors were garish, primary, rich; startling to Americans who, like our English cousins, have been subtly schooled to a pastel-hued Edwardian sensibility. The buildings themselves tended to be dark-colored, either intentionally or from the natural weathering of their wood, but their trim was disturbingly multicolored. For example, one tall building (house or commercial establishment, I could not tell) had three stories of balconies, and each balcony's railing was painted red, yellow, purple, and green. Here and there I caught glimpses of gold; everywhere as I passed I had a fleeting impression of the sinuous shapes of snakes and dragons, twined about light-posts, curling over doorways, lurking in the shadowed recesses of windows.

Meiling walked too quickly for me. I kept wanting to stop and gawk but had to keep up with her rapid pace. She walked in silence, not the least inclined to play tour guide, while I felt more like a tourist than I ever had in my life. All the signs, on shops and corners, draped in sagging festoons across streets, were in Chinese, as unfathomable as ciphers to me. Only once did Meiling speak; as we crossed a street she said, *"Tang Yahn Gai*—Sacramento Street to you." But this bit of familiarity only served to make me feel more alien.

In fact, I realized I was quite lost but was too interested in my surroundings to care. I was also interested in my companion, who moved with a swift, long, graceful stride quite unlike the locomotion of the other Chinese women. I observed that people looked at the two of us with some curiosity, but as soon as Meiling came near they averted their eyes. Did she command respect, or were they simply avoiding us? I could not tell.

The street grew narrower. I had an impression that in Chinatown the merchants kept their shops on the ground level and lived on the floors above, for one block seemed much like another. If there was such a thing as a "residential area," we had not achieved it. As the street narrowed, the shop-fronts did too; everything was more and more crowded together. And the atmosphere was darker, lights fewer and farther between.

Meiling turned into a street so narrow that we could not walk abreast, so I fell back and let her take the lead. Dark gray wooden buildings rose up four stories on either side, sprinkled with black-yawning doorways, peopled with shadows. Meiling walked even faster, and I lengthened my own stride to keep up, reaching out with my walking stick, appreciating its familiar feel in the midst of all this strangeness.

The narrow street ended in a brick wall; the brightness of its yellow paint was more than a little subdued by the dark atmosphere, and marred by flaking patches. A wooden gate of rather grand design was set into the wall; it had a rounded arch and was painted red. There were Chinese characters worked into the gate's design. I could not read them but I understood: You are entering the realm of the Family Li. Meiling, who belonged here, did not pause but went straight through the gate. I followed her with a feeling of deference as I passed through.

How exceedingly strange and beautiful this was! Down that cramped, forbidding alley one must pass, and then, if one were favored, one might enter into the spacious, all-but-hidden place of the Li's. We were in a paved courtyard of proportions that seemed vast by contrast to all I had seen of Chinatown thus far. There was a complex of buildings, long and low, spreading out around us. I had an impression of multiple, gracefully columned arcades; but as I followed the swiftly moving Meiling, I had another impression as well: These buildings had seen better days. There was a forlorn air about the place, a sense of desertion, even desperation. Or perhaps that was only my lively imagination at work.

At any rate, we passed under the peaked roof of a porch and through a great red door into a building that, I guessed, was the main house of Li. There was a kind of entry hall, its ceiling held up by dragon-entwined columns; in shadowy gloom at the far end of this hall a round brass gong caught what there was of light. Meiling plunged into a corridor off to the right, and I followed her.

The ceiling was low; on either side were many rooms. At the very end of the corridor hung a beaded curtain through which Meiling walked, the beads making a brittle shivery sound when parted by her body. They made the same sound around me, and felt like polished ice upon my neck and shoulders. There was a rich rug of flowered design upon the floor of the large room we had entered, and two white-haired, tiny women sat in chairs on either side of a long, low table. One of the women got up as we entered and, with one glance at Meiling, bowed low to the other in a servile manner and scurried away.

Meiling underwent a transformation. Her steps slowed and shortened. Her whole body somehow softened and seemed to shrink. I did not think I was capable of doing likewise, but I was certainly in awe of the ancient, ivory-faced woman who sat in her chair as if it were a throne. Meiling bowed deeply, folding her hands in her sleeves, and spoke in Chinese. The little old woman inclined her white head and said something in reply. Then Meiling straightened, and gestured that I was to approach. The two of us remained standing.

"This is my honorable grandmother, Li Kwan, wife of Li Wong. She is the head of our family now. My mother, Suyin, is not feeling well and will not be joining us. You will speak, through me, with my grandmother."

"I am honored," I said, and I bowed as Meiling had done.

A male servant appeared at my elbow, his approach so completely silent that it startled me, and gestured that he would take my things. I reluctantly surrendered purse, cape, and walking stick and was relieved to see that he did not disappear with them but placed them on an ornately carved console against the wall near the beaded curtain.

The grandmother, Li Kwan, was speaking as the servant tended to this. I returned my attention to her, and Meiling translated: "The honorable Li Kwan wishes me to tell you that something of great value has been lost to us. We believe you may be able to help us find this object."

Oh dear, I thought, knowing very well that I could not help, but I inclined my head politely. Being among the Chinese was making me more polite than a thousand lessons in deportment.

Meiling was not satisfied with the little bow; her frown conveyed that I was expected to say something. I cleared my throat, feeling the first twinge of uneasiness. "I do not know how I can help, but I certainly will try."

A brief and oddly musical exchange then occurred between Meiling and her grandmother, after which the former again turned to me. "We have learned that my grandfather came to your place of business shortly before his death. You possess a machine, and the skill to make words in English on paper with this machine. Is this not so?"

"Yes," I nodded, "it is so. You saw the machine in my office today. It is called a typewriter."

"And with this typewriter you made a message for Li Wong. Yes?"

"Yes, I did."

"You will tell us, please, what it said."

"I . . . I cannot. I would if I could, please believe me, but I cannot."

Meiling frowned at me again, but turned and reported what I had said.

The tiny old woman said one sharp word which I did not need translated: "Why?"

Meiling said, "Why?"

"Are you familiar," I asked, "with the concept of confidentiality?"

"Of course," Meiling responded, "it means to keep secret that which should be secret. But we are the family of Li Wong, and he has gone to join the ancestors. There is no need to keep the secret any longer. Therefore, you will tell us what we wish to know."

An imperious gesture from the grandmother indicated that Meiling should translate what she had just said to me. While she translated, I composed a reply that I hoped they could accept. When Meiling once more looked at me, I said, "I type things, such as I did for your grandfather, for many people. For the sake of confidentiality I make myself forget the words once I have put them on paper. Truly, I cannot remember what I typed for Li Wong. I wish I could; I have often tried, because I was so impressed by your grandfather, and so concerned when I heard that he had been killed."

I paused while Meiling relayed this, and then resumed: "I can tell you only that I have a general impression that he wanted his words set down as some sort of protection, in case something happened to him. I have an idea that it concerned some sort of business deal and in-

173

volved one, or possibly two companies. I have remembered the name of one of them, but not the other. The one I remember is Trans-Hawaiian Trading Company."

She might not understand English, but Li Kwan did understand the name of the company: She gasped, and raised her hand to cover her mouth.

"This is bad news," said Meiling.

"I am sorry," I said, wondering if the Chinese, like the Greeks, were inclined to kill the messenger who brought bad news. Lamely I added, "Perhaps I was mistaken." But I was not: That name was the one thing I had truly recalled, validated by the memory of Li Wong making a mark in the air with his finger to indicate its hyphen.

Li Kwan spoke again, and Meiling listened. I waited nervously, not liking the turn things were taking. Meiling spoke to me again. "I will now tell you of that which has been lost to us. My grandfather took from this house a valuable object which has been in the family for centuries. He did this around the time he must have come to you, a few days before his death. The object is a statue of the goddess Kwan Yin. It is carved of jade, very valuable, not only because it is old and priceless but also because Li Kwan was named for the goddess Kwan Yin and bears a special devotion to her. We want to know if he had you write about the statue, about what he intended to do with it, and if you saw it yourself."

"No," I shook my head, "definitely not. There was no mention of a statue, and he definitely did not have it with him either of the times he came to my office."

Meiling turned her head as she relayed this information to Li Kwan. I did not care at all for the tension that was building in the room. While Meiling and her grandmother became occupied in a rather lengthy dialogue, I slowly moved, half a step at a time, toward the console that held my things. As I moved, some extra sense suddenly awakened in me so that I noticed something I had not before: The three of us were not quite alone. While there was no one else in the room, there were shadowy figures in each of two visible doorways. The third doorway, covered by the beaded curtain, was behind me, and I did not doubt that it also housed a living shadow.

The dialogue between Li Kwan and Meiling had become spirited; I observed that the Chinese language was not always musical, it had some quite guttural sounds. The console was within reach—none too soon! Unobtrusively as possible, I draped my cape over my arm and took purse and stick in hand. As soon as Meiling turned again I said casually, "If there's nothing else, I'm ready to leave now."

"My grandmother does not wish you to leave," said Meiling. This was not exactly news to me; I'd been afraid of something of the sort.

I slipped the handle of the purse over my arm under the cape so that I could have a free hand. "I believe it must be getting dark out. I really must go now. I do not particularly like to be out alone on the streets after dark."

Meiling was advancing on me. The shadows in the doorways were keeping to their places—so far. "You will accept our hospitality tonight," she said. "My grandmother believes that after a night under our roof you will remember more about the statue, and about the message of Li Wong. That message has disappeared, you see. No one knows what was in it. And we must know! The honor of the Li family is at stake."

"I understand that," I said. All my muscles were tense. I had not the slightest idea what I was going to do, but I did know I was about to do something, with the greatest haste! "Nevertheless, I must refuse your hospitality with the deepest regret. Will you please tell your grandmother this? Also, please tell her that I promise if I remember, or if I learn anything about the statue, I will return here immediately and give her the information. Tell her, Meiling."

I felt both surprise and gratitude as Meiling (who knew jujitsu) stopped a yard from where I stood, turned around where she was, bowed once, and addressed her grandmother. I began to walk backward, with a glance over my shoulder. I sensed, and then saw, that the shadows in the doorways were black-garbed men who now emerged a pace each into the room.

The tiny, ivory-faced grandmother uttered a sharp command that probably meant "Take her!" I didn't stay to find out. My right thumb rubbed the silver peony blossom and its magic button.

In a smooth, practiced motion I withdrew the blade from the

sheathing base of the walking stick with my right hand, and with my left I thrust the base into the waistband of my skirt. All of my five senses were as sharp as the blade I held before me, and a sixth sense was even sharper.

When Meiling whipped around at her grandmother's command I said, my voice sounding deadly, "I will not allow you to keep me here. I have told you the truth, I have done nothing wrong, and I am leaving. Stay back, I warn you!"

Guided by my sixth sense, I whirled, snatched my cape from my shoulder, and threw it over the man I'd felt come up behind me. Tangled and blinded, he could not stop my rush through the icy glass-beaded doorway. But Meiling's legs were long, and she had two more helpers. I ran like a Fury down that endless, low-ceilinged corridor, dreadfully certain that any one or all of the doors on either side of me would suddenly spew forth something or someone to stop me.

But nothing, no one, leapt out at me. I skidded into the entrance hall, momentarily disoriented, searching its gloom for the front door. I had been right about its getting dark—the far reaches of the hall were as black as a tar pit. Feet pounded behind me; there was no time to hesitate. I plunged in what I hoped was the direction of the door. My pursuers were too close; I was going to have to stand and fight, and I knew it.

Even as I wheeled about, I had the fleeting thought that I would not like to have to use my blade on Meiling . . . but it was not Meiling who flung himself at me. "I don't want to hurt any of you!" I yelled, but I also slashed with my blade and felt a sickening elation as it connected with an arm and caused a yelp of pain. It was so dark, and I was in such a frenzy, I could scarcely see what I was doing. I slashed again, but this time my blade did not connect. I turned and ran, and thank God I ran right at the door.

How did one get this door open? Two men were coming at me, I couldn't search for a knob or a handle or whatever and keep an eye on them too. Meiling was right behind them. I let my purse slide down my left arm to my hand, grabbed its handle and hit one of the men full in the face with it—there was such force behind my blow that he staggered back and fell. The other man reached for me with both hands but I feinted with my blade, and when he jumped back I understood: They were unarmed and did not want to be cut to ribbons. They could take me only if they got close enough, and I certainly did not intend to let them do that!

Brandishing the blade in a continuous figure eight, I let my purse slip up my arm again so that my left hand was free, and reached behind me. I yelled something, I don't know what—I had gained an instant, gut-level understanding of the reason for battle cries by then—and my searching fingers found a lever behind my back. I pressed on it, and the big door opened out so suddenly that I almost fell backward.

A solitary lamp burned on the porch. With the strange, heightened clarity that comes in times of severe stress, I noted that the lamp's round red glass globe was held in the wide-open jaws of a dragon, its base the dragon's twisted, contorted body. The poor creature looked exceedingly uncomfortable!

You may be sure that I made this observation in the blink of an eye, and was off running across the empty expanse of the courtyard and under the arch of the gate. Night air, darkness—and fog. Blessed, blessed fog to hide me, to wrap me in its cool, concealing folds. That it also meant I could not see where I was going made not the slightest bit of difference at the moment. I slowed down, moved over to one side of that long, narrow alley, located by feel the wall of a building, and leaned against it with my chest heaving. When I could hold my breath I did, and listened: They were not pursuing me.

However, as long as I remained in that alley I would not be safe, not even with the fog. Meiling, no doubt, knew the alley like the back of her hand, and probably the others did too. They were doubtless gathering their forces at this very moment, arming themselves, and would soon resume the chase. I could not rest longer, nor yet put up my blade.

I began to move up the alley by feeling my way along the building. The fog had piled up thick in the enclosed space, like an insubstantial snowdrift. Every time my searching fingers encountered the emptiness of a doorway, my heart rose into my throat. But no one grabbed me.

In the course of running this foggy gauntlet, it occurred to me that Meiling's argument with her grandmother might have meant

Meiling did not agree that I should be detained against my will. I had fought hard, yes; but still I wondered whether Meiling could not have bested me if she had really tried. At any rate, she and the Li servants had certainly given me up, for I had reached the intersection of alley and street. If they had intended to follow, they would have done so by now.

Before emerging onto the street I sheathed my trusty blade, which thus became a respectable walking stick again. I tucked my blouse more securely into my skirt. Though I regretted the loss of my aubergine cape, I was glad I still had my purse. All was well. I was safe now. Jauntily—an effect produced by the continuing excess of adrenaline in my system—I set off down the street . . .

And soon realized that I was hopelessly, completely lost. In the fog, in the dark, alone, unable to read a single sign, unable to ask directions. As if all that were not enough, these streets, which had been fascinating by day, became sinister at night. The last of the adrenaline drained out of me in a whoosh and left me feeling afraid.

15.

Not Necessarily Nevermore

———⋘⋙———

REALLY, IT HARDLY seemed fair that I should have done battle and escaped unscathed (to be entirely truthful, I had rather perversely enjoyed it), only to find myself emotionally undone by being lost in Chinatown.

Fremont Jones, lost and scared to death. *Fremont,* lost? I squared my shoulders, hefted my cane, and told myself that a Fremont could never be lost! I strode off into the fog, thinking all the while that John C. Fremont, my namesake and famous explorer, had certainly never been *lost* in his entire life. Temporarily unable to identify his surroundings, yes; but he would have kept moving. His blood flowed in my veins (albeit somewhat diluted); therefore, I should emulate him.

But the streets felt like a maze, and the fog precluded my looking for landmarks. In this instance, my acute hearing seemed more a curse than a blessing, because it picked up things I would rather not have heard: strange, disembodied moans, the shuffles and thumps and grunts of a fight, a constant undertone of alien chatter, and once a strangled scream. Faceless dark forms huddled by me, feet softly pattering like huge mice. I forced myself to stride on without hesitation. What hindered me most was the constant, corrosive knowledge that I did not belong here.

Someone grabbed my arm! I cried out, and a hand went over my mouth to muffle the cry. I struggled, tried to bite the hand—

"Fremont? Stop that! Egad, it really is you!" He dropped his hand and planted himself in front of me, still holding my arm—too tightly.

179

"Justin Cameron!" I almost could not believe my senses, but it *was* Justin, all tall and pale and wearing a bowler hat. I'd never seen him wear a hat before.

"What in the world are you doing here?" he asked incredulously.

"You are hurting my arm," I pointed out. "Nevertheless, I am glad to see you, Justin. I confess I am lost, and would appreciate your assistance."

"Well, of course." He relaxed his grip. "I was on my way to a business appointment, but it can wait. I'll escort you home, and on the way I trust you'll tell me what brings you to Chinatown all by yourself at night. This is not suitable, you know. Not at all."

I forbore questioning Justin's right to determine what was or was not suitable behavior for me—though I should probably take up the issue some other time. "I believe I will hire a horse and cab to take me to Vallejo Street. If you will assist me in that, you can continue on to your appointment. Which way shall we go to find a cab?"

"This way." Justin took my elbow and steered me in the same direction I had been going. I wondered if I might have found my way out by myself. I would have preferred that, actually; fond as I am of Justin, I did not feel like talking to him, and being talked at by him, at this particular time. His peremptory tone had stifled any initial impulse I'd had to throw myself into his arms and cling to him.

"There is no question," said Justin pugnaciously, "but that I will see you to your door."

I did not argue with him, though I had no intention of allowing him to accompany me. I was feeling quite exhausted. Nevertheless, I could not resist commenting, "It's rather unusual, isn't it, for a lawyer to have a business appointment in Chinatown at night?"

"Not really."

I mulled this over and in the meantime we came to a street corner that actually had a sign in English: California Street. Justin said, "We should be able to hail a cab along here. We'll wait under that street-lamp."

There was a breeze here from the Bay that had not penetrated the crowded ranks of Chinatown. It blew the fog in swirling patches, amid intervals of clarity.

My weary mind worked well enough to put its finger on something that had been bothering me: "I had a distinct impression that you did not care for the Chinese, Justin. I'm surprised you would do business with them."

He looked down at me and shrugged. "You don't have to *like* your clients, especially if they have money. Some of these Chinese have plenty of money."

"Not—" I stopped myself. I had been about to say, *Not Li Wong's family, not anymore.* But I did not want to give Justin—or anyone—an explanation of my presence in Chinatown.

"Not what?"

"Not many of them, certainly."

"Oh. Well, you're right about that." Justin looked over his shoulder and tapped his foot. There were no hansom cabs in sight. He shoved his hands in his pockets and looked back at me. We were in a clear patch, and I could see quite well the sharp look in his eyes as he said, "You're very keen on those impoverished types, aren't you, Fremont? I'll bet old Li Wong played on your sympathy, made out like he didn't have any money, but he had plenty. He just had it hidden away."

"I did not realize that you knew Li Wong, Justin."

"Sure I did. I saw him in your office, remember?"

I remembered very well. I remembered that Justin had said he didn't know the man.

Justin raised his arm to hail an approaching cab. The horse clop-clopped to a stop. I cleared my throat. "Ah, Justin, I am going home alone. I'm grateful for your help, really, you bumped into me at precisely the right moment. And I'll be fine now."

"I know how to act like a gentleman," he said huffily, "even if you occasionally forget how to act like a lady. I am coming with you, Fremont. I will make myself responsible for your safety since you seem to have so little regard for it yourself."

He opened the carriage door and I put one foot on the step; I could not delay the driver much longer. The horse whuffled and pranced. Thin fog eddied around our feet and wreathed our shoulders.

I insisted, "I'm very tired. I only want to be by myself. I do not want to talk. In any event, your client probably won't be pleased if you fail to show up." I climbed into the carriage but, to my consternation, Justin crowded up behind me. I did not move over to make room for him. Instead, being rather desperate, I resorted to feminine wiles. In a soft voice I coaxed, "Let me go on now. I'll see you another time. In fact, I'll cook that dinner you've been wanting."

Aha! Instant success. Justin removed his foot and tipped his hat. "In that case, I'll say good night, Fremont. But I warn you, I'll hold you to that promise! Cabbie, you may drive on."

"Vallejo Street," I directed, as the horse clopped away. I was so tired that the swaying of the carriage nearly put me to sleep.

As ill luck would have it, my ordeals were not yet over that night. A light burned in the downstairs hall. Hope rose in my breast. I thought: Mrs. O'Leary has returned!

But of course she had not. As the front door closed behind me, Michael Archer came down the stairs.

I frowned and addressed him sharply: "Kindly refrain from saying whatever it is you're about to say." I went up the stairs as if he were not already on them, forcing him to retreat. "I do not want to hear it."

"You have lost your cape," he observed as I passed him on the second-floor landing. "You were wearing it when you set out this morning."

I rolled my eyes, which he did not see, for my back was to him by then. Really, this was too much! "The whereabouts of my cape are no concern of yours, Mr. Archer," I said over my shoulder. "I have had an excessively long day and do not intend to stand about talking. Good night!"

The next morning I found a letter placed on top of my newel post. One glance at my name inscribed on the envelope confirmed that it was from Michael—after what I'd been through to get a sample of it, I would never forget his handwriting! I did not want to read the letter at that moment; I wanted to keep my mind concentrated on a plan that had come to me overnight. So I thrust the envelope into my purse and continued on my way to work. While riding the cable car, I allowed myself the mild distraction of wondering how Michael's poison research was going, and if he'd poisoned anybody yet, but that was all.

I arrived at my building so early that the Sorensons were not even there yet. I unlocked the outer door, locked it again behind me, and went upstairs, where I repeated the process on my office door. Then I sat down and removed the cover from my typewriter. I was so eager that I did not even pause to take off my jacket. Positioning my hands over the keys, I flexed my fingers and closed my eyes.

I typed: *In the event of my untimely death, I wish the following to be known to concerned persons* . . . And then I stopped. I screwed my eyes shut even more tightly, and concentrated until the blackness I saw inside my closed eyelids began to turn red and I feared I was making my eyes all bloodshot. Then I relaxed a bit, but still did not open my eyes.

Come on, come on, come on; remember, remember, remember! I silently commanded myself. Surely I could do this! If my mind could not recall the words, perhaps my fingers could. With eyes shut I began to type. I tried to put myself into a trance. Surely if psychic mediums could achieve a trance, so could I, and direct it to my own purpose!

But I was, alas, no Madame Blavatsky. I opened my eyes and looked in dismay at what I had produced:

amdkot ehtke tim osoj jey theiww shif poveraltkj his t ehtime tiems the futosghdimpleksks . . .

It went depressingly on like that, down the page. I heaved a mighty sigh and ripped the sheet out of the typewriter. It was simply no use; I would never remember. I rubbed my arms; they ached from the unaccustomed exercise of slashing and figure-eighting the day before. I hoped, somewhat belatedly, that the man whose arm I'd cut was not too badly hurt. I hoped the Li's would not come after me and cut off my arm or something to get even—one hears that the Chinese are very keen on revenge.

The day passed slowly, as days usually do when one wants them to be over quickly. The one bright spot occurred when the retired professor came to claim, and to pay me handsomely for the typing of, his memoirs. They made an impressively large bulk of manuscript. He seemed most pleased, and declared his intention to have the typed pages bound. So perhaps he had known all along that his halting, ruminative style did not lend itself well to the prospect of publication. I hoped so; he seemed a nice old man, and I would not have liked him to suffer rejection of his work.

Shortly before five o'clock I heard a rustling sound outside my office door. My eyes darted to it, and at the same moment my hand reached for my walking stick. I'd thought it best to keep my weapon at my desk now. How long I would continue to feel unsafe I did not know; I hoped not for too long, as it was proving to be rather wearing upon the nerves.

I did not see anyone through the glass, which was almost opaque but with enough transparency for me to discern a human shape on the other side. Nor did I hear more rustling. Convinced that someone had been—and possibly still was—there, and unwilling to sit cowering in fear at my own desk, I took up my weapon and went to the door. Drawing in a deep breath, I jerked it open. The little bell protested with a violent ringing.

There was a package on the floor. A largish package, more or less square, wrapped in the sort of paper butchers use, and tied with string—red string. I picked it up and found it soft, yielding to the touch.

Aha! I thought, guessing at the contents. I took the package to my desk, where I cut the string and, unfolding the paper, saw my guess confirmed: my cape, my aubergine cape! I held it up, and something fluttered out: a note, on crisp ivory rice paper with a lovely Oriental design of birds and greenery down one side.

The note was from Meiling and said:

Dear Miss Jones, My grandmother did not mean you harm. She accepts what you have told us. We understand why you acted as you did and hope you will forgive us.
Yours with most humble apology, Meiling Li.

Tears of relief glazed my eyes. I gathered my cape in my arms—I really was inordinately fond of that cape—and buried my face in it. A blessed release of tension washed through my whole body. There would be no revenge, I didn't have to try to remember anymore, it was over! For me, at least, if not for the poor women of the Li family. I hoped they would find their jade statue, but I was not the one to help them. Perhaps I would read one morning that Li Wong's murderer had been captured, but I very much doubted it—too much time had gone by already. I would have liked to see Meiling again some day, but I very much doubted that, also. Certainly I would not venture into Chinatown again, not for anything. I had learned my lesson.

The telephone on my desk rang. I answered it and found myself speaking to Justin. He trusted I was well and in better spirits, and wanted to make a date for that dinner I had offered to cook for him.

The familiar sound of his voice made me smile—all was right with my world now—and I made the date for Saturday night. As I hung up the telephone I chastised myself a bit for being so curt with him the previous night. How foolish I had been! He was only acting like a typical man, after all. Most women liked being taken care of; sometimes even I liked being taken care of, just not right then. There was nothing wrong with Justin; he was a splendid example of the male of the species. And I would worry about being a terrible cook later in the week!

On Thursday afternoon I took advantage of the long daylight hours to go for a walk up Nob Hill. I carried with me, folded in my pocket, an extra copy I had typed of the page from "Damned to Darkness" that described Peregrine's house. If I could find the lighthouse from "The Man in the Glass Tower"—and I was convinced that I had—then surely I could find Perry's house. Of course, if I did, I would have to face his awful mother, who might not be so awful after all. I curbed my ranging mind and walked on. Or walked *up*. Gadfrey, this hill was steep!

After the first block I began to trudge. I was making progress in the hunt, though, because the houses were getting bigger. A thought popped unbidden into my head: *Really, these people have no taste!*

I bit my lip, said to myself aloud: "Fremont Jones, that was an unworthy thought, it sounded just like your mother." How true! I had more of my mother in me than I liked to admit. And I missed my father. Letters still arrived dutifully from Augusta, but he would not write to me. I bit my lip again and pushed sadness away.

Onward and upward. Looking to left and right. Grand and ostentatious homes of robber barons and respectable businessmen were here side by side. I wondered where they got their architects, for not a single one of these huge houses conformed to any particular style. They were a hodgepodge. I coined a new term: Gross Victorian Eclectic. I thought that had a nice ring to it, and it was highly suitable.

If nothing else, I was getting exercise and a self-guided tour of Nob Hill at one and the same time. Then I saw it: the cupola! I had reached the crown of the hill and there, across the street, the most fantastic creation of them all rose high into the air. Bizarre, Mr. Partridge had said—not quite an accurate description. Grotesque, maybe. But just as some animals—the rhinoceros, for example—are so outlandishly ugly as to be fascinating, even beautiful if you looked at them long enough, so it was with that house.

It was built in a discernible style: Gothic Revival. What made it so beautifully ugly was that all the various forms of Gothic were represented here. The main part was Perpendicular. It soared like a cathedral, with carved, pointed arches, tracery windows, and excrescences that could only be gargoyles hanging from various eaves. Off to one side was a castellated wing, all battlements and towers complete with arrow-slits and parapets. On the other side, more or less (for the house was asymmetrical), a multi-angled wing jutted up and out, adorned with oddly shaped windows and the gewgaws and intricate scrollwork of Carpenter Gothic. This wing had gone out of proportion and out of control; it towered lopsidedly over the rest of the house, like a child who has shot up too quickly and outgrown its parents. At its apex, crowning an octagonal turret, was the glassed-in cupola.

For a moment I thought I saw someone standing in the cupola, but when I squinted and looked harder, there was no one there. Perhaps it had been a trick of the light. I shrugged and returned to my examination of the incredible structure. The house had been built entirely of wood, which I found remarkable even though I knew that stone was hard to come by, whereas wood was plentiful in this region.

I crossed the street and stood directly in front of the house, looking through the iron-barred gate. The fence was also constructed of iron bars, with spikes on top. Both gate and fence were at least ten feet tall.

Peregrine's house, Peregrine's iron wall with the spiky points. My imagination broke free, and I saw before me a young boy, clinging to the gate that he could not open. His little face, pressed in the open space between two bars, ran with tears. He was a pale child, painfully thin, with dark hair and huge gray eyes. I reached out and put my hand on the gate, giving it a push. It was locked. Poor Perry. He could not get out, and I could not get in.

I backed up a step, chewing on my lower lip as I tried to decide what to do. Curse San Francisco for not having a City Directory! Well, someone would know who lived here. Mrs. O'Leary would know—but I didn't want to think about Mrs. O'Leary. I could only solve one mystery at a time. I'd given up on Li Wong, so that one was behind me. Now I'd found Perry's house; soon I'd find Edgar Allan Partridge. I could give his manuscript to him and that would be that. I would get to Mrs. O. in her turn. Hopefully, she would have returned on her own by then and would be able to tell me who had written that blasted letter!

I gave the Gothic Monstrosity one long last look, intending to imprint it on my brain. And then I turned away and started back down the hill. As I went, I thought perhaps I would let down my guard and ask Michael Archer who lived there. He would probably know—

"Wait, oh wait, please wait!"

What? I *knew* that voice. I whirled around so quickly that I nearly lost my footing on the steep pavement.

"Oh, it is you. I knew it was you. Miss Jones, Miss Jones, you've come, Miss Jones!"

I hurried. I had already gone some distance down the hill and could not yet see who called, but I heard a great rattling of the iron gate. It opened.

And there stood none other than Edgar Allan Partridge.

16.

Oh, What a Falling-off Is There!

———⊷∘⊶———

HIS DROOPING MUSTACHE was gone, and his clean-shaven face looked pathetically young. His hair had grown longer, and straggled about his shoulders. His eyes seemed too large for the emaciated face, but were feverishly alight; his whole gangling body jittered in anticipation of my approach.

"Good afternoon, Mr. Partridge," I said.

"Oh, I can't believe it, I can't believe it!" E.A.P. exclaimed, hopping from one foot to the other.

I observed that he had not lost his idiosyncratic repetitiousness. "I'm very glad to see you," I said, "as I have been looking for you for some time. You live in this house, I presume?"

"Yes, I do." He glanced fearfully over his shoulder, as if at any moment he expected someone to come out and snatch him up.

"I finished the typing of your manuscript weeks ago, Mr. Partridge. I think your stories are as excellent as they are unusual. Certainly you should be able to have them published. I was distressed when you did not return to claim them."

"I know. I, ah, I wanted very much to come. But, but . . ." He wrung his hands miserably, hunching his shoulders, and looked down at the sidewalk.

"But something prevented you."

"Yes!" He managed to inject unspeakable anguish into the one word, his black eyebrows drawing together and slanting downward over mournful eyes, bloodless lips quivering.

I felt so sorry for him. How could I ever have thought Edgar Allan Partridge a man? He was no more than a boy, he could not be much more than eighteen years old! "You are prodigiously talented, Mr. Partridge," I said warmly.

"Oh! Oh"—throwing another fearful glance over his shoulder—"do you really think so?"

"Indeed I do!"

"I am grateful for your assessment, but, but I have to get back inside. I should not be out here, but I was up in the cupola and I saw you. At least I thought it was you, and then I came down and it *was* you . . ." Another look over his shoulder, this time accompanied by a cringing that was painful to see.

"You must not go back inside," I said hastily, as he had begun to edge toward the gate, "until we arrange to get your manuscript back to you. And there is the matter of overpayment. I'm afraid I cannot return the balance that was due out of your ninety-two dollars. You see, when I began to look for you, I was at first unsure how to proceed. I thought I would test the veracity of your stories, as you claimed they were based on truth—"

"Oh, they are!" he interrupted, nodding his head vigorously, strings of hair flapping. Then his eyes opened very wide and his whole body jumped, as if startled. He grabbed my wrist and pulled me over to him and down, into a huddle. "But you mustn't say that, not on the street. Someone might hear you! And then, and then—" Edgar Allan Partridge suddenly straightened up, dropping my wrist. He had an expression of extreme puzzlement on his face.

"And then—what, Mr. Partridge?"

He rubbed at his forehead; I noticed that his fingernails were filthy. There had been, as well, a stale smell about him when I huddled near. "I don't know," he said, "I can't think. B-but they'll come for me, you know. I've got to get back inside! That's why I didn't come back, I can't leave them now. Can't leave them even for a minute, it isn't safe. Have to watch them all the time!"

190

Once more he edged toward the gate. I must be decisive. "If you can't leave the house, then perhaps you would like me to bring your manuscript to you, and the sooner the better? In fact, I suggest tomorrow."

Edgar Allan Partridge, who was not—I was sure—really of that name, clung to the iron bars of his gate. His face for a moment lit up, like the angelic ghost of a child. "Would you? Would you really do that? For me?"

"Most assuredly," I nodded. "I will come tomorrow at this time and deliver your manuscript."

"Tomorrow . . ." said E.A.P. wistfully, stepping through the gate and swinging it closed behind him.

"Yes, tomorrow. At this time," I repeated, afraid he would forget. "You will be here to open the gate for me?"

"I will, I p-promise." He gave a mighty heave on the bolt and shot it home. This action seemed to deplete his strength. He gulped air, shivered, and spoke. "You are kind, Miss Jones. I said once before and I say again, you are a godsend. It is more than I deserve." He hung his head, turned around, and plodded to the door of his monstrous house.

I raised my hand to wave good-bye, but when he reached the huge front door he did not turn. On impulse, as he pushed it inward, I called out commandingly, "Peregrine!"

His head jerked around, a wild expression on his face. "What? Who calls Perry?"

"I did. I only wanted to say once more that I will be here at this time tomorrow. Good-bye, Mr. Partridge." I smiled and waved.

He stepped backward into yawning darkness. Hesitantly he raised his hand, but the door swung closed on him before he could return my gesture.

The next day I returned at the appointed hour. Because I had been unwilling to ask either Michael or Justin, and was unable to think of anyone else, I still did not know Peregrine's last name, or anything about his family. I had toiled up the hill burdened by the weight of his stories, and arrived at the iron-barred gate quite out of breath. I felt as forlorn as he habitually looked, when I saw that he did not await me.

Shifting my burden to the other arm, I examined the gate closely. Surely there must be a bell one could ring, some sort of a mechanism whereby a caller could summon someone to open the gate!

But this was a reclusive household indeed, for there was no such mechanism. I stepped back a few steps and all but overbalanced as I looked up at the cupola. The declining sun turned the westward planes of its glass a fiery bronze. I could not see anyone inside. Well, I would just have to rattle the gate and call out. Most definitely I would not leave without getting rid of these strange stories that had resided for too long in my file drawer!

The gate was too heavy to rattle effectively—all I managed to produce was a groan of heavy metal. However, that was either enough, or Perry had been already on his way, for the front door opened and he hastened down the walk.

"I was afraid you'd forgotten," I said in relief.

"You have my stories? You really brought them back to me?" he asked eagerly. "Hand them through!" He stretched bony, beseeching fingers through the bars.

I had placed both the handwritten and typewritten pages in a typing-paper box. I could have obliged him by holding the box vertically and thus passing it through the bars, but this manner of transaction did not suit my plans. So I said, "I'll be glad to give them to you, if you will open the gate."

"No, no," he said in a near whisper, "they'll hear us. They'll *know* if I open the gate again. I must have my stories, and then I must run, I must fly!" Perry rolled his eyes so wildly that the whites showed all around. His paranoia was more full-blown than ever.

I stepped closer to the gate. Odd that he should be in such a hurry now, when he had obviously prepared for my coming. He had bathed —even from where I stood I could smell the clean scent of soap. He had washed his hair as well, for the tails of it were still wet. The nails of his avidly grasping fingers were a shade cleaner—though they were by no means manicured. Once again I felt sorry for him, but this was my last chance to satisfy my curiosity. After all I'd done to track him down, did I not deserve some satisfaction?

"Your stories are in this box, and I will give it to you as I promised. But I was hoping that you would ask me in. I would like so much to see the inside of your fine house."

"You want to come . . . *in?*" He blinked, and his expressive eyebrows arched upward in astonishment.

"Yes, if you will invite me. I would like to meet your mother, and perhaps she—or you—would be good enough to show me around. *Of course* I would like to see your house; it is one of the grandest houses in San Francisco. Surely you realize that?"

"N-n-no, no, no-no-no-no-no!" A plethora of negatives, accompanied by such a shaking of his head that the wet rattails of his hair flared out like the spokes of a wheel.

He quite alarmed me! "Very well. I will pass the box to you, Perry." I held it out, using both hands, for it was heavy and difficult to hold vertically. "Be careful," I warned. "Take hold of it securely."

In spite of my warning he snatched the box through the bars and dropped it. But luck was with him; the box did not break open at the seams.

"Oh dear!" Perry exclaimed, going down on one knee to retrieve it. When he had the box again in hand, he calmed. The temptation to have a look at his own work must have been so great that it overrode all other concerns. He removed the top and read aloud the title page I had composed on his behalf, as he had given his stories no collective title: "THREE TALES STRANGE AND TRUE, by Edgar Allan Partridge. That's me, isn't it? I had almost forgotten. It seems so long ago . . ."

"Yes, that is the name you gave me. But it is not your real name, is it?"

A look so wary it verged on madness came into his eyes. "My real name. Who knows my real name? Who knows who I really am?"

I felt a chill but I persisted. *"You* know. Your first name is Peregrine, isn't it?"

"Perry. I am Perry. At least, I *was* Perry . . ." Still on one knee, he twisted his torso to look back at the front door. He had left it open, and it yawned darkly.

"You must have a last name."

Perry looked back at me, eyes totally blank. He said nothing.

"Tell me your mother's name, then. Her last name will be the same as yours."

Slowly he shook his head, ponderously, as if the thought of his mother made his brain too heavy for his spindly neck to support.

Well, at least he was still here; my persistent questioning had not scared him back into the house. To keep him with me longer, I suggested, "Take a look at your manuscript. See how handsome it is, all typewritten!"

Perry bent his head—carefully—and fingered through page after page. Gradually a smile bloomed on his face and transformed him into a real boy. "Nice," he murmured, "nice."

Pressing my advantage, I stage-whispered through the bars of the gate, *"Now* will you invite me in?"

But Peregrine had forgotten me. He had retreated into a world all his own, most likely the world in which he had created these fantasies that had some basis in reality. I would never know exactly how much of a basis, for he gathered the manuscript in its box against his sunken chest and got to his feet. Rapidly, lightly as a child, he ran up the walk and through his front door. It crashed closed behind him.

I stood outside the gate rubbing my arms and looking stupidly at the box top, which he had left on the walk where it had fallen when he removed it. It was over. I had done my duty. Then why should I feel so unfulfilled? So . . . so unfinished?

Saturday afternoon at three o'clock I closed my office and headed for the meat market, where I bought a porterhouse steak. Earlier that morning, before going to work, I had shopped for vegetables because I recalled our cook saying that the freshest vegetables must be bought early in the day. I had some very nice mushrooms, and tomatoes, which did not have to be cooked (in this venture I was all for anything that did not really have to be cooked!); also, from the bakery on the corner I had procured a long loaf of the sourdough bread of which San

Franciscans are so fond. I had grown to prefer it myself. I returned home to Vallejo Street quite laden-down but happy with my purchases. I expected that I would make a creditable meal for Justin that evening.

I bathed and dressed with care. Using a part of the largesse from the retired professor's memoirs, I had bought a new dress—I had begun to look forward to this occasion. It was a taffeta plaid, all the rage this season, the plaid being predominantly green and blue with a thin line of black through it. The skirt was moderately full and required a petticoat, stopping an inch above my ankles to show off high-laced black shoes. I brushed my hair far longer than usual, until I had coaxed the ends to curve under. Then I pulled it back and fastened it with a gold clasp. Leaning toward the mirror critically, I tried to entice a few curls into the shorter strands at my cheekbones. I failed, of course; my hair has always been straight as a stick.

"Enough fussing!" I said firmly to my reflection. I looked quite well enough without curls. I should remember that I was not out to seduce Justin. Quite the opposite! I did not disillusion myself; I knew that Justin had not really understood my refusal of intimacy on the grounds that I would never marry. I just wasn't sure what he did think, what he wanted; and it did worry me a bit.

I longed for someone to be close to, truly close, so that I could confide in him. Or her, but there was no her. I'd had no one to talk to about my frustration at learning so few of Edgar Allan/Peregrine's secrets—not to mention my victory in tracking him down! I would even have settled for Mrs. O'Leary. Once again I pushed the thought of her from my mind and went into the kitchen to pack my dinner fixings into a bag.

I was short on real friends, and that was a problem. I would have liked to develop a friendship with Meiling, but did not know how to go about it. I might someday become friendly with the young librarian who wrote love poems—I saw her from time to time at the library and she was cordial, if shy—but someday was not now. And I was virtually certain that I would never be able to resolve all my doubts about Michael Archer, even if Mrs. O. did come back. With every day that passed, her return seemed less likely. I sighed, supposing I would have to take some steps about that soon. I did not want to. I wanted a respite, some comfort . . .

I wanted Justin, wanted to be closer to him than was proper, wanted to love and be loved by him without regard for the wisdom of it. Or the consequences.

Consequences be damned! I thought, hefting the bag. I had already exchanged my large everyday purse for a smaller reticule that hung by a gold chain from one's shoulder. I picked this up from the hall table and slipped it over my arm. Encumbered by the heavy groceries, I made my way in slow and stately fashion down the stairs. The taffeta skirt made an interesting rustle as I moved.

For once, I would have welcomed an intrusion by Michael Archer —he could have helped me with the bag. Honestly, the man was as perverse as a gremlin, always about when one did not want him and nowhere to be seen when one did! His floor was silent, deserted. I supposed that this was not unusual, as it was only six in the evening, but I had not seen or heard him in the house for the past three days. Good riddance, I thought, continuing on my way. But I did wonder where he was.

"And you said you'd never learned how to cook!" Justin rubbed his stomach appreciatively.

"I have had to teach myself the rudiments since coming to San Francisco, or starve. I'm glad you enjoyed the dinner, Justin." We sat at a small round table in the breakfast room of his house. The meal had turned out most satisfactorily.

"More wine?" He tipped the bottle over my glass, but I slid my fingers between.

"No, thank you! I've had quite enough. I shall become tipsy."

"Would that be so terrible?" Justin smiled, the bottle still poised.

"Well—half a glass."

"That's the spirit. We'll finish the bottle."

I took only small sips, having observed that Justin was tipsy enough for both of us. I felt warm and content, and decided to take a small risk. "There's something I'd like to ask you about."

"Anything your heart desires, Fremont," he said dreamily, reaching out and taking hold of my hand. He rubbed at my fingers with his thumb, sending little tremors from my hand up my arm and straight into my heart.

"Are you at all familiar with the houses on Nob Hill? Whom they belong to, I mean?"

"Why, sure. All the bigwigs live there. Stanford, Crocker, Huntington, Hopkins . . ."

"There's one house in particular, right on top, that interests me. It's huge, Gothic Revival in style. Rather a monstrosity, really, but you can't miss it. Do you know the one I mean?"

Justin's caressing fingers crept from my hand onto my wrist. The tremors deepened in intensity. "Amazing place," he said. "Seems to me . . . Why are you asking, Fremont?"

"I think one of my customers lives in that house. In fact, I'm sure he does. He, ah, he wrote some stories under a pseudonym and I typed them for him, and I was just wondering what his real name is. I thought if I could find out the name of the owner of that house, then I would know."

Justin's fingers reached the band of my bodice sleeve, and traced its edge. So lightly, so delicately. So enticingly. But his eyes were on mine, and they grew thoughtful, appraising. "He'd have to be a servant, that's my guess, so the name won't help you any. That house belongs to a widow and she's a recluse. A legend, almost. She hasn't been seen in public for years."

My heart beat faster, and for once Justin's touch had nothing to do with it. "What sort of a legend?"

"There was a scandal years back, before I was born, so she'd have to be ancient now if she's still alive. And I guess she is, since the house hasn't been on the market. Anyway, plenty of people thought she murdered her husband. But there wasn't any proof, or maybe she bribed the police. I don't recall her name, but her husband's name was Crowe, Elias Crowe. Made his fortune selling cheap shovels and mining stuff to all the Forty-niners."

"But Justin, that was more than fifty years ago."

"Yeah. Well, she was supposed to be a beauty, a lot younger than her husband, and she didn't marry him till later. Anyway, he died and

197

left the house to her, and after his death she quit going out. When I was a kid there were all kinds of tales about her being a witch, crazy things like that. Boys would taunt each other, making wagers about climbing over that fence and seeing how far you could get before she turned you into stone. That kind of thing. Crazy stuff, but I don't know if it was completely nonsense or not. It does seem odd when you think about it, her never leaving the house at all. Never having a single friend, just servants. That's why this customer of yours has to be a servant, couldn't be anything else."

"Oh." I looked down at my arm. Justin had worked his thumb under the band of the sleeve and was massaging the sensitive spot on the inside of my elbow. I placed my hand over his to stop him. But he didn't stop. Soon I would not be able to ask any more questions! "Justin, did these Crowes have any children? Any heirs to that huge house?"

"I think you're coveting the Crowe mansion, Fremont," said Justin huskily. "If you're good to me, maybe in a few years I'll buy it for you."

"So there were no children."

"None I ever heard of. Come here to me, Fremont." Justin placed his other hand behind my head and urged my face to his. He kissed me, and I forgot all about Peregrine, or Edgar, or whoever he was.

Several kisses later, I said lamely, "We should wash the dishes, we shouldn't leave them on the table like this, they'll get all hard and be impossible to get cl—" and Justin's mouth once again stopped mine.

He stood up and pulled me full against him, holding me so close that I could feel every contour of his body. I could feel how much he wanted me, and, God help me, I wanted him too. His lips plied the side of my neck, where my pulse throbbed. I swallowed a moan. Making an effort that seemed superhuman, I pulled away and said, "We haven't had the dessert. You said you were going to get a coconut cake."

"Haven't you guessed?"—he grinned rakishly, hair down in his eyes—"You're the dessert, Fremont." And he pulled me back to him.

"Coconut cake," I gasped, "is my favorite."

"Later. I got the damn cake, but we'll eat it later." His teeth nipped my ear and then his tongue plunged inside it. No one had ever done that to me before; it was most incredibly arousing!

When his tongue was free enough that he could again speak, Justin whispered in that same ear, "You know what I want. You won't refuse me, or you wouldn't have come here."

"I—I suppose you're right . . ." The moment of truth! And the truth was that I was so on fire I could hardly think, much less make a decision. It was much easier to let him decide for me. I melted against Justin, my head falling to his shoulder.

He fumbled at the back of my dress, where there was a long row of tiny buttons. Vaguely I remembered that I'd had a time of it doing them up by myself. He swore softly, and I smiled against the fabric of his jacket. I raised my head.

"Let me go upstairs and get ready for you," I said. "I need to use the bathroom anyway. I'll find the bedroom, and when I'm ready I'll call down to you."

"I'll be waiting," said Justin gruffly. He stepped back, releasing me, and thrust his hands into his pockets. The crotch of his tight-fitting trousers was enticingly distended.

Flirting, I kissed his cheek lightly and said, "I won't be long."

My ardor cooled somewhat as I struggled with all those buttons. I was in Justin's bedroom, standing near the bed in front of a low chest of drawers. I undid several more buttons, but slowly; the top drawer of the dresser was open by about an inch and had caught my eye.

I confess I am an inveterate snoop. Even as a child, my darkest secret was that I took a delicious, guilty pleasure in going through other people's things when they were not around. So I snagged the drawer and gently pulled it open another inch, making up for that by dutifully undoing a few more buttons. There were socks in the drawer. Mostly. There were also some papers shoved under the socks, as if to hide them. I undid three more buttons—only the ones hardest to reach, between my shoulder blades, remained buttoned up.

It was the red ribbon that gave Justin's game away. If that bright splash of color, so incongruous in a man's sock drawer, had not caught my attention, I would have closed the drawer and only felt momentarily guilty at prying into my lover's things. But I reached for that ribbon and pulled out a paper rolled like a scroll and bound by the ribbon. I knew what it was. My heart sank into my stomach and throbbed there miserably.

Justin Cameron had Li Wong's statement! I pulled off the ribbon and unrolled the paper, just to be sure. Yes, I knew the look of my own typewriting. And at the bottom Li Wong had signed his name, in English first and again in Chinese.

"Fremont?" came Justin's voice from below. "What's taking you so long? Can I come up?"

17.

Into the Heart
of the Fire

———◦◦◦———

MY HEART TORE, my stomach roiled; I could not tell the one from the other. I was about to be sick. More than sick: violently ill.

"Just a few minutes more," I called out, "these things take time!" Then I ran into the bathroom and pulled the chain of the water closet so that Justin would think I'd been occupied in there. The dinner I'd cooked and eaten—*for* Justin, *with* Justin—churned in my stomach. The food had become a vile mockery, an invitation to self-contempt.

But there was no time for sickness, no time for thought or emotion, or anything except survival. The sole thought in my head was that I must take Li Wong's statement away from Justin, keeping it and myself safe in the process.

My pretty taffeta dress had no pockets. I folded up the paper into a square. The ribbon hindered me, so I held it in my teeth while I lifted up the full skirts of my dress and petticoat and stuck the paper in the waistband of my underdrawers, right next to my skin. That felt secure enough. Provided, of course, that I could get away from Justin. Moving swiftly, the red ribbon still between my teeth, I rebuttoned the back of my dress at random, only doing enough buttons to keep my bodice from falling off—there was no question of taking the time to do them all. Thank goodness I had not yet unlaced and removed my shoes!

Back in Justin's bedroom, I took another of the papers from his drawer, hastily rolled it and tied the red ribbon around it, then thrust it partway under a couple of socks, and very quietly closed the drawer. My face was burning, my stomach still threatened, my hands shook, but in the very center of myself I felt a deadly, icy calm. This I trusted would sustain me.

I had grasped the banister and placed one foot upon the stair when I saw that Justin had not waited to ask again, he was already on his way up. He had removed his jacket and tie and his shirt was undone. He looked disheveled, and there was a gleam in his eye that now seemed to me more predatory than amatory.

"I have changed my mind," I announced in a strong voice, "I cannot go through with it." I continued to descend.

"You don't mean that," said Justin, continuing to advance.

We met mid-stairs. Being one step above him, and he several inches taller than I, I was able to look him dead in the eye. I said, "Indeed I do mean it. You will recall I tried to tell you"—boldly I called a spade a spade—"that I could not have sexual intercourse with you again. I admit I lost my head under the influence of the wine and the, the pleasure of your company, but belatedly I have come to my senses. Under the circumstances, I think you will agree that it's best for me to leave now."

"No," he said, laying hold of my waist, "I want you. Don't play games with me, Fremont. It doesn't become you."

Justin's complexion was mottled from drink and his speech was slowed, though not yet slurred. I hoped inebriation would also slow his reaction time. I said, "This is not a game," and brought both my fists down sharply on his forearms. His hands lost their grip on my waist and I pushed past him, hurtling down the stairs at top speed.

"Fremont!" he yelled, hanging over the banister, "what's got into you, woman? What's wrong with you?"

Oh, how I longed to turn and confront him! A part of me wanted to tell him what I'd found, ask him how he came to have it, hear him say—no matter how incredibly—that he'd acquired the paper in an honest manner. But a wiser part of me said only one word: Run!

202

My reticule and shawl hung from the newel post, because Justin had no coat tree in the hall. I snatched them up as I passed, threw the shawl over my ill-buttoned back, and continued toward the front door.

Behind me Justin thundered, "I warn you, Fremont Jones, if you leave me tonight I'll have nothing more to do with you!"

I stopped and turned around, my chin in the air, and said with icy calm, "That is not a gentlemanly attitude, Justin. I will obtain my own transportation, and I will not thank you for the dinner, as I provided it myself."

He started to come after me, and I wished mightily that I had brought my walking stick. But, being encumbered by the bag of groceries, and never for a moment thinking that I might be in danger from Justin, I had left it at home. So I gave him one last deadly stare, turned sharply upon my heel, and proceeded out the door.

When my feet hit the sidewalk, I ran. I ran without regard for my surroundings until the steepness of the hill's downside sent me hurtling headlong in a bone-rattling fall. The pain in my knees and the heels of my hands brought me out of my senseless panic. Gingerly I got to my feet, dusted myself off, felt at my waist to be sure I still had Li Wong's statement, and looked around. Justin had not followed me. I was alone on a peaceful residential street. The night was rare, cool and clear. I knew exactly where I was. As the distance was not much, I decided to walk home.

Lights burned in a second-floor window. So, Michael was there. I did not want to deal with him, and fortunately—though somewhat surprisingly—I did not have to. I went on to my own apartment unimpeded. There in my bedroom I undressed and put on my old once-viridian robe, the one I always wore when I felt unwell because its familiarity somehow comforted me. Then I sat on the bed and, at long last, was able to read Li Wong's statement in its entirety. It said:

In the event of my untimely death I wish the following to be known to concerned persons: that I have placed in Crocker's Bank, as a token of good faith, an item of great value. In my absence, this item together with the present statement, when presented to the surviving members of my family, will ensure their cooperation in a certain busi-

ness dealing. To wit: that the body of workers loyal to the House of Li will leave the employ of the Trans-Hawaiian Trading Company and become employees of the Great Atlantic and Pacific Tea Company, under the terms recently discussed but not yet legally contracted. Should I be prevented from signing said contract, the aforementioned valuable item serves as bond of my honorable intent. These things I, Li Wong, have caused to be recorded on the first day of May in the year one thousand nine hundred and five of the Western calendar, in the city of San Francisco, the state of California, of the United States of America.

Finally! I thought, and read the statement through a second time. Finally I knew what I had been unable to remember. For a few minutes I enjoyed a feeling of deep satisfaction, but then an overwhelming reaction set in and I began to shake all over. My stomach, which had behaved itself at the crucial time, once again roiled. I ran for the bathroom and threw up in the basin, again and again, until I was bringing up my own bile.

Later, though I tried to sleep, I could not. I cried tears that were as bitter as the bile, cried until my bed pillows were all wet. What did it matter, I could not sleep at any rate. My hands hurt, my knees hurt, my middle was sore, my throat felt raw, my face was puffy—I was a complete wreck. But there was far more wrong with me than simple physical pain. My faith in myself was completely shaken.

I had once read somewhere that more people die around three a.m. than at any other time. Around three that morning, I could understand why. My once high self-confidence had plummeted to its nadir. I was in despair. I felt that I could not survive on my own, I had been a fool to think I could. *Fremont Jones, Typewriting Services . . .* I sneered at the very concept of myself as a successful, independent woman. How could I succeed when I had not enough sense, enough good judgment, to choose a friend? Worse, I had wanted closeness so badly that I had made that ill-chosen friend a lover! My God, I'd given my virginity to a murderer!

Sniffing and sniveling, around four in the morning I got out my bags and began to pack. I was going home to Boston. I would humiliate myself before Augusta, beg my father's forgiveness, I would even, if necessary, marry the loathsome nephew.

But as I was packing, Li Wong's statement, which lay on the bed where I'd left it, caught my eye. I read it again, then took it with me to the window seat in my living room where I sat and watched the sky slowly change from blue-black to dark gray to the pearly shade that precedes dawn. I forgot about packing and about going home to Boston. I began to think clearly for the first time since I'd run in panic from Justin's house.

I reiterated the facts. Justin had seen and recognized Li Wong in my office and then lied about it to me. A few days later Li Wong was murdered. The statement I'd typed for him was not found until I myself found it in Justin's possession. Not long after Li Wong's murder, Justin had acquired a new client, a corporate client whose business had proven unusually lucrative. These were facts, they were incontrovertible.

And they led inexorably to certain obvious conclusions. Justin was dishonest. Justin was an opportunist. Justin was greedy. My dear Justin, he of the seemingly open and innocent face—he was most likely a murderer. For if someone else had done the deed, and done it right on the heels of Li Wong's picking up the typed statement from me—as certainly had been the case—then that statement would not have been in Justin's possession.

That the information contained in the statement had something to do with Justin's sudden prosperity I was sure, though I did not know exactly what. The item of great value had to be the missing jade statue of Kwan Yin.

Suddenly I knew what I had to do. I had to take Li Wong's statement directly to Meiling.

I never allowed myself to think for a minute that I would be unable to find my way back to the House of Li. I had set off as soon as I thought people would be up and about in Chinatown, around eight o'clock. My walking stick was in hand, my capacious purse hung by its strap over one shoulder, and I wore the aubergine cape. The precious paper was once again hidden beneath my clothing, next to my skin. I was taking no chance of losing it.

Of course I was nervous, but not especially fearful. My sense of purpose was too great for that. As the previous night had been clear, so was the morning, and in bright sunlight the gaudy colors so beloved by the Chinese glowed gaily. I strode along, marking each step with my walking stick, and did not bother to look behind me; I reasoned that if Justin had found me out, he would have been lying in wait on Vallejo Street. As he had not been, I felt safe . . . even though I had not the slightest idea what might happen after I placed Li Wong's statement in the hands of his granddaughter.

I turned into what I felt was the right alley, and was reassured when it looked more and more familiar the farther I went. There was the yellow wall, glowing golden in the sun, and the cunningly carved red gate with its rounded arch. I rapped on the gate with my stick. When a black-capped head and brown almond eyes appeared over the gate, I said, "I have come to see Li Meiling. My name is Fremont Jones. Please tell her it concerns a matter of the greatest importance."

The head bobbed silently and disappeared. I was left waiting outside the gate for what seemed a long time, and in the interval I felt as if watchful, unseen eyes had gathered all around me. But I did not look around. I kept my eyes on the gate, my hand firmly on the walking stick that had served me so well in these surroundings.

At last the tall figure of Meiling approached the gate. She opened it herself, and let me in. She was dressed differently today, in a scarlet damask tunic with black piping over black trousers. Her gleaming hair was loose around her shoulders. I thought her very beautiful.

"Thank you for seeing me," I said, remembering to bow.

"Miss Jones. Fremont," she said, bowing also. "Come into the house."

"I, ah, if you don't mind, I'd rather not. We can talk here in the courtyard." I looked around the large, clean-swept space. "We appear to be alone."

Meiling smiled. "One's eyes may deceive. In fact, there are many watching. They think you are a white she-devil, but you command their respect. They will keep their distance unless I give them a signal.

So. What brings you here? The servant who came to the gate does not speak much English, but recognized the word 'importance.' "

"I found something you have been looking for, and I will give it to you. Allow me a moment; it is hidden beneath my clothes." I tucked my walking stick under one arm, unbuttoned my blouse, and withdrew from my chemise the folded paper. Without comment I handed it to Meiling.

She unfolded the paper. I watched her while restoring my blouse to rights. Her eyes widened as she read, and she expelled an audible breath. "So," she said, scanning Li Wong's words a second time, "that is what has happened to the Kwan Yin! Fremont, you cannot imagine how important is the information in this document!"

"I think I understand some of it, but I would be grateful if you could explain the entirety to me."

"First, I would like to know where you found it."

I cleared my throat; tears stung at my eyes. It would be a long time before I could speak of this without feeling pain. I told Meiling about Justin. I did not hold anything back, not even my own poor judgment of the man. "I believe," I finished haltingly, "that Justin Cameron must have been the person who murdered your grandfather."

"He does not know that you have found this paper."

"Not yet."

"You did not go to the police?"

"No, nor anyone else. I came straight to you."

To my embarrassment, Meiling bowed deeply to me. "You have done us the greatest service, Fremont Jones. My family and all connected with us are in your debt." She stood tall again. "Now I will explain. The item mentioned will prove to be the Kwan Yin. To know that my grandfather took it for the noble purpose of insurance restores him to honor in the eyes of all. Now we will be able to reclaim the statue."

"Will it still be in Crocker's Bank?"

"I am sure that it is. If your former friend Mr. Justin Cameron had managed to obtain and to sell it, we would have heard of this in our extensive search. What is more important than the Kwan Yin is the knowledge of this business arrangement. I will take this statement to the Great Atlantic and Pacific Tea Company and sign the contract for the House of Li. This will release our people from a situation in which they have been worked like slaves, or worse than slaves, like beasts of burden!"

"I am more than glad to hear it. But why, Meiling, is that information worth killing for?"

"Same as always, since the beginning of civilization: money. Li Wong was honest, he wanted our people paid honest wages. The Trans-Hawaiian Trading Company is run by criminals, and they will lose much profit when our people are freed from their employ. They pay very low wages. Sometimes they promise to pay later, but do not pay at all. Or they pay in poppy, which is almost worse."

"Poppy?"

"Opium. They make addicts, people without a will. When they can no longer work because the opium has made them sick, the criminal bosses kill them, get new workers, start over."

"How horrible!"

"Yes. My grandfather, Li Wong, had a reputation for being—what is the word—incorruptible. During the Tong Wars . . . You have heard about the Tong Wars?"

I nodded.

"A very bad time. My grandfather went into hiding here, in this house; as you have seen, it is very large, with many secret places. The criminals, the bad bosses and bad Chinese, were in control then, and there was no choice for poor people but to work for them. When Li Wong once more took control of our tong's affairs, there was reason for the criminals to be displeased. They would lose money, much money; the worst of them might have met with harm in mysterious ways. That is our justice, you see."

"I understand," I said grimly.

"You do not love this man, this Justin Cameron?"

"I thought I did, but I do not. I made a very bad mistake."

"I ask that you do not go to your police. That you let the House of Li deal with this. We will obtain the truth from Justin Cameron, we have our ways, and then we will administer justice for the death of Li Wong. Will you agree to this, Fremont Jones?"

I swallowed a lump in my throat. Then I said, "Yes, I will, Meiling Li."

She reached out and touched my hand. "Your gods will smile on you, Fremont. I will see you again some day."

"I hope so," I said, smiling myself. I felt that the smile of the gods —any gods—would be most welcome. Then I bowed and went out through the gate.

I was thinking about Justin, about how ironic it was that his name sounded so much like "justice," and about the kind of justice that would be his, when a man stepped out of a doorway into my path. I had never liked those damned doorways!

Immediately, swift and natural as a reflex, I unsheathed my weapon. In the next instant I recognized Michael Archer. I said coldly, "You followed me." And I did not put the weapon away.

"Yes, I did," he replied, slipping one hand into a pocket of his jacket. "I advise you to watch what you do with that blade, Fremont. I have a gun, and I will not hesitate to use it."

18.

Doom, Doom, Ulalume!

I SIGHED AND inserted the blade back into the base of the walking stick. "I was thinking just the other day, Michael, that you are like a gremlin."

"I won't even ask what you mean by that," he said, dark eyebrows arching up. His sensual mouth curved with disdain. "I will ask instead what business you have in the place you have just been."

"Hah!" I stuck my chin in the air and resumed walking. "As if it were any of your business whom I see or where I go or what I do!"

Michael walked along beside me. I could feel him looking at me with great intensity, but not for the world would I have turned my head and met his eyes. When we reached the end of the alleyway I entered the street without hesitation.

"I suppose you must know whose house that was," said Michael, matching me step for step.

"And I suppose you have a reason for following me."

"I do, and I am forced to think it may have become something different from what I had originally thought."

"You're talking in riddles, but then that's nothing new for you. Is it, Michael Archer?"

"I've had enough of this, Fremont," Michael said in a low voice. Its degree of control was menacing.

My own small measure of control was nothing compared to his, and I felt it begin to crack. But resolutely I marched on. There was exotic music coming from somewhere, the Chinese chattered all around us, flashes of color burst at the corners of my eyes. I could not respond to Michael, or I might say something I did not want to say.

Suddenly he grabbed my arm and pulled me sideways, pushing me through a door. We were inside a restaurant whose ceiling was hung with red-tasseled lanterns. "Sit down!" he commanded. Not letting go of my arm, he forced me into a chair.

I sat, and glared at him as he did also.

A waiter pattered over, bobbed, and Michael ordered something. In Chinese. "Your linguistic talents have no end," I said.

"I am known in this establishment," said Michael. "We can talk here. Talk to me, Fremont."

I said nothing, glaring my refusal.

"What were you doing in the Li compound?"

Suddenly I was interested. I thought I might draw him out. "So you know who lives there?"

The waiter placed a fragrant pot of hot tea on the table, and a plate of small cakes. "Yes. I knew Li Wong's son, Meiling's father, rather well. I have been in that house many times."

"In that case, why didn't you go to them long ago? Or perhaps you did, and did not bother to tell me what you learned." I tasted the tea—it was delicious, and my empty stomach demanded more.

"I did not go there because Meiling's mother hates me. She's an unfortunate woman, Fremont. Since her husband's death she has become addicted to rice wine and seldom is sober enough to see anyone. Not that she would see me in any case; she holds me responsible for his death."

"Well," I said acerbically, "knowing you, you probably *were* responsible." I nibbled at a cake and discovered it was delicious too.

There was a lengthy silence. Finally, in a curiously resigned tone, Michael said, "If you can think that, then you have not come to know me at all. Just as I have begun to think that I do not know you at all. I'm confused, Fremont, I admit it."

"You surprise me, Mr. Archer."

"No more than you continue to surprise me, Miss Jones."

I considered him thoughtfully. He did look somewhat at a loss;

212

and I sensed an air of sadness in him that touched me even though I did not want it to. "You have followed me before," I guessed. "Why?"

"For the same reason I followed you this morning. I've been concerned for your safety."

"Is that all?"

"Yes."

I believed him. But then, I had also believed Justin. With a sudden flash of insight I realized that I had *wanted* to believe Justin, and I had made innumerable excuses to myself in order to maintain that belief.

"I must remind you," Michael said, "that you promised me you would let me know of any further developments regarding Li Wong. You did not keep your promise, and I would like to know why."

"Because I stopped trusting you. I had my reasons."

"Oh." Michael's sadness increased; his face took on a worn look, as if he'd heard that, or something similar, far too many times. He fussed in his pockets for money to leave on the table. Saying nothing in his own defense, he asked, "Shall we go?"

Michael had not eaten, whereas I had finished the entire plate of cakes. "Certainly," I agreed.

Now that I'd been fed, I wanted nothing more than a quiet room and a long, long sleep. I was extremely grateful that Michael did not attempt conversation on the way home.

The House of Li was swift with its justice. Monday morning's *Chronicle* headlined on the front page: RISING YOUNG LAWYER SLAIN. And a subhead: Strangled with Scarlet Cord.

I sat at the table in my office and read the article through to the end. They didn't get the red cord connection, but I did. They got another one, though, that I hadn't known about—an underworld connection. They had obtained Justin Cameron's client list, and it contained several names that the reporter labeled suspect. I shook my head back and forth, trying to sort out my feelings.

Predominantly I felt a keen sense of loss. Not just personal loss, in that I'd lost a relationship I had invested a great deal in, no matter how foolishly. But also loss for Justin, in that he'd had a good education, he

213

could have gone in any direction he wanted; yet he had chosen crime, and fast money. It was such a shame, such an awful waste.

At any rate, there was no way I would be able to work today as if nothing had happened. I made a sign for my office door: CLOSED DUE TO BEREAVEMENT, and I went home.

In our house on Vallejo Street, Michael Archer sat on the stairs. He was reading the newspaper—the same one I had just finished. He looked over the top of it at me, and to my astonishment and humiliation, with no warning, I burst into tears.

"Fremont! Oh my God, you know! You've already seen it." He jumped up, letting the paper fall to the floor, and came to my side. He pulled a clean handkerchief out of his pocket and thrust it into my hand.

Tears were blinding me, sobs prevented speech.

"I'm so sorry. What a brutal way to learn about the death of a friend." Michael put his arm around my shoulders, bracing me.

"H-he wasn't a friend," I blurted, tears still streaming down my face, "I only thought he was. And I knew already, I expected this, so I, I—" I broke off, choking and gasping, and Michael rubbed my back until I could continue. "I don't know why I'm going all to pieces this way!"

"You knew already?"

I nodded, sniffing, wiping my cheeks only to have them drenched all over again. Michael pulled me into his arms and gently pressed my head into his shoulder. I continued to cry, and he stroked my hair, making some sort of soothing noise that I only half-heard. It felt good to be in his arms. Even if he was a traitor, or worse.

"Feeling better?" he asked eventually.

I pulled back, wiped my face on his handkerchief a last time, and said, "Yes. Thank you."

"We should talk, if you feel up to it. Do you?"

I supposed I might as well talk to him. I certainly had nothing else to do. I said, "All right."

"My place or yours?"

"Yours. It's closer."

I settled on Michael's couch and refused his offer of brandy or coffee or both. He pulled over a chair and sat, crossing his legs.

"I would be grateful," he said, "if you would elucidate on your statement that you 'already knew.' "

I sat up very straight, because the telling of it would require every inch of backbone I possessed; then I proceeded to tell Michael exactly what I had told Meiling. All of it. He did not interrupt.

When I had finished, he said quietly, "My God. To think of what you've been through, and all alone, when I might have helped you. Fremont, didn't you read my letter?"

"Letter? What letter?" But in a flash I remembered and exclaimed, "Merciful heavens! I forgot all about it. I must still have it in my purse somewhere." And with that I retrieved my purse from the floor and dumped the entire contents on the couch next to me.

Michael chuckled. "I can well understand how you might lose track of what you have in that motley collection."

I felt my cheeks go pink; I have always been rather sensitive about my tendency to let things pile up in my purse. However I did have his letter, though in a rather smudged and crinkled state. I opened it and read silently:

My dear Fremont, I must go out of town at the end of the week. I would prefer not to leave at this time but cannot avoid it. I have learned something of importance concerning your friend Mr. Cameron that I feel obliged to relate to you before I go, if you will be so good as to take the time.

When I had done reading, I looked over at Michael. "I'm sorry," I said. "I had a good many things on my mind last week. What did you learn that you wanted to tell me?"

"I was concerned about your relationship with Justin Cameron. When he brought you home that night I thought I had seen him somewhere before. I was not sure where, but I believed in a suspicious context. So I investigated the man. I discovered that he came from a bad background—"

215

"But he told me that his father was a professor at Berkeley, he grew up across the Bay!"

"I'll wager you never met his parents, did you?"

I shook my head. "No."

"He made that up, Fremont. He went to college and then to law school at Berkeley, but his mother was a prostitute. His father, whose name I was never able to learn, must have paid for his education. Certainly Justin was a bright young man, but he either did not want to, or simply could not, escape from the life he'd had as a child in the more unsavory parts of San Francisco. Justin most likely grew up with a working knowledge of the underworld. He would have known immediately the significance of Li Wong's presence in your office, and how he could put his knowledge to good advantage. Finding the statement must have been like icing on the cake to him. He sold the information to the Trans-Hawaiian Trading Company, of course. That was where I'd seen him, the day I went nosing around there myself. You may recall, Fremont, telling me you remembered that company's name."

"Yes, I do remember." My suspicions of Michael Archer were fading with every revelatory word, and I was glad to let them go.

"I think you may be able to understand that when I recalled seeing Cameron at Trans-Hawaiian, I wondered if he had anything to do with the Li Wong affair. Especially knowing of his closeness to you and your own unwitting involvement. Then, when you did not respond to my letter, and in addition seemed suddenly so hostile to me, I began to wonder if your involvement were really unwitting. May God forgive me, I thought you might be in league with Justin Cameron, feeding him information."

"How *could* you?" I cried, anguished.

"The same way you stopped trusting me."

Checkmate. We looked at each other for a long time. It was so quiet in the room that I could hear the clock ticking.

"It is my fault," said Michael at last, with a deep sigh. "I'm sorry, Fremont."

"No, it's not your fault. I have been a fool."

He uncrossed his legs and leaned forward with his forearms on his knees. "You aren't a fool, Fremont. Far from it. You are young, that's all. But you learn quickly. Good lord, I've trained men for weeks to get them to pull out a blade as rapidly, as automatically as you did against me in that alley yesterday! I was filled with admiration."

"Thank you," I said. I felt a smile tug at the corners of my lips. "Trained men? You've given yourself away, you know. You really are a spy."

He smiled, eyes clear and very blue. "Are you suggesting that we should have no more secrets?"

"Indeed I am. So tell me what you did with Mrs. O'Leary."

Of course I no longer thought Michael had done anything with our landlady. He was astonished to learn of my former suspicions in that regard, but when I'd told him my reasons, we fell into an agreeable Holmes/Watson-type discussion on the subject. I did not, of course, divulge my escapade under his bed—some things are best kept to oneself! I had to pay a price for keeping mum: There was no way I could satisfy my burning curiosity about Michael's poison research.

We concluded that since Michael had not written the letter for Mrs. O'Leary, one of her friends must have done so. I provided the information that most of her friends seemed connected to her church, and Michael volunteered to visit its priest at the first opportunity. This he did the next day, and learned that the priest himself had written the letter. Mrs. O'Leary had been informed of her sister's serious illness by telegram on Sunday morning, and left that same afternoon. No doubt she would return as soon as she could.

Before leaving off our Watson/Holmes-type discussion, I had told Michael about the afternoon I'd answered several telephone calls at my office and found no one on the line. This had bothered me for a long time; also I would have liked to know who had broken in. His opinion was that Justin had done both, and I supposed he must be right. Since Justin was dead, there was no way I could ever know for certain; on the other hand, there had been no more episodes of that sort, so I resolved to let it go. In fact, I resolved to let the entire past go, to devote myself solely to my typewriting business, and to take a fresh lease on life.

As if to confirm the turning over of a new leaf, a few days later I received a letter from my father. He wrote in a breezy style; one would have thought I'd come all the way across the country with his blessing and he had been writing all along. I responded in the same fashion, inviting him and Augusta to visit me in San Francisco whenever they were pleased to do so.

However, all was not well with me. In spite of my resolution, in spite of my joy at having heard from my father, I felt something hanging over me. I did not know what it was, yet I could not get rid of it. I was often restless and uncomfortable. I began to wonder if I had taken this Sherlock Holmes business too much to heart—if I had become, like the great detective, excessively restless when there was no game afoot. This would never do! Holmes's solution to such restlessness was cocaine, in which I most certainly could not emulate him!

Resolving anew to be content with my thriving business, I consulted my bank book, and went out and bought the rug I had long desired for my office. Though I would have liked a Kirman or, better yet, a Kilim, I restrained myself and chose instead a large square of Wilton carpet in a gray-green color. The results pleased me. But I was still restless, still dissatisfied. Why?

After two very uncomfortable weeks, my subconscious mind provided the answer: I dreamed about Edgar Allan Partridge, or Peregrine Crowe, or whatever his name was. My dreams were ominous, foreboding, frightening—like his stories. So vivid, so real were the dreams that I was forced to pay attention. I could not help recalling the disastrous ending of "Damned to Darkness": Peregrine, believing himself possessed by the demon his mother had made him swallow in the form of a black toad, went insane and killed himself. He slit his wrists and bled to death on the floor of the Black Room.

Pursued by the bad dreams, I became obsessed with a need to return to the monstrously Gothic house on Nob Hill. Day after day, I walked by it after work, always hoping that Perry would see me and come out. But he never did. The place had a forlorn, deserted air. I began to wonder if he had made his story come true, if he had killed himself. I knew my obsession was unhealthy, but it had such a hold on me that I worried over Peregrine's fate night and day.

To preserve my own sanity, I decided that if I could not get Perry to come out, I would have to find a way in. Investigating in earnest one late afternoon, I made a complete circuit of the iron fence surrounding the house. This revealed a back gate, which was also locked. But here behind the house the fence had not been as well cared for, and the iron bars were rusty. Aha. Rust weakens iron, I thought. I had an idea, an idea born out of obsession.

Desperate situations call for desperate measures, I told myself for reassurance. And I proceeded to buy a hacksaw of the kind that will cut through metal. I had no elaborate plan, I simply had to get into that house!

I went early on a Sunday morning, as that seemed the time I would be most likely to operate undisturbed. I had never told Michael about my obsession with Peregrine because it seemed bizarre, even to me; and besides, he had not read the stories and it would have required a great deal too much explanation. So I set off alone, with only my great determination to keep me company.

The hacksaw made a rasping noise loud enough to wake the dead, or the neighbors, but did not raise an alarm. It did, with a great deal of effort on my part, cut through the rusted bar. This created a gap that I was able to squeeze through. Once within the perimeter I circled the house, looking for a means of entry.

There were numerous outer doors in the huge facade, but they were all locked. Keeping close to the walls, I had made one complete circle of the house before I noticed a partially open window in the back of the central part. It was on the first floor, but due to a slope at the rear of the lot, I had to climb upon a ledge in order to reach it. This activity made me wish again for trousers like Meiling's. At least I had intentionally worn old, soft-soled shoes that made no sound when I walked and were good for scrambling about. I achieved the ledge with little problem and went through the window. It was a long window, of the sort that is only a foot or so from the floor, and hung with a heavy velvet curtain. I concealed myself behind the curtain while I peered around it to get my bearings.

I was at the end of a very long and exceedingly gloomy hall. Its ceiling was vaulted and fan-ribbed, giving the appearance of some forgotten passage in a moldy old monastery. I listened keenly and did not hear a sound. Well, I thought, I am here. Now I must find Perry.

More than once I lost my way in the vast surroundings. I thought about poor Perry, doomed by fate to grow up in such a place. It might have made a good Museum of the Most Strange, but as a place to live, romp, play, be a child, it had nothing whatever to recommend it. I was reminded of *The Hunchback of Notre Dame,* or the underground caverns of *The Phantom of the Opera,* or *The Castle of Otranto,* or even (without the humor) of *Northanger Abbey.* I shivered; I was scaring myself.

I had been up and down numerous stairs, some narow and winding, some wide and sweeping; through doors and archways; in and out among various pillars; and I had looked into many, many rooms—all of this without seeing a living soul—when at last I heard a voice. I was on the second floor of the part of the house that was, on the outside, Carpenter Gothic. The voice, which rose and fell in a chanting rhythm, came from above me. I followed, and found myself in the base of the octagonal turret. I had to open five doors (each of the eight walls had a door, most of which opened onto nothing but a blank wall; what an odd room this was!) before I found stairs that went upward.

As soon as I opened the door to that stairway, the chanting voice grew louder. It was unfamiliar. That was not Perry's voice, not the Perry I knew. I wished I had my walking stick with me—I'd not brought it because I had thought it would encumber me, and it would have. Yet I much desired some form of protection other than my wits. Chills of an almost supernatural foreboding rippled through me; I shrank from placing my foot upon the stair. But I had not come this far to stop now.

I climbed up one floor. The voice grew clearer; it was deep and masculine, with a striking resonance. Now I could make out the words:

The skies they were ashen and sober;
The leaves they were crispéd and sere—
The leaves they were withering and sere;
It was night, in the lonesome October
Of my most immemorial year;
It was hard by the dim lake of Auber,
In the misty mid region of Weir—
It was down by the dank tarn of Auber,
In the ghoul-haunted woodland of Weir.

I knew those words from somewhere! A poem—I could not place it. I continued to listen, spellbound.

And now, as the night was senescent
And the star-dials pointed to morn—
As the star-dials hinted of morn—
At the end of our path a liquescent
And nebulous lustre was born,
Out of which a miraculous crescent
Arose with a duplicate horn—
Astarte's bediamonded crescent
Distinct with its duplicate horn.

Gooseflesh rose on my arms. I knew the author now. Though the voice still sounded strange to me, I had no doubt that I was hearing Peregrine read from the work of his inspiration, Edgar Allan Poe. Yet still I could not recall the name of this particular poem. I leaned upon the frame of the still-closed door that would admit me to the room, waiting as he read, waiting to identify the poem that had me as much in thrall to the weaver of those words as Perry himself had ever been.

. . . we passed to the end of the vista,
But were stopped by the door of a tomb—
By the door of a legended tomb;
And I said: "What is written sweet sister,

On the door of this legended tomb?''
She replied: "Ulalume—Ulalume!—
'Tis the vault of thy lost Ulalume!''

The voice cried, hanging in the air on a mournful echo that chilled
my soul: *Ulalume!* That was the name of the poem. I would not
interrupt, would wait until the end before putting in my appearance.
As I waited, I tried to prepare myself for whatever might happen when
I entered the room. But the words of the poem, as it drew to its
chilling conclusion, intruded into my preparation and seized my mind:

Said we, then—the two, then: "Ah, can it
    Have been that the woodlandish ghouls—
    The pitiful, the merciful ghouls—
To bar up our way and to ban it
    From the secret that lies in these wolds—
    From the thing that lies hidden in these wolds—
Have drawn up the spectre of a planet
    From the limbo of lunary souls—
This sinfully scintillant planet
    From the Hell of the planetary souls?''

He stopped. There was silence. I opened the door and stepped into
the eight-sided room.

There were four people inside—four people and an atmosphere so
heavy that one could have sliced it with a knife. Only one of the
people appeared to note my entrance. I said, as normally as possible,
"Hello, Perry. I have come to visit you, and to inquire how your
writing is going."

He had greatly changed in the few weeks since I'd last seen him.
He had ceased shaving and had grown a patchy black beard. His pale
eyes were darkly ringed in a death-white face. His hair was as long as a
prophet's. He sprawled in his chair, wearing a shirt with its tails out,
ruffled at the neck and sleeves, a shirt that had once been white and
fine but now was grime-gray. If he recognized me, he gave no sign.

He did not move at all, except to balance his book upon a black-clad knee.

"It is I, Fremont Jones, Perry," I said, walking a few steps into the room. There was a strong, medicinal smell to the air, with an underlying stale fustiness that I could taste. It tasted horribly unpleasant. A mental image suddenly leapt to mind: the old priest at the Mission Dolores, and I recalled his words: "Those who are fascinated by Evil all too easily fall prey to it themselves."

No one moved, no one spoke. I ventured a step farther.

"I hope you have been well," I said, a conventional remark that I realized at once was bizarre in the circumstances.

Perry laughed, a wild cackle, and leapt to life. His book fell with a crash to the floor. "Well? Oh certainly, we have been well, as well as can be expected! So you have come to call?" He danced in a circle around me. His voice, higher pitched than when he'd read, sounded more like the voice I knew as his. But nothing else was like; I did not have to be Dr. Freud to see that poor Perry's mind was gone.

He stopped his capering and peered into my face. I tried not to flinch from his stinking breath as he asked, "I know you, don't I?"

"Yes, you do. Why don't you introduce me to the others?" I had not yet really looked at them, my eyes had been on him, but I thought it odd that none of them had reacted to my uninvited presence.

"Oh, of course." He turned, and my eyes followed him. And then I knew that I had indeed entered Hell—what were the words of the poem?—*the Hell of the planetary souls.*

They were dead, quite, quite dead. Their eyes stared, their skins were a waxy yellow, and the horrible odor in the room was from something he'd tried to do to preserve them.

"This is my mother, the sorceress," said Perry, sticking out his tongue at her and leaning down into her stony face. "And this," he said, continuing on with a sweeping bow, "is her henchman, Hubert, erstwhile friend of my childhood. He went berserk, poor man, thought he was a werewolf. But then, my mother does that to people. Ruins them. Puts spells on them. Or at least she used to, but I rather think she can't do that anymore." He giggled. "I stopped her, you see. That over there"—he jerked a dirty thumb in the direction of the other woman, who I now saw wore the black-and-white of a domestic servant—"is of no account. Her name's Isabelle or Esmeralda or something like that; I had to kill her too or she would have *told*. Can't have anyone telling, can we?"

"I should certainly hope not," I said, wiping my cold, sweating palms on my skirt and all the while thinking, Oh dear God, dear God, help us now!

Suddenly Perry's shoulders drooped and he began to shake. He was crying!

I overcame my revulsion, went to him and gently took his shoulders in my hands. He felt like a skeleton, but he cried living tears and I could feel his sorrow. Softly I said, "Tell me, Perry. Tell me what happened."

"I did it!" he wailed in the voice of a child, "I'm very awful, I'm very, very bad!"

At that moment he did not seem like an insane killer. I urged him to walk with me back to his chair, and before he sat down I turned it away from that awful tableau of death. I urged Perry into the chair and knelt beside him. "You need help," I said with the strength of conviction, "and I'm here to help you. That is the real reason I've come."

Stammering and sobbing, poor Peregrine Crowe told his story. "I-it wasn't me, not really, it was the D-demon inside me. He gets very strong sometimes, s-so strong I can't control him, and then he comes out. I can't stop him coming out. B-but I didn't want to do the bad things anymore for Mother, the things in the Black Room . . . SSssh!" He rolled his eyes, startled out of his tears.

"It's all right, Perry, I know all about the Black Room. I know it's a secret. Now go on, tell me everything that happened."

"You're sure?" he whispered.

"I'm sure."

"I, uh, uh, I called the Demon out of me on purpose. Mother's evil, you see—oh I know I'm evil too but she's the worst of all, and I never meant to be evil, it's only that I can't help it"—he was talking so rapidly that his words tripped over one another and I had to attend very carefully as he went on—"and she's the most evil of all, so I called out the Demon and I told him to kill her. And he did. It was easy, all he had to do was put some poison in her tea, and we have lots of poison all over the house. For the rats, you know."

"Ah yes, for the rats, of course."

"But that was after what she did to Eubie. Eubie, that's Hubert, he was my friend, he wasn't really evil, and after a long time, years and years, he left. He went away, he got a job, a real job. He used to write letters to me and he had the maid— Not that one, another one, she left too, everybody always leaves except me, I can't, I tried, I *can't!* He had the maid smuggle them in. That's the right word, isn't it? Smuggle?" His eyes were wide and innocent with the question.

Perry's madness was stunning. Heartbreaking. He was like two people, the one an innocent, odd young man who'd never quite grown up, and the other the Demon that had killed three people. I hoped I would not have to meet the demon. With a little nod I replied to Perry's question: "Yes, smuggle is the right word. You're telling it very well, Perry."

"Eubie wrote me letters all about his job and the lighthouse where he lived and how free and open and fine it was, really wonderful. But then *she* found out. She found the letters, and it was my fault she found the letters, and she forced me to help her put a spell on Eubie, from the Black Room. I didn't want to do it, but I had to. *I had to!* I tried to help Eubie, really I did, I even ran away and took a lot of money and I found him and, and everything . . ." Once again he broke down, sobbing.

"You did help him"—I rubbed the skeletal shoulders—"you really did."

"No, I didn't! Because the spell worked and he really was a werewolf, and, and . . . And she scried us in the lighthouse on Point Reyes, and she, she sent people after us . . ." Perry rolled his eyes until only the whites showed; he began to rock back and forth; I was afraid he was going into some kind of fit. But his voice still came out, keening: "She did something terrible to Hubert, worse than being a werewolf. I don't know what she did because she kept me locked up for a very long time. She did something to his brain and he wasn't Hubert anymore. He wasn't my friend anymore. So I had the Demon kill him too."

Perry stopped his rocking. He sat very still, looking at me. Slowly, as if a filmy curtain were being drawn back, I saw sanity take shape in Perry's eyes. He said, "Hubert was my only friend, Fremont. Except for you."

"I'm glad you think of me as a friend." The sudden sanity was jolting, almost worse than the madness. For how could the two exist, side by side, in the same person?

He continued to speak sanely for a minute longer, but in the midst of his speech he turned mad again: "I killed them, or the Demon did, sometimes I'm not sure—but I couldn't bury them like ordinary people because they weren't ordinary. I knew the bad magic could bring them back again. She can do that you know, from the grave she can do that, *she can come back!* But not without her whole body, not without her heart and her lungs and her stomach—I know that from the Egyptians, from a book in the library. So I took that book, all about the Egyptians and embalming and I went out and I got what I needed and I did what it said, I took out their organs—except the brains, I couldn't do that no matter how hard I tried—and I put them in jars. So now I don't think they can come back, not even *she* can come back, but still I have to watch them all the time. Maybe I didn't do it right because all I had was glass jars. Here, I'll show you."

Perry led me by the hand and showed me. I did not want to look, but I did—with horrible fascination. I saw that he had told the truth. He had done a brilliant, twisted, demented thing.

I could not let this go on any longer. Interrupting Perry's continuing tale, which in any case had deteriorated to jibberish, I firmly took his hand and said, "You're coming with me now, Perry. We're going where there are people who will be your friends and who can help you. It's all over now. You don't have to watch them anymore. You can rest, you can sleep. You'd like that, wouldn't you?"

Step by step, Perry jibbering and protesting and pulling back all the way, I got him down the stairs. I prayed to the Force in the Universe that I call God, asking for guidance out of that house because I never could have found the way on my own. We found it. I opened the huge front door, turning the key that I found in the lock, and locking it again behind me.

The Demon came out of Perry as I locked the door. He roared, a guttural bellowing sound loud enough to break the eardrums. He pulled away from me and, with one superhuman blow to the side of my head, knocked me down. I expected him to fall upon me and batter me senseless, but he did not. Instead he ran off, roaring, around the house.

I tried to get up, and fell back. Through the ringing in my ears I heard a shout, a scrambling as of feet, and with blurred vision I looked. Michael! Michael Archer had vaulted over an iron fence ten feet tall!

"You should know by now, Holmes," he said as he pulled me—none too gently—to my feet, "that Watson does not take kindly to being left behind. Shall we both save the explanations for later?"

"Yes!"

"You run around that way, and I'll go this way, and between the two of us we will catch that fellow. Agreed?"

"Yes!" I exclaimed again. I was sure he was right—between the two of us we could do anything!

I insisted on going to see Peregrine in the hospital when the police finally decided that they were through with us, and Michael insisted on going with me. We'd had quite a long day and were both exhausted when at last we alighted from a hired carriage in front of our house on Vallejo Street.

The front door opened, seemingly by itself. And a voice boomed out: "Well, well, it's themselves. Wotcha doing out so late, the both of ya?"

Epilogue:

The Strangest Peregrination

I RECEIVED THE summons to the hospital on my office telephone and obeyed it posthaste, putting a sign—CLOSED FOR EMERGENCY—on the door. I was able to hire a cab on Sacramento Street and so arrived quickly at the private hospital run by the Sisters of Mercy. They had been merciful with poor Perry, though he was kept of necessity in a straitjacket most of the time.

"Something has happened?" I asked the Sister who stood guard outside his room.

"I'm afraid so," she said in a hushed voice that went with her medieval garb. "We don't know how he did it. He strangled himself. We thought we'd found him in time when we called you, but I'm sorry. We couldn't save him. He's gone."

Couldn't save him. That was the problem, wasn't it? No one could save him. I said, "I'd like to see him anyway."

The nun pushed open the door and stood back, allowing me to enter alone.

Peregrine Crowe, whom I would always think of as Edgar Allan Partridge, lay purple-faced in his bed. His hands were crossed on his chest in an attitude of reverence.

On the pillow by his head sat a black toad with red eyes.